Never Have You Ever

Never Have You Ever

THE LOVE GAME: BOOK ONE

ELIZABETH HAYLEY

WATERHOUSE PRESS

*To Robyn, for the constant support
and help you provide to us.
You're the best.*

Chapter One

SOPHIA

"Carter."

He didn't answer, even as I put my hand on his shoulder to shake him. It felt weird to touch him—like I was invading his privacy—even though he was lying on my bed, drooling from the right side of his mouth onto my Vera Bradley comforter. It didn't get more intimate than that.

"Carter!" I whisper-screamed into his ear, and he jolted. "You gotta get out of here."

He rubbed a hand down his face, which was somehow still boyishly handsome even though the right side held indentations from where my sheets had bunched under him.

"Sorry, Sophia. I must've fallen asleep."

"It's fine. I think the other girls are still asleep. It's early."

Looking at his watch, he said, "Let's go back to sleep. I don't have class for another two hours." He let his head fall back onto the bed, eyes already closed, his floppy light-brown hair falling over them.

I grabbed his hand and tugged, trying my hardest to pull him off the bed.

1

"Get up!" I tried one more time with all my strength but was only able to slide his body a few inches. Damn athletes. It was like trying to drag a bag of rocks.

He flashed an impish smile, and I gave him a shove.

"I'm serious. Aamee's gonna kill me if she sees you here."

"Screw Aamee."

"She'd like you to do that, I'm sure," I said with a chuckle.

"I'm not interested."

"Don't tell *her* that. Don't tell her anything. Just get out before she sees you."

Finally, he seemed ready to comply, his long limbs spreading into a morning stretch. He moved around the room—albeit slowly for a wide receiver—packing up his bag with the books we used last night.

"What's the big deal? We were studying."

"*I* know that. Aamee will think differently, though, if she sees you leaving in the morning instead of last night."

"Aamee, Aamee, Aamee," he said with a laugh. "She doesn't even spell her name right. Who cares what she thinks?"

I tried my best to convey the severity of the situation through my expression, but Carter Blaine wasn't known for taking much of anything seriously other than football and Bud Light.

"I do. She's the sorority president."

"It's not like she can kick you out for having a guy spend the night. Coed sleepovers are like . . . one of the foundations of Greek life."

"They're really not," I said dryly.

I opened my door a crack, listened for footsteps, chatter, or the sound of the water running in the bathroom. When I didn't hear anything, I grabbed his hand again and ushered him toward the hallway.

We were halfway down the stairs when Aamee walked from the kitchen to the front door and spun to face us, her dark-green eyes narrowing and her blond hair whipping around. "Just what do you think you're doing?"

I looked to Carter, his bright-blue eyes widening as he looked from me to Aamee and back again. "Sorry."

"For what exactly?" Aamee asked.

"For . . . coming over so early. When I left last night, I thought I understood all that psychology stuff. Then I got home and realized I'd forgotten most of it. So I came back over here super early. I didn't mean to wake anyone up, but we have a test today—"

"Bullshit." Aamee crossed her arms.

"We do. You wanna see the syllabus?" Bless Carter's heart for trying. He was already going into his phone to log in to the course.

All she said to him was "Don't bother" before turning to address me. "I'll talk to you after Carter leaves."

I tried to disguise the heavy sigh, but my defeat was evident. And to further cement my spot at the top of Aamee Allen's Shit List—a real list she kept on her phone—Carter gave me a kiss on the forehead and said, "Thanks for last night."

Xo

I'd done my best to avoid Aamee for the remainder of the morning, and thankfully, when I'd returned from class this afternoon, only a few of the other girls were in the house.

I was Aamee-free until she got home from work around five p.m. I'd expected her to be thrumming with excitement as she prepared herself to dole out my consequence, but instead she said she was going to take time to think about it. I had a feeling that had more to do with her wanting to cause me anxiety than it did her need to give it any serious thought, but I was happy not to speak to her all the same.

I was lying on my bed with my headphones on when my roommate, Gina, came in and sat down on her bed. "I heard about what happened this morning with Carter."

"Well, with how news travels in this house, I'm not really surprised," I said with a laugh.

"Right." She took a brush from her bedside table and began running it through her long dark hair. "Well, Aamee's a bitch."

"Obviously."

"She's worse with this stuff when it comes to guys, and she's liked Carter for four years, since they were freshmen. I bet it'll all blow over once she moves on to whatever or *who*ever she has an issue with next. Just give it a little time."

I let out a humorless laugh. "I'm not so sure. She told me she was going to think about my consequence and she'd let me know what kind of trouble I'm in later tonight."

"Ugh." Gina lay back against her pillows and stared up blankly, like she was trying to make out the solution to my problem in the popcorn ceiling. "I wish she'd calm down with this shit. She's not making any friends by pointing out every little thing all of us do wrong."

"She still has her groupies." I shrugged.

"Ew, don't call them that. She's not Justin Bieber."

At least Gina always had a way of making me laugh, even if I might not be laughing later when Aamee dished out my punishment like a crotchety grandmother serving someone's second helping of dinner. She really wouldn't give a fuck whether I wanted it or not.

"I gotta admit," I said, "I'm actually a little scared. Aamee is no doubt going to make me pay for this."

"Maybe she's gonna make you walk naked through the streets while we all point at you and yell, 'Shame,' like you're Cersei Lannister from *Game of Thrones*."

I laughed again. "I think I might actually prefer that to what Aamee probably has in store for me."

Gina looked over at me, her expression serious for the first time since she'd entered our room. "Seriously though, what's the worst that can happen?"

X_0

"Sophia Mason, you are here in the presence of your sisters to atone for your sins."

"I think 'sins' is a little extreme, Aamee," someone said.

It might have been Gina, but I couldn't be sure. I couldn't see anything in the dark room except the blinding flashlight of Aamee's iPhone shining in my face.

"Shut up, Gina," someone confirmed.

Aamee got closer to me, bringing the light with her. It was like I was heading toward my inevitable death, but instead of feeling a peaceful calm as I sat surrounded by loved ones, I was battling a power-hungry college senior who was permanently PMSing.

I moved back and turned my head to the side so the light wasn't directly in my eyes. "Can we turn that thing off and have a normal conversation about this, please?"

There was silence for a few moments until the light shut off and a lamp turned on instead. "Fine," Aamee said, "but the process is still the same."

Some of the girls were looking at their nails in between eye rolls, seemingly siding with me on the ridiculousness of this. Others were nodding as Aamee spoke, though I wasn't sure if it was because they agreed with her or were just too scared *not* to.

"Can we just get this over with?" I asked.

I knew Aamee was pissed about Carter, but after my conversation with Gina, I'd let myself get my hopes up that my punishment began and ended with her silence toward me over the past two days. It was a consequence I was happy to accept since it was more of a reward than a punishment.

Aamee flipped her blond hair behind her shoulder and pursed her red lips together. They were so plump, I'd once asked if she'd done "whatever Kylie Jenner had done." I'd quickly identified that question as a mistake, but it was too late to take it back. And thus began her hatred of me.

That night she'd announced the addition of my name to her Shit List, and I'd only moved up in rank since then by doing little things like using her toothpaste or disconnecting her phone from a charger so I could charge my own.

"Then let us begin," Aamee said. "On the fifteenth of September, you, Sophia Marie Mason—"

"My middle name isn't Marie."

"Sophia Elizabeth—"

"Nope."

"Ann?"

I shook my head.

"Whatever. Like…ninety percent of the female population has one of those. I just guessed."

"Well, you guessed wrong."

"Do you plan to tell me what it is?"

I pretended to think for a second. "No, I think I'll leave you in suspense."

Aamee composed herself, though she looked like she was ready to explode. Which, after picturing it, I realized would've been amazing to watch. Long strands of yellow hair painted red from her blood, her spray-tanned orange skin splattered all over the walls like some sort of abstract painting.

Unfortunately, my Aamee fantasy was interrupted by her voice. "On the fifteenth of September, you, Sophia—"

"You should probably include the year," Gina said, sounding like she was choking back a laugh. "I mean, if we're being formal about all this."

Aamee's lips looked like they were ready to pop when she pressed them together. "Any other requests?" She looked around the room.

"You do you, sweetie," Bethany shouted. "You're doing great."

"On the fifteenth of September, you, Sophia . . . Something Mason, were caught harboring a male student in your room during nighttime hours."

My eyebrows raised. "Harboring? Really? You make him sound like a fugitive."

"That's enough of the interruptions. May I continue?"

I gestured with my hand, though I knew I didn't exactly have a choice.

"According to the Zeta Eta Chi handbook, which our founding sisters created at the induction of this chapter, and I quote, 'No male shall be permitted to spend more than four consecutive hours in the house, and those hours must not be between dusk and dawn for the sole purpose of preserving the organization's reputation of integrity, honor, and respect.

Any member found to have disobeyed this regulation shall, at the sole request of the chapter president, be evicted from the house immediately.'"

Aamee closed the book and waited for a reaction. I didn't give her one.

"You're citing a manual from almost a hundred years ago."

"The age is irrelevant. What matters is the content. Do you dispute the fact that a male was in your room overnight?"

"No. Do you dispute that one was in yours a few weeks ago?"

Aamee appeared flustered for a moment but regained her composure quickly. "Good thing I'm the president."

"Way to abuse your power. You're really going to kick me out of the house for this?"

"Punishment fits the crime if you ask me. If you can't abide by house rules, you can't live in the house."

"Oh, come on. Let's call it like it is. You're pointing a finger at me because the 'male' who stayed over is someone you have a major crush on. And while a big part of me wants to lie and say I slept with him so I could watch you raze this house like Carrie, the truth is all we did was fall asleep studying. So hop down off your moral high horse before you break your hypocritical neck."

She was eerily quiet, staring absently for so long it made me wonder if I'd put her into some sort of catatonic trance. It also made me wonder if my points had been valid enough to make her second-guess my punishment, though I doubted it. More likely, it was simply the calm before the storm. A few more seconds passed before Hurricane Aamee spoke.

"My decision stands. Don't do the crime if you can't do the time."

"Any more clichés you'd like to toss out? You're not going to tell me if I don't have anything nice to say, don't say anything at all?"

Aamee laughed. "Actually, I don't care what you have to say one way or the other. I just care that you leave."

This time it was Emma who came to my defense. "Aamee? You know Sophia's mom is Kate Macland, right? She was president. We can't kick Sophia out of the house."

"Of course I know who her mom is. How do you think she got in?" Aamee fixed her eyes on me. "Besides, it's not like she's out of the sorority completely...yet," she added with more hostility in her tone than had been there previously. "You should probably start packing your bags. You have twenty-four hours to get out."

"Thanks." I gave her a sickeningly sweet smile. "But I'll probably only need a few hours."

She laughed like I was kidding, but when I got all my stuff into boxes and suitcases with the help of Gina, Emma, and a few other girls who weren't attached to Aamee's tit—and left without making a big deal of it—I was certain Aamee's curiosity about where I'd gone might kill her. Too bad I wouldn't be there to see it.

I arrived at my brother's a half hour later with a hastily packed bag of clothes, shoes, toiletries, and various electronic gadgets. I hadn't called Brody to give him a heads-up, but our dad was paying for the place, so he couldn't exactly turn me away at the door.

We'd never been what I'd call close, but maybe we could be now that we were on the same campus and I'd be bunking with him—at least until I figured out how to get back into the sorority house.

Brody, a fifth-year senior, had been attending college halfway across the country—largely to get some space from our parents and me. But now, four and a half years and dozens of lost credits later, he was closer to home and trying to climb out of whatever hole he'd dug himself during his years of partying.

That our father had let him transfer again had been a shock to both of us. I'd thought for sure he'd make Brody throw in the towel and figure his shit out before he burned any more of his money at institutions of higher learning. But when Brody promised that a change of scenery and living by himself would help him focus, our dad agreed to give him one more shot before he pulled the plug on his education. I guess he had more faith in Brody than the rest of us did. Brody included.

It occurred to me, as I shifted my bags at the door of Brody's apartment situated above a small bakery, that I should've at least checked to see if he was even going to be home. For all I knew, I could be spending the next five hours waiting for him to get back from class.

Thankfully someone opened the door when I knocked. Instead of my shit-for-brains brother greeting me, it was a handsome stranger.

Guess my brother had already made some friends. Hot ones.

"Hi, I'm looking for Brody. Is he here?"

The guy opened his arms wide and plastered on a smile. "You found him."

What?

"I'm sorry, is Brody here?"

"I'm Brody. Can I help you with something?"

"You're not Brody."

He jerked his head back like the accusation was absurd, and for a brief second, I wondered if I'd somehow entered the Upside Down and was in some sort of parallel universe where nothing made sense and my brother was a gorgeous stranger who looked happy to see me.

I pushed past him without waiting for an invitation. "Brody! Brody!" I called as I moved through the apartment.

"I'm right here. I'm sorry, *who* are you?"

"The better question is who the hell are you? Because I'm Brody's sister, and you're sure as shit not Brody."

Chapter Two

SOPHIA

"Have you lost your goddamn mind?" I asked Brody as soon as he picked up his phone.

"I feel like I get asked that a lot."

"That should probably tell you something, then. Where are you right now?"

"At home, why?"

"Home as in Mom and Dad's?"

"No. My apartment. Why? What do you need, Soph? I'm trying to study."

I was still looking through the apartment like I was going to find Brody bound and gagged in a closet somewhere, which made absolutely no sense since I was currently talking to him. Meanwhile, the man claiming to be Brody was following me around, trying to talk to me. I continued to ignore him.

"You know how I know you're not at your apartment right now?"

"How?" He sounded skeptical.

"Because *I'm* at your apartment right now, and there's

some guy here pretending to be you. You wanna tell me what the fuck is going on?"

"Why are you at my apartment?"

"I feel like you're missing the point!"

"What *is* the point?" He seemed calmer than the situation called for. I sounded like a victim from *Saw 2*, and he sounded like fucking Gandhi.

"The point is that I got kicked out of my sorority house, and I came here so I could stay with you for a little while, but you aren't here." I looked at the Brody imposter. "Some weirdo is, and... You know what, I'm calling the cops."

"No! Wait! Don't hang up. Don't call the cops."

I was happy he sounded frantic now too. "What am I supposed to do? You're missing, and there's some person claiming he's you."

"I'm not *missing*."

"Then where are you?"

There was a pause so long, I took the phone away from my ear to see if I'd lost the call. I hadn't.

Finally, after a deep sigh, he said, "Italy."

Now it was my turn to pause. "Italy? I really hope you just forgot to put the word *Little* in front of it and you don't mean you're actually in Italy, as in another country on another continent."

Brody's silence confirmed it was the latter.

"Oh my God! What are you doing in Italy?"

He let out one of those long, pained sighs, like all the air inside him had been released, leaving him completely deflated. It made me feel like it would be a good idea to sit down for the rest of the conversation, so I walked to the couch, lowering myself carefully onto it like the movement might disturb some imaginary sleeping person.

"You can't tell Mom and Dad," he said. "Promise me."

"Jesus, Brody. I'm not gonna rat you out." I was more hurt by his insinuation than I cared to let on.

"Right. I guess not. Because then I'd tell them you got kicked out of your sorority house."

I rubbed the bridge of my nose in frustration. "Do we always have to talk in threats? We're not kids anymore. Can't we just help each other because we're family? Just tell me what's going on."

"It's not really that complicated. I just couldn't do the whole school thing. I thought I could, but I went for like three days before I needed to get away."

"You're such a douche." The comment slipped before I could think about its effect.

"See? Why would I tell you anything?"

It was a valid question. "I'm sorry. Really. I just... I thought you were finally committed to going down the right path."

"Well, the right path for you may be the wrong path for me. The idea of staying there, trying to become what Dad wants me to be was ... It was suffocating, Soph. I needed to get away."

Oh, the drama. He should've been a theater major.

"What are you gonna do about your classes? Dad'll find out you've been dropped from every course because you haven't shown up."

"That won't happen."

I laughed out loud. He'd really lost it. "How could it not?"

"Because my teachers think I'm showing up to my classes."

My eyes locked with the person who'd claimed to be Brody, and suddenly it all clicked. I pulled the phone away from my ear.

"What's your real name?" I asked the stranger. "When you're not pretending to be my brother?"

He hesitated like the admission might cause him serious harm.

"Drew Nolan."

Now my attention went back to Brody. "And how much are you paying Mr. Nolan to live your life for you while you're across an ocean drinking wine and eating pizza?"

"If that's all you think Italians do, *you're* the one who should be traveling." When I didn't reply, he spoke again. "I'm not paying him. Just giving him a place to stay and a chance to learn something about business. It was kind of a mutual exchange."

"Right. So you get to travel around Europe, and Drew gets to learn macroeconomics. Seems like a fair trade."

Drew was pacing now.

"I don't need to justify my choices to my little sister."

"No. I guess you don't. But you'll need to justify them to Mom and Dad when they find out what you're doing. And they *will* find out eventually. I get that you're new to this campus, but you actually think that your teachers won't notice another person pretending to be you?"

"They haven't yet. He looks enough like me to fool people who've only known me a couple of days."

"And what about your social media accounts? You think when Drew meets friends here they aren't gonna check out his Instagram and see that there's another person on there?"

"Have you been on lately?"

Of course I hadn't been. I wasn't even sure why I followed him. I didn't care what he was up to. "No." I put him on speakerphone and pulled up his Instagram page. All I saw were pictures of places, sporting events, other people. There were a few of Brody, but they were from far enough away that he could've easily been Drew, or vice versa, especially to someone who didn't know them well. "You really deleted all the pictures of yourself?"

"Yeah. I'm not an idiot. Reckless and impulsive maybe, but not an idiot."

I couldn't help but laugh. "Reckless and impulsive are a definite, not a maybe."

"I won't argue with that." We were both quiet for a moment, and then Brody said, "Guess you can stay there if you don't have any other place to go."

"You think I'd want to live with you if I did?"

"Well, it's a good thing I'm not there. I don't exactly wanna live with you either. I'm sure Drew'll see what I'm talking about soon enough."

"He's not staying," I said adamantly.

"Ha! You say that like it's your choice. Just because you don't have a place to live doesn't mean Drew shouldn't. It's not his fault you don't know how to play nice with your little girlfriends. And it's not my fault either. I'm not letting your fuck-ups ruin a perfectly good arrangement I have going."

"I didn't 'fuck up.' A guy fell asleep in my room when we were studying, and apparently there's some ancient rule about—"

"Sounds totally understandable. I'm sure when Dad finds out you can't follow simple rules, he'll find you a nice place of your own."

"Like he did for you?"

There was silence on the other end. I'd hit a nerve. And I was happy about it.

"Drew stays," he finally said. "We gotta help each other out and all that, remember?"

Damn it. I hated when a person used my own words against me. And I hated it more when that person was my asshat older brother.

"Fine. He can stay."

"You're still acting like it's your decision."

"Brody!"

He let out a long sigh. "Okay, okay. You can even have my room, and Drew can take the couch. I'm not gonna have my little sister sleeping in a common space with a guy walking around at all hours of the night."

"Thanks," I said softly. And I meant it.

"You're welcome. Just don't fuck the place up, okay?"

It might've been the most welcome Brody had ever made me feel.

By the time I hung up with Brody, Drew looked even more panicked than he had before, if that was possible. He kept shoving his hands in his pockets and then taking them back out again to rub them together.

"Are you trying to start a fire?"

He looked up at me, and I noticed how dark his eyes were—almost black. "Huh?"

"I was referring to the way you're rubbing your hands together." I was suddenly embarrassed, though it shouldn't have been me who felt that way. "Never mind. It was a stupid joke."

"Oh." He laughed, but it came out as more of an exhalation than an actual sound. He put both his hands on the top of his head and stood with his elbows out as he rubbed up and down his head nervously. "So... What's the plan? Is he coming home?"

His worry surprised me, considering how relaxed he'd been when he'd insisted he was Brody. I laughed too this time, an overly exaggerated sound to tell Drew how ridiculous his question was.

"No. I highly doubt that."

"Good."

"Good? So you *like* living his life?"

He shrugged, and when his shoulders fell, he looked a little more relaxed. "So far, so good, I guess. Well, until you showed up. Brody didn't tell me he had a sister who went to school here."

"Of course he didn't. I'm Sophia, by the way."

Drew walked closer to me and held a hand out, creating a formality that didn't quite match the situation.

When I took his hand, he said, "Nice to meet you."

"You too, I guess." I smiled, hoping the gesture would help me relax. It didn't. "So, Brody told me I could take his room."

He smiled back. Unfortunately for both of us, it wasn't for very long. "Yeah, sure. I'll get out of your way soon. I just need a few minutes to move some of my stuff." He pointed toward the small hall that led to the bedroom. "And I'll change the sheets for you."

"Take your time," I told him, suddenly feeling a little bit bad about how accommodating he was being. Though it wasn't *his* apartment, so he should be accommodating. Then again, it wasn't mine either. And I was sleeping in what should be my brother's room in his apartment, and the guy who was supposed to be him was sleeping on the couch.

God, this was already such a clusterfuck.

DREW

Was this chick crazy? She had to be. No girl in her right mind would voluntarily share a living space with a guy who'd lied about who he was immediately upon meeting her.

She wore a light-pink shirt that hit just above the waist of her jeans, and her long dark hair, which had been curled into loose waves, matched her dark eyes. With light-olive skin, a round face defined by pronounced cheekbones, long lashes, and a bottom lip that was slightly plumper than the top and begging to be kissed, she was quite attractive. From what I could tell, she didn't *appear* insane. She looked totally normal.

"Why are you looking at me like that?"

Damn it. How the hell had I managed to impersonate someone for this long with absolutely no problem, but now someone I just met gets a read on me within minutes?

"Like what?"

"Like I'm crazy. Or maybe like *you're* crazy. I'm not sure which."

"Can it be both?"

We held one another's gazes for a second before bursting into laughter.

She began to unpack some of her belongings.

"You need any help?" I looked around and realized she'd only brought two bags. "Do you have anything else back at the sorority house?"

"First thing you need to learn if you're gonna pretend to be Brody is that he would absolutely *not* offer to help me do anything."

"Noted." I couldn't reconcile the laid-back, friendly

guy I'd known from the bar I worked at with the guy who wouldn't offer to help his sister and forgot to even mention her.

"And yeah, I have a few things still there, but Aamee will probably send me to the gallows if I step foot in there again. I think a few of the girls can bring the rest over later."

"Who's Aamee?"

"The sorority president. Picture like a really sweet, selfless person who's down-to-earth and beautiful inside and out." She paused for a moment before continuing. "Then picture the opposite of everything I just said. That's Aamee. She's the reason I'm here right now, and I will take her down or waste my entire junior year trying. Well, after I'm done studying and going to class. I'm not Brody."

I nodded. "So this is what college life is like, huh?"

"Guess it can be. You sorry you signed up for this?" Then she said with furrowed brows, "Why *did* you sign up for this?"

I didn't really feel like getting into any of it now, so I just said, "A lot of reasons, really. And who can pass up a tiny one-bedroom that smells like chocolate chip cookies?"

"Clearly neither one of us."

At the mention of the cookies, I offered to go down to the bakery and grab us a few, because once I had them in my mind, it was impossible to get them out unless they ended up in my stomach.

When I returned with a small bag of cookies from downstairs and two lattes from the coffee shop on the corner, Sophia was sitting on one of the barstools at the kitchen counter, scrolling through her phone.

"I guess I should've asked if you drank coffee," I said, setting the cup down in front of her.

"Of course I drink coffee. I don't trust people who don't."

"Well, we have at least one thing in common." I raised my cup to give her a casual toast.

"Make that two things," she said, reaching into the bag of cookies before tapping her cup against mine.

There was a knock at the door a few minutes later, and after wiping the crumbs from the counter, Sophia said, "I'll get it. Two of the girls are supposed to be bringing over some more of my things."

The door opened, and three girls walked inside. Two carried boxes, and one carried nothing but a cell phone. "We brought the last of your stuff," one of them said as she set the boxes on the floor.

"Thanks. But you also brought *her*," Sophia replied, her eyes focused on the tall blonde who was heading toward me like a lioness who'd just spotted a gazelle.

"We tried to stop her," one of the girls said.

Sophia's eyebrows narrowed like she thought that story was unlikely. "Well, you obviously didn't try very hard. She had no idea where I was going, so that means one of you must've either told her the address or given her a ride."

"Emma drove me," the lioness said without looking their way.

"Seriously, Emma?" Sophia said. "How could you bring Aamee here?"

Ahh, that makes so much sense now. "Aamee," I said with a smile. "I'm Sophia's brother, Brody. I've heard so much about you."

"I'm sure you have," she said. "But if it came from Sophia, most of it's probably a lie."

Sophia rolled her eyes. "It's time for you to leave."

"Hang on. I just wanted to introduce myself and see your new place. So, you're Sophia's brother?"

"I am."

"Sophia didn't tell me she had a brother."

This was the strangest family.

"And a cute one," Aamee added. "So what was it like growing up with this one? Did you have to hide all the Twinkies and tell her how great she was constantly?"

"She was a great kid."

"Not so much as an adult, though, huh?" Aamee tilted her head in a way that made me think she felt sorry for me. "Do you have any embarrassing stories?"

"I sure do," I said.

Sophia glared at me like she'd cut off my nuts if I told Aamee anything of the sort.

In an effort to assert our sibling bond, I said, "But Fifi would probably kill me if I told you any, and I'm too nice of a big brother to do that." I thought the nickname was a nice touch.

"Fifi?" Aamee and Sophia said in unison. Though their tones could not have been more different. Aamee was practically vibrating with excitement, while Sophia looked less than pleased, to say the least.

"Brody, you know I can't stand when you call me that," Sophia said much more sweetly than she obviously wanted to.

"Sorry." I tried to give her an apologetic smile, but no apology could change the fact that Aamee had already heard it.

"Fifi," Aamee said. "It reminds me of a small toy poodle."

"All toy poodles are small," Sophia told her.

"I think toy poodles are cute," the other girl said.

"You're not helping, Gina."

Gina mouthed a *Sorry* to Sophia before addressing Aamee. "We should probably get going and let Sophia get unpacked."

Aamee looked genuinely confused. "She owns like six things, and all of them should be donated to Goodwill."

Of course that wasn't true. I'd seen some of Sophia's clothes already, and a few still had the tags on them. I wasn't sure who would pay sixty-eight dollars for a tank top. Apparently those people existed, and I was now sharing an apartment with one of them.

I couldn't say I was particularly surprised, though, because from what Brody had told me, the Masons were wealthy. Brody was set to take over his dad's company if he could figure out how to finish his business degree. Hopefully I wouldn't fuck all this up for him. Or myself. Or for Sophia, for that matter.

"All right, well, it's been real . . . I'm sure Sophia wants to finish unpacking." When no one budged, I added, "And I need to shave my balls."

Emma started giggling like a second grader, and Gina and Aamee looked disgusted and were already heading toward the door. Since that was the point, I was proud of myself for my quick thinking.

"I guess I'll see you around," Aamee said to Sophia. "Though not at the sorority house, obviously."

"Well, I'm still allowed there. I'm not kicked out of the sorority."

"Right," Aamee answered, and it looked like it pained her to do so. "It was a *pleasure* meeting you, Brody."

The way she said "pleasure" gave me the chills—and not the good kind.

"Nice to meet you too."

Once the three of them had left, I closed the door and locked it. Sophia and I didn't say anything right away. We just looked at each other, both fighting back smiles until we couldn't any longer.

"I'm not sure whether I should address the ball shaving first or the fact that you basically gave me a nickname that's associated with one of the most annoying breeds of dog ever."

I shrugged. "I've never been great under pressure."

"I can see that," she said, but thankfully she was still smiling. "This is going to be an interesting living situation."

"You can always go back and live with Aamee."

"Technically I can't," she said.

"Then I guess you're stuck with me for the foreseeable future."

"Guess you're stuck with me too."

Chapter Three

DREW

I opened the door to Brody's apartment, only to find every light off and total silence. Sophia was either a hardcore partier or she was already asleep. My bet was on the latter. Not that I could blame her. I'd have loved to have been sleeping at almost three a.m., but I had a job to maintain.

While being Brody had some advantages—namely taking business courses for free and not paying rent—there was also a distinct disadvantage: having to maintain my job as a bartender so I could pay my other bills and feed myself.

Burning the candle at both ends would've been harder had Brody not stacked most of his classes in the afternoons. The guy might have been in school longer than some doctors—and didn't even have a bachelor's degree to show for it—but he wasn't a total idiot. Getting up before noon was overrated.

I toed off my shoes and left them next to the door. No way did I want to track the grossness from the bar into Brody's apartment. As I tried to find a lamp, I banged into an end table, causing the plastic legs to screech across the floor. I reached out to steady it, and my hand connected with the remote.

Figuring the TV could provide some light, I felt around for the large button near the top and pressed it. Music blared from the Bluetooth speaker, and I jumped, causing me to knock into the table again.

"Shit, shit, shit, shit." I tried pushing the same button again, but the music didn't stop. I think it actually got louder.

Panic began to set in. I smacked the remote into my palm repeatedly, as if assaulting the damn thing would get it to do what I needed it to. When that didn't work, I moved toward the speaker, only to stub my toe on the couch three steps into my journey.

In a move that would've impressed a seasoned ballet dancer, I twirled around on my good foot while holding my other and landed on my back on the couch, which made a loud thump when all my weight came down on it.

"Fuck my life. And this couch."

As I lay there groaning and clutching my injured toe, a light flipped on, and I craned my head around in time to see Sophia turn off the speaker before putting her hands on her hips and glaring at me.

She really had the "if looks could kill" vibe down. I'd bet she could deter a mugger with the force of that look alone.

"Are you auditioning for the circus in here? Seriously, what the hell? It's the middle of the night."

I laboriously moved around on the couch until I was sitting up. "Sorry. I just got home, and it was like a comedy of errors on the path to disaster."

"Comedies are funny. Making so much noise it sounds like the apartment is being ransacked isn't funny."

"I said I was sorry."

She stared at me for a second longer before taking a deep breath. "Listen, I know what you do is none of my business, but I have a GPA to maintain. Also, marketing majors are a dime a dozen, so I have to stand out. And I'm assuming part of the deal with my brother is that you actually *pass* his classes. So maybe being out till all hours of the night isn't your best move."

Despite the fact that I was being lectured at, what she said gave me pause enough that I didn't immediately defend myself. While it had never occurred to me *not* to pass Brody's classes, Brody had never actually requested that I pass them, probably because he wasn't used to passing any himself. He'd made it clear that I had to go to class, but he never said I had to put any effort into it beyond that. His complete lack of concern for his future was almost enviable.

"Whatever," Sophia muttered as she spun to go back down the hall toward her room.

I must've taken too long to respond, and she'd taken my silence for the "screw you" I kind of wanted to say out loud because what the fuck?

"Wait," I called.

She stopped short and slowly turned around, as if she was doing me a big favor by listening to me. They must teach rich girls this shit in etiquette school.

"I wasn't out at a rave. I didn't stumble in wasted. I had to work tonight, I'm exhausted, and it was pitch-black when I came in. I was trying to be quiet, but I'm not the most graceful guy in the world. It won't happen again." After I thought about my last statement for a second, I amended it. "Well, it might, but I'll try to avoid it."

Even though I shouldn't give a shit what this girl thought about me, I felt myself waiting for her response like it mattered.

I couldn't figure out why it was important to me that she knew I wasn't some immature punk. Sure, we'd be living together, but I didn't have any intention of getting to know her. Not really. But it *was* important, and I watched her anxiously as I waited for her to reply.

"I didn't realize you had to work. I'll try to remember to leave a light on for you so you don't wake the whole neighborhood next time you come home."

It wasn't the most bountiful of olive branches, but I'd grown up with enough crazy sisters to know I'd better accept it for what it was—insulting wrapping paper with a small apology nestled inside.

"I'd appreciate that."

She nodded once at me before turning and going into the bedroom. I heard the snick of the lock on the door after she closed it. She clearly still hadn't ruled out the possibility of my being a homicidal lunatic.

That was okay. We'd get there. Or not.

SOPHIA

I'd lain in bed for what felt like hours after I'd given Drew a hard time. The truth was, I'd had a mini heart attack when all his noise had woken me up, and the fear had turned to anger when I'd seen him writhing around on the couch.

I'd immediately assumed he'd come home drunk, which was all I would've needed. This situation was messed up enough without having to share a small apartment for the foreseeable future with a reckless partier.

When he'd said that he'd been at work all night, guilt had

crept in and diffused my irritation. I really hated when that happened. Being angry was much easier than feeling bad.

I'd finally fallen asleep, but it seemed like my alarm went off minutes later. Of course, Drew's late-night interpretive dance in the dark had to happen when I had my earliest class of the semester the next morning.

I'd dragged myself through a shower and stopped to grab the biggest coffee I could before hauling ass to class. I hadn't remembered to reset the alarm with an earlier time that would accommodate my longer walk, but I still managed to make it to class before the professor.

I felt all kinds of discombobulated when I slid into a seat and dug through my bag for my laptop. As I struggled to make room on the small desk for my MacBook, my phone, and the coffee that I wished I could mainline into my body, I registered someone taking the seat next to me. Once I had everything settled, I looked over casually and then did a double take when I saw Emma sitting beside me.

"What are you doing here?"

"I have a class down the hall and I saw you walk by, so I thought I'd come say hey."

"Okay," I replied, drawing the word out in my confusion. "Hey."

"Hey." Emma held eye contact with me but didn't say anything more.

After a few seconds, I started to get weirded out. "Did you take an entire bottle of NoDoz again?"

"No. I was just trying to figure out who you are. Because you're not the Sophia I thought I knew."

I exhaled loudly and slumped in my chair. "I can't do"—I waved my hands in front of her—"whatever this is today. Just come direct."

She leaned closer to me like she was about to impart state secrets. "Why would you never tell your best friends how hot your brother is? It's like . . . girl code."

"It's really not."

"Well, it's something, and Gina and I feel some kind of way about it."

This conversation was a mental minefield I was not caffeinated enough to handle. Lying to my best friends in the sorority wasn't something I was keen on doing, but I couldn't trust them either. Emma would never intentionally betray my confidence, but she simply wasn't built to keep secrets. And I could *not* risk the truth getting back to Aamee. She'd burn Brody and me like we were Salem witches.

"He's my *brother*," I said, hoping that would explain it.

"Please," Emma said as she flipped a strand of her auburn hair over her shoulder. "Just because you're related doesn't mean you can't see what's right in front of you."

I want to be literally anywhere else right now.

Because, yeah, I could have objectively evaluated my brother's attractiveness. Was Brody hot? Sure, if you were into underachieving guys with Peter Pan Syndrome. But my sorority sisters were suckers for a boy with a pretty face, even if he didn't come highly recommended. And the fact that the guy she was really referring to wasn't even related to me was even worse because it meant I had to tread more carefully.

I'd ordinarily have had no qualms about remarking on the hotness that was Drew Nolan. From his long, lean frame, to his slightly lopsided smile that made him look like he was up to no good, to the way he at least seemed to be a decent person, there was a lot to remark on. But I couldn't resort to my usual girl talk about him. He wasn't some stranger I'd stumbled upon—even if they didn't know that.

So I had to keep my urge to gush about how sexy he was firmly within the confines of my inner monologue. And I couldn't have them sniffing around trying to hit on him either. So I did what anyone would do in my situation.

I panicked.

"He likes dick!" I blurted out loud enough to cause the entire room to abruptly stop what they were doing. I cleared my throat and whispered to a bug-eyed Emma, "He's *gay*."

Just then, I noticed my professor standing by the doorway, staring at me. My male professor . . . who had a husband at home. Fuck. My. Life.

Emma slid out of the chair. "I'm just gonna . . ." She motioned over her shoulder.

I nodded as she practically sprinted from the room. Dr. Cranston regained his composure and walked over to his desk, dropping his bag and some other items onto it.

"Okay, let's get started," he said. "Take out your copies of *Crime and Punishment*, which you should have completed by today. I want to review an important section on page two seventeen. Sophia, you seem to have a lot to say this morning. Would you read the first paragraph on that page that highlights the main character's abnormal behavior for us?"

I'd honestly thought the day couldn't have gotten any worse. Until I realized I'd forgotten my book.

Chapter Four

SOPHIA

I barely processed anything during class. I was too busy obsessing over whether I should address the gay elephant in the room. While my instinct was to run away, drop the class, and never return to the liberal arts building for the rest of my academic career, I couldn't leave with one of my favorite professors thinking I'd been gossiping about him. So I hung back while everyone filtered out at the end of class.

Dr. Cranston was classically handsome, with his styled dark hair and chiseled jaw. His intelligence and wit only enhanced his appeal, and I really hoped I hadn't decimated his opinion of me.

"Excuse me, Dr. Cranston? Could I speak to you for a second?"

He glanced up at me briefly before checking his watch. "I have another class, but I can spare a couple of minutes. What can I do for you?"

I opened and closed my mouth a few times, unsure of where to begin. Finally, I just let words fly out of my mouth and hoped they made sense.

"I'm sorry about what happened at the beginning of class. I wasn't talking about you."

He lifted one brow slightly.

"I know what I said was insensitive either way. Vulgar, really. But I promise it wasn't about you. My friend was... God, this is an awkward conversation." I muttered the last words as I wiped my hand down my face.

Somehow my honesty pulled a laugh from him, and the sound broke the tension.

"It's really okay, Sophia. I was just a little...thrown by your outburst. But it's reassuring to know that you at least weren't talking about me."

"No, I know. I just didn't want you to think I was gossiping about you behind your back. I'm a much more up-front gossiper." I smiled.

"Good to know. Though I have to say, it did sound like you were gossiping about *someone*. And depending on his circumstances, they may not want that information shared with a room full of undergrads."

"It's not a secret." *It's not even true.* "My friend was interested in my brother, and I had to make it clear why she didn't have a shot with him."

"Ah," he said, his smile wide. "Well, I think his sexual orientation is abundantly clear to everyone now. I'm glad he has you to fight off the female populace for him."

"I don't think he's nearly as glad as he should be, but I'll let him know you said he should be more grateful."

He gathered up his things. "Enjoy your weekend, and I'll see you next week."

"You too, and I'll be here."

I watched Dr. Cranston walk out the door, and as soon as he was out of sight, I dropped my hands onto the desk and bent over, taking deep breaths through my nose and releasing them through my mouth, as if I was staving off an anxiety attack.

Where's a paper bag when I need one?

When I'd finally collected myself, I made my way out of the building and into the sunshine, thankful for its warmth. I didn't have a class for another hour and a half, so my plan was to grab a snack and hang out in the quad to enjoy the weather.

There was nothing I loved more than being outside on beautiful days, and Lazarus University was the perfect place to enjoy the sunshine that made the well-manicured lawns gleam and the flowers bloom even wider. As I walked down the maze of walkways that joined the Gothic-style buildings, I dodged clusters of students talking about who knew what, but their voices provided a steady soundtrack to my journey across campus.

I hiked my bag up higher on my shoulder before heading in the direction of the on-campus coffee shop called Rise and Grind. I don't think I made it twenty feet before I heard my name being called.

By the time I located the direction the voice was coming from, Carter had already jogged up beside me.

"Hey," he said. "I meant to text you, but football's been crazy. How'd everything go with Aamee?"

He fell into step beside me as I spoke. "Oh, it went awesome. Up until she held some kind of pagan ritual and kicked me out of the sorority house."

That caused him to stop suddenly. "Wait, are you fucking serious? She kicked you out because I fell asleep? She can't really do that, can she?"

"Apparently her Royal Highness can do whatever she damn well pleases. But don't worry. I plan to scour the sorority's code of conduct and find a way back in." I hadn't really thought of doing that up until the words had left my mouth, but as I processed them, I felt the conviction in them. There had to be a loophole or a rule somewhere that would get me back into the house.

"Man, she's a savage. I didn't think she'd be that extreme."

"Eh, I kinda did. She's been shaking her milkshake in your direction for four years in an attempt to bring you to her yard. I knew she'd be pissed."

Carter looked thoughtful for a moment. "That's probably the least sexy reference to that song I've ever heard."

"Being the least sexy is kind of a hobby of mine."

He laughed and bumped his shoulder against mine. "Yeah right, princess."

My face scrunched up. "Don't call me that. I hate nicknames."

I heard a throat clear behind us. "Is that so, Fifi?"

Carter and I whirled around to see Aamee standing behind us. I had no idea how long she'd been standing there, but judging from the smug smile on her face, I doubted she'd heard much. She'd have been plotting how to make my death look like an accident if she'd heard me tell Carter about her milkshake.

"Fifi?" Carter asked.

"Say it again and you can find a new psych tutor." Then I turned my attention to the evil spawn masquerading as a sorority president. "Aamee, to what do I owe the pleasure?" My voice was saccharine and my smile so broad, I could've been portraying the Joker.

Lazarus's campus wasn't enormous, but it was big enough that the odds were against my running into the two people who caused my eviction. Fate seemed to be having a great time at my expense lately.

Aamee waved her phone in front of me and said, "I just wanted to come check in on the newest internet sensation."

"What the hell are you talking about?" Had she been huffing glue? Surely there was a Zeta Eta Chi bylaw against that.

"You're all over Instagram saying your English professor likes dick. I'm surprised at you, Sophia. You always seemed more open-minded and . . . proper than that."

It took a few seconds for her words to fully sink in, but when they did, I would've sworn my heart actually dropped out of my body. "I didn't say that."

"Oh, I think you did. I have the video to prove it."

"That's not at all what happened." And why the hell was someone filming me anyway? Though I knew the answer. Some students were too lazy to take notes and filmed the classes instead. I'd likely been caught on film accidentally.

"It kinda looked like what happened," Carter added.

I shot my gaze to him. "You saw it too! Why didn't you tell me?"

"I meant to. It's how I knew where you were. Then I got distracted."

"Jesus Christ," I muttered. "I wasn't talking about Dr. Cranston. I just had bad timing."

Aamee took a step closer to me. "Whoever you were talking about, you didn't sound as accepting as I'd expect a Zeta Eta Chi sister to be. I'm not sure we have any room for bigots in our house."

The heart I thought I'd lost moments ago began pumping blood furiously throughout my body as anger took over. Pointing a finger at Aamee, I warned, "You better not twist this into something it's not. I was talking to Emma. She'll vouch for me. I wasn't saying it to be negative. I was merely stating a fact."

She scoffed. "Of course your little lapdog would vouch for you. But the video doesn't lie."

I wanted to yell at her that of course the video fucking lied because I'd lied in the video about Brody. Or Drew. Or ... Whoever.

"I swear to whatever demonic god you worship that if you try to kick me out over this, I'll—" I caught myself before I said something that would actually *warrant* me being kicked out of my sorority.

"You'll what?" she asked.

"I'll fight you tooth and nail on it," I said, more calmly this time. "You're letting your personal feelings toward me influence your actions as president. It's unfair and an abuse of your position."

"So says you."

"You're being ridiculous. My saying someone is gay isn't even offensive."

"It is when you say it like it's a disease. And when you're gossiping about a professor."

"I already told you I wasn't talking about Dr. Cranston." I'd never wanted to hit someone as badly as I did in that moment. She was being deliberately obtuse, twisting the narrative to fit the plot she'd already created.

She cocked her hip and rested her hand on it. "Then who were you talking about?"

"How is that any of your business?"

"I doubt it was the business of your English class either, but it didn't stop you from announcing it to them."

"Oh really? Did you hear a name mentioned on that video?"

"I should sell tickets to this," Carter interjected. "How would you girls feel about wrestling in pudding?"

I looked at him, bewildered. "Why are you still here?"

"Why would I leave? This is awesome."

"Yeah, well, I'm done entertaining idiots today." I pointed to Aamee's phone. "Do your worst with that. You'll be laughed out of the room."

To emphasize a confidence I didn't feel, I whirled around with purpose and walked directly into a firm chest. Two hands shot out to grab me and keep me from losing my balance. It wasn't the exit I'd pictured, but I could work with it.

"Excuse me," I said as I started to move around the person I'd bumped into. Before I made it a full step, I let my eyes drift up to see who it was. "What even *is* my life right now?"

"Hey, Sis," Drew said. "Funny seeing you here."

"Hilarious." I eyed the cast of characters surrounding me. Each of them represented how terribly off course my life had drifted. When had my entire existence become a Shakespearean tragedy?

"Hey, Brody," Aamee said, practically purring. It was gross.

"Oh, uh . . . hey. Gina, right?"

Aamee's face looked like she'd just sucked on a lemon. Score one for Drew. I didn't know if he'd intentionally dissed her or if it had been a legitimate mistake, and I didn't care.

"It's Aamee," she corrected.

"She spells it with two *a*'s and two *e*'s. Wild, right?" Carter explained before extending his hand. "How's it going, man? I'm Carter."

Drew accepted the handshake. "Brody. Sophia's older brother."

Carter looked back and forth between Drew and me. "I can see the resemblance."

I looked at him like he'd grown an extra head.

"We get that a lot," Drew said.

"I don't think you look anything alike. You could be a model, Brody." Aamee moved closer to him and lifted her hand as if she was about to rub it down his arm. Or some other body part.

"Oh my God, stop flirting with him. He's the one I was talking about in the video."

Aamee jerked back and then froze in place, clearly surprised.

Drew, who still had his arm around me, turned his head so he could look down at me. "You were talking about me on video?" He looked nervous, which made me realize he was worried I'd been talking about his real identity.

I opened my mouth to say something that would reassure him, but Carter beat me to the punch. "Huh. Never would've guessed. That's cool, though. I'm all about equal rights and shit."

"Um, thanks?" Poor Drew looked so lost, and I felt bad that I'd made his life more difficult.

"You're really gay?" Aamee blurted out.

Drew's head recoiled a bit. "I am?"

I elbowed him slightly.

"I mean, I am. Yes. Have been for a while now."

Jesus Christ.

Aamee looked like she was ready to breathe fire. Not only had she lost her shot with my "brother," but the video that she thought would be my undoing was useless.

Game, set, match, bitch.

"Sophia never mentioned she had a brother. What year are you?" Carter asked.

Drew looked a little lost for a second before he fell back into his role. "Yeah, she doesn't like to mention me because I'm so much better at everything than she is. Jealous little thing. I'm a senior. A very *senior* senior."

"He should be graduated and gainfully employed," I corrected. It was what I would've said to Brody, and Drew *had* just called me jealous, so he had it coming. Though I had about three dozen shots coming if we were keeping score. Outing a straight man had to put me pretty far in the hole.

"I feel ya, man," Carter said. "Thank God for redshirting. What's your major?"

"Business."

"I'm a communications major."

Drew nodded like Carter had announced he was reversing climate change. "Very cool. We always need people who know how to talk."

The look Carter gave Drew was full of admiration. As if someone finally *got it.* "Real shit, man. No one talks anymore. It's all about Facebook and Snapchat and all that bullshit. I'm going to bring conversation back to communicating."

"Right on, man," Drew said before moving into some bro backslapping thing with Carter. Maybe Drew *was* gay. He'd certainly established a bromance pretty damn fast.

"Okay, well, I'm going to go . . . anywhere else," I said. "See you guys around. Unfortunately."

"Are we still on for our study date Monday?" Carter asked me.

"Yeah, sure." My voice sounded resigned, but the truth was, I didn't mind helping Carter. I guess, deep down, I had a fondness for nice guys with no aspirations. "We should probably meet at the library, though."

"Ugh, I hate the library," Carter complained. "Librarians creep me out."

"Librarians?" I held up my hand. "Forget it. I don't want to know."

"I do," Drew supplied.

Carter opened his mouth to explain, but I cut him off. "Library. Six. Be there."

"I don't wanna," Carter whined. "Come to my place instead."

"No. I told you last time I was never coming back over there. It smells like feet and semen."

"Ew," Aamee murmured. At least we agreed on something.

"Come to my place," Drew said. "Well, *our* place now."

"Wow, really? You sure?" Carter asked.

"Totally. You can tell me about your librarian-phobia."

Carter shivered. "It's the stuff of nightmares. But you're on. Soph, can you text me the address?"

"Sure." I had to push the word out through gritted teeth.

The last thing I needed was people further infiltrating the cocoon of lies we were spinning.

Chapter Five

DREW

After I left Sophia and the others, I had to book it to my next class. I'd probably get an earful from Sophia later. She hadn't looked too thrilled that I'd invited Carter over to our place, but I hadn't even thought about it at the time.

My mom had always told me I had the gift of gab. It was what made me a great bartender. Unfortunately, she'd also told me that my mouth would get me into trouble one day. She was probably equally right about that. Good thing Sophia's mouth had gotten her into trouble today too. Maybe she'd go easy on me.

I entered the room my—well, *Brody's*—business ethics class was in and nodded to a few people who looked my way. I took a seat near the front, like I always did, because I was here to learn something.

Bartending had been a gig I'd kind of fallen into, but I had to admit, it suited me. I was good with people, and I was responsible and competent enough to handle running a business. All that was missing was knowing *how* to run a business.

The situation with Brody had been a giant stroke of luck. Getting to take some business courses would take me one step closer to opening my own bar one day. And I was going to take full advantage of the opportunity, whether I had to pretend to be gay or someone else entirely. Or both.

I didn't come from a family of overachievers. My parents' definition of success was to be able to stock up on groceries and have enough left over to buy themselves cigarettes. They weren't bad people, but they never supported us the way they should have. They never pushed me or my siblings to be better, to work harder, to achieve more, to *be* something. It was why I didn't talk to them much anymore.

The professor, Dr. Sherman, came in shortly after me and started class. I wrote down almost everything she said. A lot of people typed their notes on laptops. Brody had left me his MacBook, but I wasn't quick enough at typing. I was an old-school guy in a new-school world. So pen and paper it was for me.

When the professor asked questions, I did my best to participate when I could. There was no denying I was missing some background information, having never taken any of the intro courses, but I was getting by. It required a bit more research on my part, but that was okay.

Toward the end of class, Dr. Sherman set her papers aside, leaned back against her desk, and crossed her arms over her chest.

"As we discussed at the beginning of the semester when I reviewed the syllabus, there is a group component in the requirements of this class. Now that we have sufficient background into the ethics of business, you're ready to delve into that group project. I will allow you to choose your groups, but be sure to choose wisely. It is a team effort and a team grade.

"Once you've put yourselves into groups of four, you'll peruse the cases I've posted online, choose one, and as a group, you'll tackle the case questions that accompany it. You'll present your findings during the last week of classes. The format as well as an example are provided for you on Blackboard. Any questions?"

When no one spoke up, Dr. Sherman smiled. "All right. Once you've signed up for a case and worked out the logistics of working with your group, you're free to go."

Most of the other students jumped up and got into groups with their friends. It all happened quickly, and it fascinated me how people were typically drawn to others like them. It was the most homogeneous grouping process I'd ever seen—not that I'd seen very many.

But then there were the outliers. The wallflowers, the mutes, the geeks, and the rebels who were too cool for group work—sort of like a collegiate *Breakfast Club*. I let my eyes drift over them for a few seconds before I got up from my seat and approached a pretty girl with thick-framed brown glasses and curly hair. She looked like she'd rather burn her bra than pair up with any of the giggling girls in her vicinity. I had to have her in my group.

"Hi. I'm Brody. Can I be in your group?"

She looked around. "I don't have a group."

"Can we start one?"

"Are you in a frat?" she asked.

"Nope."

"Do you play a sport for the school?"

"Uh-uh."

"Can you read above a seventh-grade level?"

"Sure can."

She shrugged. "Looks like we're starting a group."

"Sweet. Come on, he's next," I said as I pointed at a guy in a button-down shirt and khaki pants. He always participated in discussions, and I'd bet my left nut that he'd already read all the cases. He was looking around anxiously, clearly too shy to approach anyone.

The girl, whose name I hadn't gotten yet, looked at me curiously but gathered her things and followed me over to him.

"Hey, wanna join our group?" I asked him.

He stood up quickly, almost causing his chair to fall backward. "Me? I mean, yes, uh, yes. Absolutely."

I extended a hand toward him. "I'm Brody."

"Toby," he replied as he took my hand.

"Why didn't you offer to shake my hand?" Mystery Girl asked me.

"Because you looked like you were seconds away from gutting me where I stood."

She seemed pleased with this answer. "I'm Aniyah."

"It's great to meet you both," Toby said, smiling wide. "I guess we need to find one more."

I scanned the room and zeroed in on a guy in the corner who was hunkered down in his seat and appeared to be sleeping. I wasn't buying it. Granted, I hadn't seen him take a single note since I'd been in the class, but the guy always handed in his assignments on time, and Dr. Sherman didn't seem the type to let someone get away with dozing through class. I had a good feeling about him, and I was used to trusting my gut.

"Him."

Aniyah and Toby looked at where I was pointing. "Really?"

Aniyah asked. "Him?"

"Trust me."

"Yes, because I just love trusting complete strangers," Aniyah muttered, but she and Toby followed me over to where the guy was sitting.

"Need a group?" I asked him.

He wore a knit beanie that was pulled down almost to his eyebrows, but I could still see some of his shaggy blond hair under it. He opened his eyes and let them rove over our group before sighing deeply in what sounded like defeat. "I guess."

"Great. I'm Brody, this is Aniyah, and that's Toby."

"You can call me Slayer."

"Nope. That's not going to work for me," Aniyah said.

A small smile quirked "Slayer's" lips before he pressed them back into a firm line. "Dragon?"

Aniyah gave him an annoyed look.

"Warlord?"

Aniyah looked at me. "There's got to be someone else. *Anyone* else."

"Fine, fine, my name's Xander," he conceded.

"Welcome to the group, Xander," I said. I clapped my hands together and asked, "Has anyone looked through the cases yet?"

Toby didn't disappoint. "I have. And I did a little preliminary research to see which might yield the most information."

"And which would that be?" I asked.

"The Polaski Mine. It's a gold and copper mine that would bring in a lot of jobs and could financially rejuvenate an area. But it's within the limits of a city, so it would necessitate the relocation of houses, schools, and businesses. Not to mention it'd be a freaking mine in the middle of a city. There's a lot to consider, and I think it would be interesting to dissect."

"Any objections?" I asked.

"Nah, that would've been my first choice too," Xander said. "Though the Chiquita Banana case also looked cool."

Aniyah's eyes widened as she looked at Xander like he was an alien. She clearly hadn't expected that he'd have looked into the cases already. But that had been something I'd been banking on. He presented as a slacker, but I bet Xander had some serious brainpower under that beanie. The kind that didn't require note taking.

I had a great feeling about this group.

Chapter Six

DREW

Sophia and I had been living together for over a week, and it was different from anything I'd ever experienced. I would've thought growing up with three sisters would've prepared me for all the makeup and lotions and body sprays and perfumes and *hair*—so much hair!—in the bathroom, but I'd either forgotten about how...female everything was, or I'd blocked it out like some sort of estrogen-fueled PTSD. I was suddenly getting flashbacks of disposable razors and leave-in conditioner.

Every time I went into our bathroom to shave or take a shower, more of Sophia's beauty products seemed to have appeared on the sink, which was already struggling for space in the tiny bathroom. Though I guess I was partially to blame for her things ending up on the sink because I only kept two of my own items out—deodorant and my toothpaste. Even my toothbrush was put away in the medicine cabinet. No way I'd risk getting a long dark hair stuck to it.

I slid some of the bottles toward the back of the sink

against the wall like I'd done the past few days, knowing damn well they'd return to some other random spot. They were like drunk college kids who slept wherever they happened to land.

"Why do you have charcoal in the bathroom?" I called.

"Huh?"

Sophia had been in the kitchen, but she suddenly materialized in the bathroom doorway.

"This." I held up a gray tube. "It says it has charcoal in it."

"It's a charcoal mask," she said, like the answer was the most obvious thing in the world.

"You put this on your face?"

"Yeah, it cleans out your pores and gets all the gook out."

"That's disgusting." I noticed a hair stuck under the lid. "Have you tried not putting gook *on* your face? Maybe you wouldn't have to get it all out."

She'd already grabbed the container and was opening it. "That's not how it works. And don't knock it till you try it. It's so satisfying when you peel it off. You'll see."

If she thought I was putting that black shit on my face, she had another thing coming. "I'm not putting that on my face."

"You'll feel like a new man," she said, already dabbing a little on her finger. "You can thank me later."

Before I could make a move to stop her, her hands were on my face.

"What the hell? I didn't consent to this!"

"Stop being a baby," she said, still applying the cold paste to my skin. At least I had some facial hair that Sophia had to work around as she applied it.

"Fine, but while it…does whatever this does, can we move some of this stuff off the counter? Like whatever you don't use every day or something?"

She looked confused. "I use all of it."

"You put this shit on your face every day?" I pointed to the gray plaster of paris she was smoothing over my flesh.

"Well, not *every* day, but enough that I don't want to put it away."

I was tempted to point out that my toothbrush, which I used multiple times a day, was never left out, but it was a pointless argument and I knew it. "So how long do I need to keep this on?"

"Twenty minutes. I've got class in a half hour, so I'm leaving in a few minutes, but just wash it off with warm water, towel dry, and put this on." She held up some sort of intense moisture serum and then scooted me out of the bathroom so she could get ready for class.

I shuffled over to the couch, plopped down, and got comfortable. I hadn't realized I'd fallen asleep until a knock at the door woke me up.

"Coming," I called, heading to the door. I pulled it open to see Emma standing on the other side.

"So it's true, then?" She sounded sad, but I had no idea why.

"Um, what's true?"

"The whole *gay* thing." She whispered the word *gay* like some sort of homophobic government agency had tapped the apartment and she didn't want me to get waterboarded until I spilled all the secrets of the LGBTQ community. "I've been wondering about it since Soph told me, but I refused to believe it. Maybe it was wishful thinking." She sighed and gave me a shy smile, probably feeling embarrassed by her admission.

"Wait, how do you know it's true?"

"What do you mean?"

"Do I give off like a gay vibe or something?" I was suddenly very concerned about it. I know had to pretend I was gay, but I *wasn't* gay. Until now, I'd never had someone look at me and assume that I liked men.

She brought a finger up slowly to point at me. "You're in a charcoal face mask."

"Shit." I rubbed a hand over my face, feeling where Sophia had mummified it before she'd left. I would kill her if this didn't come off. "I actually don't usually do these, but Sophia made me put it on before she left for class, which was like"—I looked at my watch—"an hour ago."

"That's cute. Did you let her do that when you were little? Like practice her makeup skills and stuff?" I could practically see the lightbulb appear over her head. "Oh my God, is that why you're gay?"

"What? No!" Was this how she thought sexual orientation was determined? "I just like men. That's all." I'm not sure how my life had become . . . whatever this was. "Are you staying or going? I need to get this stuff off my face before it eats away at my flesh."

SOPHIA

I'd been sitting in psychology class for less than twenty minutes when my head started pounding and my stomach began to twist. "Are you okay?" Carter asked when my insides made a noise that sounded like a lion sitting down to devour its recent kill.

Since there was no pretending it didn't come from me, I said, "Yeah, just hungry."

I knew that wasn't it. I'd eaten a bagel and cream cheese an hour ago, and the thought of food made my stomach turn in a way that made me wonder if I'd ever have an appetite again. I swallowed hard, took a small sip from my water bottle, and silently prayed to the vomit gods that they'd find someone else to punish today.

Not only did I absolutely *not* want to get sick in front of Carter and the other twenty or so people in our class, but I didn't want to be out of commission in the middle of the semester. I *couldn't* be out of commission. I had a GPA to maintain, and a stomach bug—or whatever this was—might mean time away from class and falling behind in my work.

"You want some of my protein bar?" He was already reaching into his backpack to pull out a chocolate peanut butter bar.

"I'm really okay," I said, but my stomach still said differently.

It was gurgling and cramping, and I knew if I didn't get the hell out of here soon, whatever was inside me would be coming out. I didn't even get a chance to say where I was going before I jumped out of my seat, grabbed my belongings, and bolted to the nearest bathroom.

Not much satisfaction came from vomiting in a public restroom. Even though I should have felt some sort of relief, the thought of having my face dangerously close to a seat where countless people had placed their asses was enough to make me want to throw up all over again.

I didn't leave the bathroom until I was certain I had nothing left in my stomach, and by the time I made it back to the apartment, I felt like my body had rid itself of every ounce of fluid it had. I was desperate to replenish it.

Opening the fridge to grab a bottle of water, I couldn't have been more thankful that Drew was working this afternoon. The last thing I needed was for him to see me like this. God only knew how much worse this would get before it got better.

Already sure I had a fever, I couldn't think of anything other than my bed. I couldn't even bring myself to text Carter and ask him to tell the professor I'd left because of a sudden illness. Sophia Mason wasn't someone who left class abruptly without an excuse.

Though evidently I was.

I don't even remember falling asleep, but I must have. I woke up two and a half hours later with a splitting headache. Other than that, I felt much better. I was at least sixty percent. And that was like fifty percent better than I'd felt when I'd left class.

I took a long drink of water, feeling the liquid make its way through my body and hydrate me almost immediately. I just needed to brush my teeth and take a shower, and I'd probably be up another five percent.

I was still a little dizzy as I made my way out of my room, or *Brody's* room, toward the bathroom. Stopping at the hall closet, I grabbed a clean towel before pushing open the bathroom door the rest of the way.

But the thought of a hot shower was squashed as soon as I saw Drew standing in front of the toilet.

"Oh my God!" I quickly backed out of the bathroom and shielded my eyes like I'd witnessed a murder and was scared I'd be killed if I'd been caught watching it. "Why didn't you shut the door?" I yelled once I was safely outside.

"I didn't know you were home."

I heard the toilet flush, the sink turn on, and a few

moments later, the door swung open.

Don't look at his... Jesus, look up.

What the hell was wrong with me? It was like I half expected his penis to still be out when he exited the bathroom.

"Did you wash your hands?" was the only thing I could come up with.

"Of course I washed my hands. I'm potty trained."

"Oh, um... I'm sick." I pushed past him, and once I was inside, I locked the door and turned on the shower.

What the hell had my life become?

DREW

To say I felt awkward about what had happened was an understatement. It wasn't that I cared that Sophia saw me peeing. She'd only seen me from behind, so there wasn't much to see anyway, but her response to it was causing me anxiety. And I wasn't an anxious person. She clearly wasn't feeling well, and I probably hadn't helped.

She was in the shower close to forty-five minutes when I finally got up the nerve to knock and ask if she was okay.

"Yes" came her terse response.

"Okay, just checking. Is there anything I can get you?"

"No."

I was silent for a moment. "Is there still hot water left?" Did that make me sound selfish? I knew Brody's hot water didn't last long, so it surprised me she was still in there. "I'm not asking for myself," I clarified. "I just wanted to see if you were comfortable or..."

I needed to stop talking. There wasn't anything I could do,

and my questions were probably hurting more than helping.

"I'll be out soon," she said, and we both left it at that.

About ten minutes later, she came out of the bathroom wearing sweatpants and an oversize Zeta Eta Chi T-shirt.

From the couch, I could see Sophia walk over to the refrigerator and pull out some Gatorade. Then she opened a pill bottle, popped a few into her mouth, and swallowed them down with a drink. It was obvious, at least to me, that we were intentionally trying to avoid eye contact.

"Don't feel weird about what happened," I said.

"I don't."

Unconvinced, I nodded, even though I'm sure she couldn't see me.

"Do *you* feel weird?" she asked.

"Not really. I guess just a little bad that you seem so disturbed by it." I almost laughed.

"I didn't see your . . . " Now she was facing me, one finger gesturing toward my lap before she seemed to realize it only made the situation more awkward to point to my dick and dropped her hand. "Thingy."

"The anatomical terminology is 'enormous wang,'" I said, hoping to make her laugh.

She smiled, but it seemed to be more out of embarrassment. "Since I didn't see it, I can neither confirm nor deny the size of it."

"Guess you'll just have to take my word for it, then."

She rounded the small bar in the kitchen and came over to sit in the chair next to the couch. "I was thinking it might be a good idea to establish some ground rules for living together."

I'd heard worse ideas. "What'd you have in mind?"

"Well, for starters, probably closing and locking doors if

you don't want someone coming in."

"I wasn't the one who minded you coming in," I said, and she gave me a look that was somehow both cute and chastising. "Okay, so I'll make sure to close and lock the bathroom door when I'm in there."

"Thank you."

"It just feels cramped sometimes with all of the lotions and things all over the place," I teased.

"Hey, there aren't *that* many in there."

"I counted no fewer than sixteen the other day."

"You counted them?"

She sounded incredulous, but I couldn't be sure if it was because she didn't believe I'd counted them or because the number sounded so high.

"You don't need all those, you know?" I wasn't trying to tell her how to live, though I knew it probably sounded like that. "I just mean you look nice without all the makeup and face creams and stuff."

She was beautiful, really. A smooth complexion, skin that looked soft and smelled like citrus and vanilla. I'd seem like a real psycho if I said any of those things, so I kept it simple.

When she gave me a small smile, some of the tension seemed to evaporate. "Thanks."

"You could probably narrow it down to ten or eleven and that would be plenty," I joked.

"Noted," she said. "Anything else?"

"Uh-uh, it's your turn." There was no way I was getting myself in trouble by listing all the things she did to annoy me, even if that list was a short one.

"You leave all your half-filled glasses of water around. I feel like I'm living with that girl from the movie *Signs*."

"Well, you'll thank me if aliens ever attack."

Laughing, she said, "Shut up."

"Okay, I promise to try to put my dishes away if you promise to stop drinking and eating everything I bring into the apartment without asking."

She looked taken aback. "I don't eat and drink *everything*."

I raised my eyebrows. She knew as well as I did that was exactly what she did.

"At the sorority house, we all chipped in equal amounts and we'd take turns stocking up on certain things."

"Then maybe you should do more stocking up. Because right now, it's like living with a teenage boy minus the bad hygiene."

"That's disgusting."

"So is the tuna you made the other day that's still sitting in a bowl in the fridge uncovered."

"Hey! I thought we were taking turns."

I chuckled. "Sorry."

"Okay, last one and then we'll be even."

I nodded.

"You need to stop walking around without a shirt in the morning."

I hated wearing clothing at home but was forced to at least wear pants because I was cohabitating with a female. I looked down at myself quickly before returning my gaze to her.

"I am wearing clothes."

She breathed deeply and then let out a long sigh, her eyes avoiding mine for a moment before she looked back up at me.

"Are you really gonna make me say it?"

"I honestly have no idea what you're about to say, so yes."

"It's because you're sexy, okay? You're hot. You have abs

and broad shoulders"—she gestured around my body—"and a muscular chest. I shouldn't be looking at you like I do or thinking the things I'm thinking. You're supposed to be my brother. My very *gay* brother. So can you please just keep on as much clothing as possible?"

She let all of that out in what seemed like one gigantic breath. When she was done, she inhaled loudly again, like she was trying to extract all the oxygen out of the room at once.

"I guess I can do that," I said.

But hearing Sophia admit she found me attractive didn't make me want to put clothes on. It made me want to take more off.

Chapter Seven

DREW

I'd been at the library for over two hours, and my eyes were beginning to blur. When I'd written—literally by hand—my paper a few nights ago, the words had flowed fairly easily. So easily, in fact, that my handwriting appeared barely legible now that I was forced to read it back to myself.

Typing on Brody's laptop at home had been taking forever, so I thought coming to the library and using a desktop like I had in high school would make the process quicker. I was wrong. I'd been typing for well over an hour but only had a few pages done.

Who the hell wanted to read ten pages from every student in class, anyway? Teachers were just as crazy as I remembered them being in high school.

I was pecking at the keys, my head bouncing back and forth from the page to the keyboard, when someone took a seat beside me.

"You look like my grandmother trying to learn to text."

I recognized the voice but didn't look over, afraid of losing my place. I did smile, though. When I finished typing the sentence I was on, I settled back against the chair and brought a hand to the back of my neck to massage it a little.

"I've never been compared to somebody's grandmother before."

"Glad I could be the one to take your grandmother virginity," Sophia said.

"That sounds . . . Don't ever say that, okay?"

She laughed. "Seriously though, why are you typing like that?"

"Because I suck at typing. It was an elective in high school, but I never thought I'd use it, so I took things like transportation technology and art and stuff like that. Add it to the list of poor choices I've made in my life."

Sophia laughed again, scooted closer, and leaned down to look at my notebook. "Who wrote this?"

Strange question. "Me."

"Do you speak whatever language this is in, because I'm pretty sure it'd be easier to decipher cave drawings than read your handwriting."

"I'm starting to think the same thing. I've been at this for hours, and I've barely made a dent in it."

She was still looking at the paper, bringing her face closer to the page and then away again like she was trying to focus a camera lens so the image wasn't blurry.

"I don't think I've ever known anyone who's handwritten a paper before they typed it."

I knew she was teasing me, but the truth was, I wasn't the typical student in more ways than one, and I seemed to be constantly reminded of it. The only thing I could do was keep plugging away however I knew how and hope for the best.

"Scooch over," she said, patting my arm as she studied the notebook and screen.

"What? Why?"

"Because watching you try to type might be more painful for me than it is for you."

I shifted over into the next seat. "I highly doubt that."

"Does this say 'blood'?" She pointed to a word that even took me longer than it should have to decipher.

"'Greed.' I think."

"You *think*?"

"It's a business paper. Greed definitely makes more sense than blood."

She finished out the sentence and then handed me the notebook. "I'll type this for you, but you're going to have to dictate it for me if you want me to finish it before the semester's over."

My eyes had to have shown my relief. "Seriously? That'd be awesome! This would've taken me all night. You're the best!"

Without giving it a second thought, I reached over and wrapped Sophia up in a huge hug. Then, when I evidently didn't think that was enough, I kissed her on the cheek.

"Aww, that's sweet," I heard someone say from behind us.

I turned to see Emma walking toward us with Gina and a girl I didn't recognize. Her large front teeth were gleaming with a smile so wide, she reminded me of a beaver who'd just eaten a bag of shrooms.

"You guys are so cute," Emma said. "My brother would never kiss me in public."

"Well, I wish mine wouldn't either," Sophia said through gritted teeth.

"Ignore her. She likes to pretend she's not related to me,"

I explained. I wasn't sure why I liked getting under her skin so much, but there was a certain thrill to it.

She rolled her eyes and sighed, probably knowing I'd just continue if she responded.

The other three girls laughed.

"Sorry, I'm Sophia's brother," I said to the new girl. "Brody," I added almost as an afterthought. It still felt strange to say the name aloud or respond to it, and I figured no amount of practice would change that.

"Macy." She extended her hand to me with a smile as she shifted her books from one arm to the other. "Sophia didn't tell me she had a brother."

This seemed to be a common theme.

"Are you older or younger?" she asked.

"Older. I'm a senior," I said proudly.

"A second-year senior," Sophia said.

Macy didn't even seem to realize Sophia had spoken. Her brown eyes were still on me, and I'd noticed her hand was still in mine.

"Why didn't you tell me you had such a cute big brother?" Macy asked, but she hadn't bothered to divert her attention from me.

"Because he's her big *gay* brother," Emma said. "None of us has a shot with him."

This was going to be a long-ass year if people kept bringing this shit up. Couldn't she have at least made me bi?

"Right," I said sadly. "I'm gay. Super gay."

None of the girls responded, and the silence was awkward…until Sophia said, "You should wear a rainbow cape with a giant G."

Maybe after all this was over, I'd have her make me one.

I'd certainly earned it.

SOPHIA

Once Emma, Gina, and Macy had left, I went back to typing Drew's paper. Or *Brody's* paper. Whatever.

"Are we allowed to eat in here?" he asked.

"They've never said anything to me. I usually bring something if I plan to be here for a while."

"Okay, good. I'm starving." He dug through his bag and pulled out a cardboard box with two slices of cold pizza in it.

"Are you serious?"

He took a bite and asked through a mouthful, "Want some?"

I shook my head slowly. "How long have you had that in there?"

He shrugged. "A few days." When my eyes widened, he said, "I'm kidding. I threw it in my bag right before I came here. I had an ice pack in there with it."

"Don't you ever get sick of pizza?" I'd noticed he'd eaten it almost every day this week. Sometimes for breakfast, lunch, and dinner on the same day.

"Nope. Not Marco's. Have you tried it?"

"No, but they should give you some kind of discount with the amount of money you spend in that place."

He swallowed his bite and laughed. "Or a job. They offered me one the other day because I already know everyone who works there and most of their menu."

"That's . . ." I didn't exactly know what to call it, so I went with "impressive," though that sounded more complimentary than what I'd been going for.

"Thanks. So is that Macy girl in your sorority?"

"Yes." I typed a few more sentences. "You can't hit on her."

"I wasn't asking because I was interested in her. Just wondering if she's Aamee's friend or yours."

"Aamee doesn't have friends. She has minions who follow her around like a bunch of ducklings scared to cross a street alone."

"Interesting."

"Interesting?" I stopped typing and turned to him. "Did you forget you're supposed to be dictating your paper to me?"

"Sorry. I got sidetracked."

"By what?"

"I was thinking about how to get Aamee back. Have you come up with anything? Asked any of the other girls in the house?"

There was no getting back at her, at least not that I could think of. I didn't have a house I could kick her out of, so as far as I was concerned, I'd just have to sit this out until next year, when I could move back in.

I hoped with the start of a new year and Aamee graduated, we could all agree to live in peace.

"My hands are tied, Drew."

"No way. There's gotta be something you can do. When my buddy stole my girlfriend in eleventh grade, I filled his whole car with those little Styrofoam pieces that come in packages." He looked like that was a fond memory, which was surprising considering the transgression he was retaliating against.

"I don't think filling her car with Styrofoam is the answer."

"Maybe not. But it would be funny as hell."

I shook my head, but I couldn't deny I found the image

funny. It was a shame I couldn't do something like that, if only for the entertainment value alone.

"Anything I do will only make things worse. Aamee's the president."

"So?"

I knew this was his first time in a college setting, but the implications of Aamee being president seemed pretty clear to me. "So *what*?"

"So what if she *wasn't* president?"

Chapter Eight

SOPHIA

"But she *is* president. And she will be until she graduates in May," I said. This was a pointless conversation because there was no way to go back in time and campaign for someone who wasn't a power-hungry monster who ruled with estrogen and an iron fist. "I just wish someone had opposed her last year. They probably would've won."

Drew stood abruptly and began walking around pensively, like he was more frustrated than I was at the whole situation. I figured most of his emotion had more to do with being bored in a library while I typed and less to do with his actual concern for me getting back into the house. Unless...

"Wait," I said. "You want me to move back into the sorority house so you'd get Brody's room back."

Not that I wouldn't understand that. Having his bachelor pad invaded by a pretend younger sister who told everyone he was gay had to be cramping his style. It wasn't the college experience he'd probably hoped for when he'd agreed to switch lives with my brother.

"No!" He looked momentarily shocked, but the surprise seemed to slide off his face as quickly as it appeared. "I mean, I won't deny that sleeping in a real bed again would be a nice by-product, but it's not my main motivation. I'd actually like to help you. What Aamee did to you was fucked up, and I'd love to see her face if we could find some sort of loophole or something that would allow you to move back in."

Drew looked so determined. I felt bad I didn't feel the same passion. Well, I had when it had all first gone down, but since living with Drew hadn't turned out to be a hardship by any means, my initial anger had dissipated quickly. Still, I had to agree that the injustice of it all was difficult to ignore, and I'd love to prove Aamee wrong on principle alone.

"Maybe there *is* a loophole," I said. "I never checked the Zeta Eta Chi handbook."

Drew's face lit up. He stopped pacing and looked at me. "Is that the one Aamee cited to kick you out in the first place?"

"The very same."

"And you never bothered to look at it to see if there was some way to get back in?"

When he put it like that, it sounded ridiculous. But at the time, there was no debating what the rule said. Sure it was unfair that *I'd* been the one to get called out on it, but I'd broken it all the same.

"It occurred to me the other day," I said, "but I forgot all about it, to be honest. It's just one of those stupid handbooks that probably hasn't ever been changed. Every girl gets one emailed to her, but no one ever actually reads it."

"Except Aamee," Drew said with that goofy smirk he had.

"Very funny."

He leaned against a nearby table and folded his arms

across his chest. "You think it breaks any rules if *I* read the handbook?"

"I guess it doesn't if no one knows about it."

"Can you email it to me? I'll look it over while you type."

"I can barely read your handwriting, remember?"

"It'll be fine. Just put what you think it says, and I'll read it over and correct anything before I turn it in," he said, obviously not letting the suggestion go.

I sighed heavily, shaking my head at him. "What's your email address?"

DREW

I picked a computer about five seats down from Sophia so as not to disturb her any more than was necessary. She was doing me a huge favor, and the least I could do was help her find a way to take down Aamee.

As I scanned through the sorority handbook's Table of Contents, I couldn't shake the optimism that I would find some way to help her.

My eyes locked on Bylaws and Code of Conduct, but both proved to be unhelpful. Other than Sophia calling attention to Aamee's transgressions—which would be difficult now that she wasn't living with her—I couldn't find anything useful.

Until I began reading up on Officer Transition. "I think I got it!" I could barely hide my excitement, and I didn't try to.

Sophia seemed less enthused. "What is it?"

"You said you can't do anything to Aamee because she's president, right?"

Sophia's raised eyebrows let me know I should continue.

"Well, there's a clause here, or whatever you call it, that says if a current president ran unopposed, she can be challenged by another member of the sorority if that member was previously ineligible to run."

I was reading from the screen, but I couldn't wait to see Sophia's expression when I finished. She'd probably be so ecstatic that she'd immediately begin campaigning. Or maybe she'd run over and throw her arms around me in a grateful and much-welcomed embrace.

In reality, she looked like I'd been lecturing her on how to properly install a car transmission or something else she couldn't give a shit less about.

"Why do you look like that?"

"Like what?"

"Like . . . not as smiley as I'd hoped."

"Because I can't run for president," she said simply.

"Are you in a sensory-deprivation tank? I just said you can."

"I heard you. And I'm thankful you're trying to help me out. I am."

I wasn't sure if she was trying to convince me or herself, but she definitely didn't seem thankful. She seemed . . . dejected. Defeated. And I hated to see her like that, especially when I thought if she ran against Aamee, it wouldn't be Sophia who'd experience the feeling of defeat.

"But?" I asked.

"But I have absolutely no desire to be president."

"Why? You'd be great at it."

Of course I didn't know that for sure. I'd only known Sophia for a few weeks, and I'd only been in college slightly longer. But while I admittedly knew little of Greek life, I knew leadership potential when I saw it. And Sophia definitely seemed to outshine Aamee in that department.

"No offense," Sophia said with an expression like she already felt bad for what she was about to say, "but do you know what it takes to be a sorority president? It's a ton of work, and you need to know the ins and outs of pretty much everything and every*one* in the sorority. I don't think I'm cut out for all that, and more than that, I don't want to be."

"That's how you know you're a true leader."

"I have little faith in myself?"

That made us both laugh. "No. You're humble. And granted, everything I know about Greek life I learned from *Animal House* and a sorority handbook I got ten minutes ago, but I think you have what it takes. You don't seem like the type of person to shy away from something just because it seems difficult. You tutor Carter in psychology, for Christ's sake. I don't even know if he knows it starts with a P."

I was glad when that made her smile.

"Well, that doesn't say much for my tutoring skills."

"I'm serious, though. I think you should at least consider it."

Her expression told me she wasn't going to. "And you should consider looking through the handbook some more. I'm not running for president."

I mumbled a "Fine, but I think you'd be good at it," before turning back to the computer to continue my mission.

There were other possible loopholes that I found— like Aamee not giving Sophia written notice of what she did wrong—but Sophia would've had to request that before the initial meeting. Sophia's eviction should've also been cleared with the dean of students, but since Sophia technically had broken the rules, that likely wouldn't help her case.

I'd almost given up when I stumbled across something that I knew would pique Sophia's interest. I read through the paragraph to make sure it was feasible before I alerted her to my findings.

A stupid grin spread across my face. "You can appeal it."

Immediately Sophia's attention was on me. Her eyes locked on me before she bolted up from her seat and hovered behind me.

"Really? What does it say exactly?"

"It's right here." I pointed to the spot on the screen and selected the text with the cursor. "If the decision was made in bias, you have a right to appeal that decision and ask the other sorority members to vote."

"Oh my God! You're a genius! This is amazing!"

Sophia was practically dancing behind me. When she stopped, she spun the chair I was sitting in so I was facing her. Then she leaned down, grabbed my cheeks, and brought her lips closer to mine than a sibling ever should.

I was torn between fearing someone would catch this near-intimate exchange and hoping she'd do it.

But for now, the excitement on her face was enough for me.

"That bitch is gonna get a taste of her own medicine," she said.

I grinned proudly. "Fuck yeah, she is."

Chapter Nine

DREW

I wasn't sure if inviting such an odd group of people into a one-bedroom apartment was a good idea, but it was too late to reconsider now.

When my business ethics group had wanted to meet in a place to study where we wouldn't have to worry about our decibel level and could spread out in a more comfortable way than we could in the library, I'd offered my place. Well, Brody's place.

Xander enthusiastically seconded the suggestion, but Toby had asked if we could meet later. It would be an added distraction to have to play gay big brother to a beautiful debutante who was having her own study session with a guy who seemed to have been bashed in the head ten times too many, but I hadn't wanted to rescind my offer.

"How many people did you say were coming?" Sophia asked me.

"Three."

She gave me a long-suffering look. "You're lucky you

found the appeal thing yesterday. You practically walk on water to me right now."

"Want me to go fill the bathtub so I can show you I can *actually* walk on water?"

She smiled a little too sweetly. "Not unless you want me to drown you in it."

"That's no way to talk to your savior."

She opened her mouth to reply, but before any barbs flew out, there was a knock on the door. "Carter won't be here for another half hour, so that has to be one of yours."

"One of mine? I feel like a cult leader," I said as I strode to the door.

"If the Kool-Aid fits."

I laughed as I swung open the door. There was Toby, wearing khakis again but with a blue sweatshirt and a timid smile.

"Hi. I'm not early, am I?" he asked.

I opened the door wider and gestured him inside with a sweep of my arm. "Nope. Right on time."

He took a few steps in but stopped when he saw Sophia. "Oh. He— Hello."

After I shut the door, I moved to his side. "This is my sister, Sophia. Soph, this is Toby."

"Nice to meet you," she said, giving him a warm smile.

He returned her greeting in a quiet voice, his face a bit redder than when he'd first arrived.

I made a decision then and there that in addition to our group project, Toby was going to be a personal project for me. I'd need a month tops to get this kid laid.

"Want anything to drink?" I asked him.

It seemed to take a minute for him to realize I'd spoken

to him. "Oh, no. No thanks. I have a water bottle in my backpack."

I motioned to the sofa. "I figured we could spread out in there."

"Sounds good to me." Toby went over and began setting up what he needed for the project on the coffee table. He seemed much more comfortable in work mode than he did having to be social. Maybe I'd need two months.

Just as I was about to follow Toby, there was another knock on the door. I swung it open and saw an annoyed Aniyah and a smirking Xander with his left arm around her shoulder.

She slowly panned to look at the offending appendage before looking straight ahead again. "If you have even the tiniest desire to keep that arm, you will remove it from my body."

Xander's cheeks looked ready to burst with holding back his laugh. He was clearly trying to get under her skin, but I thought he'd maybe want to choose a less volatile adversary next time.

"It's cool," he said. "I'm right-handed anyway."

"Xander," she warned with a clear desire to murder him.

He withdrew his arm. "Everybody's so touchy. Or, more accurately, not touchy." He stepped inside the apartment, and Aniyah followed after, rolling her eyes.

After I shut the door, I quickly introduced Sophia, who said pleasant hellos before excusing herself to her room.

Aniyah took in the apartment. "Nice place."

I shrugged. "I like it."

She looked around but didn't ask any questions, and then she and Xander followed Toby's lead and prepared to get to work.

"Anyone have anywhere particular they want to begin?" I asked.

Toby cleared his throat. "I think it would be useful for us to answer the ethical dilemma questions first. Then we can have a solid foundation from which to evaluate our case."

"Makes sense to me," Aniyah said.

"Me too," Xander agreed.

So that was what we did for the next hour or so until a pounding on the door interrupted us.

Sophia rushed out of her room to answer it. "Sorry," she said to my group. She threw open the door and planted her hands on her hips. I imagine the glare she sent Carter matched her stance. "Why are you banging on my door like you're trying to break it down? And where the hell have you been?"

"Dude, you would not even *believe* what the last hour of my life has been like." Carter skirted past Sophia like she wasn't radiating anger and hoisted himself up on a ledge in the apartment. "Have you ever been at the wrong place at the wrong time?" he asked everyone in the room.

"Every second of my life, man," Xander replied without looking up from what he was typing on his laptop, his beanie pulled low.

"Carter," Sophia said as she grabbed his arm and tugged on him. He didn't budge an inch. "They have their own work to do."

"No, we don't," Xander said. "Not until we hear why Carter was late."

"My car wouldn't start, and when I finally got it going and started to reverse, there were nuns in my rearview mirror. And I'm not gonna tell some nuns to move, so I just let them continue with their conversation, but I'm pretty sure one of them said 'Fuck you,' so I don't even know if they were real nuns. They could've just been some chicks in costumes—"

"Okay, you can take him now," Xander told Sophia.

Sophia grimaced. "And we need to get started if you're going to pass the quiz tomorrow."

"I don't know why he has to quiz us every week," said Carter. "Like, what's the psychology behind the stress he puts us under? It's gotta be damaging, right?"

We all looked around at one another. He kind of had a point.

"Maybe you can ask him tomorrow," Sophia answered. "I'm sure that'll go over well. Now come on. We can study in my room."

"Fine, fine," Carter muttered before sliding off the ledge and retrieving his backpack where he'd dropped it. He cast another look at us and then did a double take. "Hey, wait, you're that guy," he said, pointing a finger at Xander.

Xander squirmed, looking uncomfortable under the scrutiny. "I am a guy, yes."

Carter rolled his eyes. "No, you're *the* guy. The one who tried to set the library on fire."

My brow furrowed, but it seemed everyone else knew what Carter was referring to because they stared at Xander, mouth agape.

"That was *you*?" Toby asked, his voice sounding accusatory.

"Holy shit," Aniyah breathed. "You're not just pretending to be an asshole. You actually *are* one."

"Hold on a damn minute," Xander barked as he put his laptop on the ground and sat up straighter. "One, I'm not pretending."

"I know, that's what I just said," Aniyah quipped.

Xander stared daggers at her. "And two, I didn't try to set the library on fire. It was a cycle of unfortunate mishaps that nearly collided to form a devastating disaster, but thankfully this school's security team isn't a bunch of asshats, and everything worked out just fine."

"The top floor of the library was closed for a whole semester. We lost an entire section of primary sources about the Balkans," lamented Toby.

"Oh," Xander said. "Then you're welcome, because that sounds boring as fuck."

"What the hell are we talking about, libraries?" My question was treated as if it were rhetorical, but I truly wanted an answer. None came. "This is why you didn't want to meet there to work on our project, isn't it?"

"It's not as much about my *wants* as it is about school-mandated restrictions. They refer to it as probation, but I like to consider it more of a guide for avoiding prison. They said in exchange for my complete cooperation, they'd keep my identity under wraps, but"—Xander raised his hand in Carter's direction—"apparently not."

"I know everything," Carter explained. "It's a gift."

"How'd they find out it was you?" Sophia asked. "Were you caught in the act?"

"It was the librarian, wasn't it?" Carter asked. "She framed you."

"Framed in the sense that I was in the frame of the camera they have monitoring that floor," Xander answered. When everyone continued looking at him in silence, he groaned in frustration and rubbed a hand over his face. "It was an accident. Sometimes I get a little . . . frazzled. It's hard to turn my brain off. But I've found that watching a flame flicker can help me zone out. It's like meditation."

"No, being a pyromaniac is what it's like," Aniyah said.

Xander shook his head like he was used to people not understanding. "I don't usually even set things on fire. Watching the flame of a lighter is typically enough, but it ran out of fluid, so I had to use matches. The librarian must've seen what I was doing and came up the stairs screaming. She startled me—"

"Damn librarian in that section's a nuisance," Carter chimed in, his voice dripping with disdain, like it was her fault the library almost burned down.

"Yes," Xander said, clearly happy to have someone on his side. "She is. Not for this, necessarily, but she's not an innocent. I'm pretty sure she makes voodoo dolls of students when she's not stirring her cauldron and collecting cats. Anyway, the match dropped onto a notebook I had on the floor, the paper caught fire, and I panicked, so I kicked it toward the stacks. Since she was focused on yelling at me, she didn't notice what was happening at first, and I froze for a second. That's all it took for the fire to spread to the shelves and the Balkans were history. Literally. It was a total accident."

"I can't believe they let you stay enrolled here after that," Sophia said. "No offense."

"None taken. And they wouldn't have, except my dad said he'd pay for the repairs and a few other upgrades. And hey, it gives him another way to tell me I'm a fuckup every time we speak. It's a win for everyone."

"Doesn't sound like much of a win for you." Aniyah's voice was low and soft. She sounded almost . . . compassionate.

Xander shrugged. "I get to stay in school."

"True."

"Well, in my opinion, you didn't do *enough* damage." Carter walked over and held out his fist for Xander to bump. "Not all heroes wear capes, my man."

Xander looked at Carter's fist curiously before giving it a soft bump. "Thanks. I think."

"Okay, Carter, story time's over," Sophia admonished. "We have work to do."

"Coming, Mother," Carter whined as he winked at us. "You guys going to be here a while? We can hang out after Professor Scrooge is done with me."

"Hey, you're the one who wants *my* help, jackass."

Carter turned to look at Sophia. "Can we be real here? When I asked you to study with me, what I meant was will you let me copy your homework, write all my papers, and let me look over your shoulder on quiz and test days? I never expected any of this actual studying crap."

She put both hands on her hips. "Why would I ever agree to that?"

"Because I'm a football player and you're super hot."

"How do either of those things translate into me doing all your work for you?"

"It's unwise to ask questions you don't want answers to," Aniyah warned.

Sophia put her hands up. "You're right." She squeezed the bridge of her nose and turned back to Carter. "Just...we either do this my way, or you can find a new study partner."

Carter sighed. "It's too late. All the other smart girls are taken already." He looked truly devastated by this fact. "See you guys later," he said to us as he made his way down the hall.

"This campus has some really interesting characters," Aniyah said.

"Yup," I said. And it seemed I was destined to meet them all.

SOPHIA

Carter kept staring at the door like a puppy who needed to go outside to relieve himself.

I smacked him on the arm. "Come on. Focus."

"I'm trying."

"You're not usually this all over the place."

"I know, but I had a shitty day, and the people in the living room seem way more entertaining than learning how my brain developed. Who even cares, as long as it works, right?"

"You need to stay eligible," I reminded him.

"I know," he replied miserably.

"Tell you what. Give this your undivided attention for twenty more minutes, and then we'll go out there and get a drink."

"Yeah?"

I nodded before pointing to his notebook. "Now read over your notes again and tell me what doesn't make sense."

And that was how we passed the next twenty minutes. Carter wasn't a dumb guy, despite the things that came flying out of his mouth. He just didn't *care* about psychology. He was only trying to fill a general requirement, and for that reason, he resented having to put so much effort into understanding the material.

When we emerged from the room, it seemed Drew's group was also taking a break. Carter immediately began mingling with the others, and I sidled up next to Drew.

"How's it going?" I asked.

"Really well. We all have similar beliefs in terms of the role of ethics in business, so that's making the process a lot easier."

"Ah, you're the good guys, huh?"

Drew looked surprised by my assessment. "How do you know we're not ruthless future moguls?"

I tapped a finger against my top lip. "Hmm, let me see. That guy looks like he's going to spend his life driving only electric cars and have solar panels on his roof, and the girl, while slightly intimidating, seems like she's going to be a crusader for Greenpeace."

"What about Xander? He almost burned down a library."

"As a form of meditative therapy," I pointed out. "What a shark."

Drew snorted out a laugh at my assessment, which made me smile in return. "And then there's you."

"Me?"

"Yup. A guy who goes to school all day, soaking up every bit of information he can, while also holding down a full-time job and helping hapless sorority girls out of bad situations. Total monster."

When Drew didn't reply, I turned my head to see him watching me, a weird look on his face that I couldn't decipher.

"What?" I asked.

He shook himself slightly as if he'd been in a daze. "Nothing."

Before I could press for a real answer, Aniyah walked by us and stared at a painting on the wall. "This is fascinating. Who's the artist?"

Her question was directed at Drew, and he shoved his

hands in his pockets and stared at the painting on the wall like it was going to rip his face off. "Oh, that. It's uh . . . "

"God, you don't remember anything," I teasingly scolded him so I could save him from having to answer. "It's a Paul Castle. His work is amazing. I stumbled across his Instagram page a couple of years ago and had to own some of his work. I bought this for Brody last Christmas."

My story was true. I'd bought Brody the vibrant painting on a whim but later worried it might get buried in a closet somewhere. Work like Paul's was created to be displayed, and it would've broken my heart a little to think that no one would get to see it. When I'd moved in and found it hanging on the wall, I was pleasantly surprised.

And as I stood there admiring the painting with Aniyah and Drew, my body filled with affection for my brother who knew fuck all about art but had hung the painting anyway. Maybe it was because he thought it made him look cultured, but I preferred to think that he hung it because I'd given it to him.

"I'll have to look him up," Aniyah said before moving back to where everyone else was congregating.

Drew held his palm up in front of me. "Thanks for the save," he said.

I quietly slapped his hand. "Anytime." I possibly should've been worried about how much I meant it.

"Sophia," Carter called. "What's going on with Aamee? Have you figured out a way back into the sorority house yet?"

Aniyah's head whipped in my direction. "You're in a sorority?" Her tone was a mix of accusation and disbelief.

"Yup. Zeta Eta Chi." When her face scrunched up, I asked, "Not a fan?"

"When I was a freshman, my roommate rushed with them. I went to some parties with her, but . . . it's not for me."

I nodded. I got it. For how close most of the sisters were, some didn't always extend that friendliness to outsiders. Hell, some didn't extend it to their sisters either—hello, *Aamee*. Cattiness sometimes went looking for a target, and I wouldn't have been surprised if freshman Aniyah had been one before she'd built all that armor she cloaked herself in.

To answer Carter's question, I said, "I think I found something that'll get me back in the house." I left out Drew's new hobby of scouring sorority handbooks in his free time. "I'm going to call for a meeting to discuss it. Fingers crossed it goes in my favor."

"Well, I hope it works out for you," Carter said. "Let me know if there's anything I can do."

"Thanks. I will." I cast a look at Drew, who was giving me a smile I couldn't help but return. It was nice of Carter to offer, but I had a feeling I already had all the help I'd need.

Chapter Ten

SOPHIA

"This meeting will come to order," Aamee shouted over the chatting sorority sisters who were all gathered in the large living room.

The day after the cramped study date at Brody's place, I'd sent Aamee and Macy, our sorority secretary, an email requesting a formal meeting. I knew Aamee would try to block the meeting, which was why I'd also sent it to Macy. A formal request had to be taken seriously, and she was gung ho about her secretary role in the sorority.

Macy then sent an email to all my sisters, telling them to mark their calendars for Tuesday of the following week. Everyone was told to make every effort to be there.

Once everyone was quiet, Aamee continued. "Sophia Mason requested this meeting, but she hasn't shared what it will pertain to. Though I'm sure we can all guess." Her smile was smug, and I couldn't wait to wipe it off her face. "So at this time, I'll turn the floor over to Sophia so we can all get back to our lives."

Aamee walked over to a chair that she banned anyone else from sitting in during meetings. She considered the floral upholstered monstrosity some kind of throne.

I moved to the front of the group. "I know everyone has other commitments, so I'll be as brief as possible. You're all aware that I've been removed from the house due to a misunderstanding and an arcane rule that has been unfairly enforced."

"Here you go with this again."

I could practically hear the eye roll in Aamee's words.

"But as it turns out, Zeta Eta Chi isn't a tyranny," I continued. "The rules don't begin and end with the president."

Aamee sat up straighter in her chair, her lips pressing into a thin line.

"A sister has the right to appeal a decision if she feels she's been treated unjustly."

Aamee scoffed. "And you think appealing to me will get me to change my mind?"

I turned to look at her. "No. I don't appeal to you. I appeal to them." I gestured toward the roomful of women. "My sisters can reverse your decision if they feel it was made with bias."

Aamee launched herself from the chair so quickly, I expected to see a jetpack attached to her ass. "This is such horseshit. You know you were in violation of the rule. There's no arguing that."

I shrugged. "Lucky for me, I don't have to, because the first motion I would like to make is for us to hold a vote as to the merit of that rule." I turned toward my sisters. "We've all had boys in our rooms. The fact that Aamee chose to enforce it only with me shows her clear bias against me, which guarantees me the right to appeal her decision. But rather than putting all of you into the awkward position of overruling her, I'd rather turn our focus to striking the rule from the handbook entirely. It would come down to a simple majority vote."

Aamee stepped closer to me, rage emanating from her. "And just who the hell are you that you think you can go around changing rules that have been in place since the founding of our chapter? Your mother would be appalled."

Her words stung, but I refused to let it show. The fact was, my mother *would* be appalled. As a former president, she held high regard for the position, even if a complete nitwit was currently occupying it.

"Rules change as the world does. When that was written, it would have been scandalous to have been caught with a boy in your room. Now it's a common occurrence. There's no reason it can't be amended or disregarded entirely."

Aamee glared at me for another few seconds before I watched her entire body relax. She turned toward our sisters and smoothed a hand down her white blouse before clasping her hands in front of her.

"I would like to remind all of you that any change to our code of conduct needs to be brought to the attention of the dean of student affairs," she said. "And from there, news of the change will no doubt spread. I can just hear the rumors now. That we're running some kind of brothel over here. Is that what we want people to think of Zeta Eta Chi? That we're a bunch of sluts whose bedrooms have revolving doors of men coming and going at will?"

My sisters looked at one another, reluctance all over their faces. Even though sorority girls were often labeled as judgmental bitches, we often were also judged harshly. It was already difficult to overcome the stereotype of being vapid whores, and Aamee was playing right into that fear with her monologue.

"Do we even need to vote on it? Or is it clear where we stand?" Aamee's voice was smug as the girls looked around at one another as if torn on what to do. But no one called for a vote, and Aamee took that silence as the victory it was.

"I still have the right to appeal your decision," I said.

Sighing, as if I was a nuisance as insignificant as a fruit fly, Aamee turned to look at me again. "If they appeal my decision, they'll basically be doing what they've all just decided they don't want—changing the rules to allow boys to sleep over in our rooms. Overruling me shows that they're okay with me not enforcing the rules, which ultimately makes the rules worthless. I think that's a slippery slope. Don't you?"

"You've never enforced the rule before. Doing so only with me shows your bias against me."

"Maybe I just never caught anyone before. Don't forget, I've only been president since Abigail graduated in May. And since no one was around all summer..." Aamee let her words die off. The implication was clear.

She stepped into my space and smiled wolfishly. "You'll never win against me," she whispered. "Haven't you embarrassed yourself enough?"

Anger coiled in my stomach as if it were a jack-in-the-box. One more turn of the crank would send it shooting outward. And of course, if anyone was going to crank it that last bit, it would be Aamee.

"Or more importantly, haven't you embarrassed the legacy of your *mother* enough?" Aamee turned away from me after delivering what she thought was the death blow.

"I think we can dismiss this meeting unless anyone has any other issues they'd like to raise."

When no one said anything, everyone began to get up from their seats.

"Wait!" I called. "I have another motion."

Aamee looked pissed off as the girls looked at me expectantly. I cleared my throat. "The rules allow someone who was previously unqualified to be president to run when that qualification is met *if* the previously elected president ran unopposed. As a sophomore last year, I wasn't allowed to run. But now I'm a junior, and therefore eligible. And since no one opposed you, I'm now allowed to do so."

"That's not how that rule works," Aamee argued.

"No? Because that's what it says. As soon as I became a junior, I was entitled to run."

"But..." Aamee seemed to flounder for words. "I've already begun my presidency."

"If you're as fit for the office as you claim, you should win by a landslide."

Aamee was looking a little pale, but she kept her shoulders square and her head high. "This is ridiculous. You're creating drama for no reason. None of our sisters will support someone rocking the boat like this."

I looked at her with determination I didn't feel. "I guess we'll see, won't we?"

Chapter Eleven

DREW

Rafferty's wasn't as packed as I'd ever seen it, but I'd been pouring drinks steadily since my shift started at eight. Our regulars littered the bar, while a few groups gathered around the pool tables and dart boards.

"Drew, how those college classes been treating ya?" Max, one of our regulars, asked. He was a widower who lived a block away and came in for drinks a few times a week. He always took an interest in my life, and I appreciated the man for it.

I picked up his empty glass and wiped down the bar. "Pretty well. I haven't gotten anything lower than a B yet."

"Attaboy. My Olive was a schoolteacher. She always wanted to become a professor, but the timing was never right, and then we were out of time." He paused for a second, his shoulder hunching a bit. "Anyway, good for you for working hard and bettering yourself. I'm damn proud of you."

A lump formed in my throat. It had been a long time since anyone had said they were proud of me, if it had ever happened at all.

"Thanks, Max." I cleared my throat. "Want another?"

"I think I'm going to order some food. Maybe just a water and a menu for now."

"You got it." I grabbed a menu and poured his water. When I turned to deliver them, I had to blink to make sure I was seeing clearly.

Sophia slid into a chair near Max and plopped her head into the arms she had crossed atop the bar.

Max and I shared a look as I set the items in front of him.

"Well, this is a surprise," I said to Sophia.

Her only response was to lift her head slightly and thump it back down onto her arms, a motion she repeated a few more times before stopping.

"Rough day?" I rested my own arms on the bar so I could lean closer to her. "Did the meeting not go well?"

She raised her head and looked at me, her expression showing exhaustion. "I messed everything up."

"Why? We went over your arguments, and they were all good ones."

"I underestimated Aamee. She had a counterargument for everything."

"So I guess I won't be helping you move back into the house this weekend?"

She shook her head miserably. "No. But you can help me launch a winning campaign for president."

I bolted upright. "You challenged her?" A smile overtook my face. My Sophia had balls of steel. "Good for you."

She massaged her forehead with her hand. "The only reason I'm doing it is to piss Aamee off. That's not a good reason to want to be sorority president, but it was the only thing left for me to do."

"The fact that you feel that way already shows you're better equipped to have the job than she is."

"That's not saying much. A trained seal is better equipped than her."

"But you're the only one with the guts to do anything about it," I argued.

She shook her head and looked depressed as hell. "I'd take it back in a second if my pride would allow it. I don't have guts." She sighed heavily. "Would you make sure that goes on my headstone when the stress of this gives me a fatal ulcer? Sophia Mason: Gutless Sorority President."

I smirked. "See! You're already giving yourself credit for the win."

She didn't return my enthusiasm. "You can add delusional to my headstone. And stop encouraging me. It's not conducive to sustaining my pity party."

"Oh, come on. If your big brother won't encourage you, who will?"

She narrowed her eyes at me.

"I didn't realize this was your sister," Max interjected, his face brightening.

"She's not," I explained. "It's an inside joke."

"If jokes weren't funny, this one would be epic," Sophia muttered.

Max looked confused but didn't ask for clarification.

"You want a drink?" I asked her before a realization dawned on me. "Wait, are you even old enough to drink?" Some fake big brother I was. My question did get a smile from her, though, so I guess my ignorance was worth it.

"Yeah, I turned twenty-one in April."

"Okay. So what'll it be?" Rafferty's policy required me to

card anyone who looked under thirty, but I wasn't going to add insult to injury by making it seem as if I didn't trust her.

"Guess you can't do a shot with me, huh?" she asked me.

Shaking my head, I said, "Sorry. No can do." If it had been closer to closing, I could've gotten away with it, but if my boss, Sean, saw me hitting the sauce this early in my shift, he'd send me packing.

Sophia looked disappointed, but when she turned her attention to Max, she looked more hopeful. "What about you?"

It took Max a second to realize she'd been talking to him. "Me?"

"Yeah. I don't like to drink alone."

Max held up a hand, and it was clear he was going to decline, but then Sophia added a drawn-out "Please."

He looked at her pouting face for another moment before grumbling, "Ah, what the hell? What are we having?"

"I'm not picky. Whatever you want. It's on me." She opened a small purse and pulled out a credit card, which she handed to me. "Keep it open."

I nodded as I took the card from her and waited for Max to choose a drink.

"You got Sambuca back there?" he asked.

"Chilled and ready to go."

Sophia clapped her hands. "Yes! Sambuca party." She wiggled around in her seat, doing some kind of uncoordinated chair dance.

Max chuckled, clearly charmed by her antics. As I moved away to pour their shots, I heard Max ask, "So what is all this about a sorority?"

SOPHIA

The first shot had been a great idea. The second one might have even been as well. But there was no doubt I'd be regretting the third and fourth tomorrow, even with the amount of water Drew kept forcing me to drink.

I had also eaten about half of Max's fries, so hopefully the grease would soak up some of the alcohol. Did grease do that? My hazy brain wasn't sure.

"Listen," Max said. "I've never met this Aamee person, but if you will excuse my language, she sounds like a real asshat."

"Yes," I replied, relieved that he saw it my way. "She is. She *so* is."

"It's obvious you're the better choice," my other new friend Bill added. He'd come in as Max and I were throwing back shot number two and had joined us from there. Then Dave had wandered in at some point after that.

I loved these guys. They were supportive as hell, and I was in desperate need of that.

"Is it obvious?" I asked. "I'm really not sure. It feels like *anyone* would be a better choice, but are they? It's not like Aamee is slaughtering virgin pledges or anything."

"More water," Drew said, pushing my glass toward me. "Lots more water."

I rolled my eyes but did as he asked. I'd had so much liquid, it felt like my stomach was about to drown. "Can stomachs drown?" I asked.

"And food," he added. "Want anything in particular?"

"Justice with a side of revenge."

"That's the spirit," Bill said, sounding proud.

"To eat, Sophia," said Drew. "What do you want to eat?"

"The entrails of those who wrong me," I said to a chorus of laughter from my new friends. "But a cheesesteak will do for now."

"Coming right up." Drew left to put my order in, and I slumped back on my barstool.

"What kinds of things do you have to do to become president?" Dave asked.

That was a damn good question. "I have no idea. I'll have to do some research and maybe ask around." *I could ask my mom*, but . . . no. Bad plan. Bad, bad plan.

"How would your mother know?" Bill asked.

Oh, so I'd said that bit aloud. "She was the president of my sorority when she went here."

"Then why would it be a bad plan to ask her?"

"Because I'm not doing this the conventional way. I'm basically stirring up a shit ton of drama because a girl was mean to me. My mom would *not* be impressed." I took another sip of my water. "If, by the end of this year, I told her I wanted to run for next year, she'd be all over it. But basically dethroning someone—do you dethrone presidents?" I shook my head to dismiss the unrelated question before continuing. "Nah, she wouldn't be a fan."

"Even if the person you were removing from office wasn't the right person for the job?" Max asked.

"Well, then I'd have to explain that she wasn't the right person because she kicked me out of the house for having a boy in my room overnight. My mom would lose her shit. And probably side with Aamee." That gave me pause. I dropped my head and stared at the way the wood swirled on the bar as I thought about my circumstances.

"Should she side with Aamee?" I asked. Maybe I was wrong. I mean, I knew I was technically wrong according to the rules, but had what I'd done warranted the punishment I'd received? My mom would probably think I deserved what I'd gotten. And while sober me definitely didn't think that way, drunk me wasn't so sure.

"No," Drew said, sliding my cheesesteak in front of me and then propping his hands on the table. "Aamee *is* abusing her power, Soph. Anyone who sides with her over you in this is flat-out wrong."

My eyes pricked as tears threatened to spill. Drew was so strong as he stood there. So resolute. There wasn't an ounce of anything that would indicate he didn't wholeheartedly believe what he was saying. And Jesus, did I need that kind of confidence right now. If I didn't feel it myself, maybe I could lean on his until I did. Maybe he could prop us both up until I got my feet under me again.

I'd had a lot of friends in my life. But the warmth I felt staring at *this* particular friend—one I never would've found if it hadn't been for my dumbass brother—was unlike anything I'd ever felt before.

Or maybe it's the Sambuca. Christ, drunk me was a real downer.

I took a long, deep breath and decided to trust in Drew's words. "Then I guess we fight for what's right," I said.

"Hell yeah," Dave said, and Max and Bill chimed in with similar words of encouragement.

But I kept my eyes on Drew, who only smiled and nodded. And that was all the encouragement I needed.

Chapter Twelve

DREW

Even though she was probably only a hundred and twenty pounds soaking wet, drunk Sophia was surprisingly difficult to maneuver. "Just a little farther," I grunted as I tried to prop her up with one arm and unlock our door with the other.

"Tonight was so fun," she practically yelled as she threw her arms back.

"Shh, people are sleeping."

"This is college. Everyone can sleep when they're alive. Or ... wait ... that doesn't sound right." She was momentarily still as she contemplated where she'd gone wrong in her statement, which gave me the time I needed to twist the key and push the door open.

I then grabbed her with both arms again and led her inside. It probably would've been easier to throw her over my shoulder and carry her that way, but I was worried being upside down would cause her to throw up all over my back. When we arrived at the couch, I let go, and she plopped down onto it.

She immediately spread out as much as she could. "It's so

comfy here. Maybe I should take the couch and give you the bed."

"I'm ready to switch when you are," I muttered as I turned on a few lights.

She rolled onto her side and nuzzled her face into the pillow. "It's like velvet."

It was more like polyester, but there was little point in arguing.

When she tired of rubbing herself on the pillow like a cat, she moved to her back again and looked up at the ceiling. "I should drink more often. Everything's so pretty."

Like a moron, I glanced up at the ceiling to see what she was talking about. It was solid white, like most ceilings. "I bet in the morning you'll be vowing to never drink again."

She threw an arm over her eyes. "Nah, I needed it. And I made friends. I love friends."

I shook my head and laughed. She was damn cute like this—all loose-lipped and smiley. I also liked how she considered Max and the gang her friends. Granted, she was wasted, but she sounded like she truly valued the men she'd met tonight.

It was easy to look down on guys who spent their free time in a bar, but the truth was, those guys were just looking for people to pass some time with. They weren't deadbeats but rather dependable men with good hearts, and I liked that Sophia recognized that about them.

I gave myself another second to watch her sprawled out on the couch before I extended a hand in her direction. "Okay, Drunk Spice. Get off my bed and go to yours."

"I don't wanna," she whined.

I reached down and took hold of her hand and gently

pulled. "Come on. Up ya go."

"I'm not a baby," she grumbled, but she made no move to get up.

"If you don't get up, I'm going to shave your head while you sleep."

Her eyes opened slowly. "You don't have the balls."

"You really want to test me and find out?"

"Kind of, yeah."

I couldn't help laughing. "Dude, get up! Or else I'm going to roll you onto the floor and leave you there."

"Like I'm scared of a floor," she muttered, swaying upward slightly as if she were attempting the world's lamest sit-up.

I pulled her hand as she started to drift back down toward the couch and managed to wrangle her to a sitting position.

"Okay, making progress," I said.

She cut her eyes to me in a withering look before beginning to lie back down. "But I like the velvet couch," she wailed when I pulled on her hand again.

Had I really thought she was cute a few minutes ago? She was a pain in the fucking ass. I moved my hand down so I was gripping her wrist and gave her one more pull to get her on her feet.

I hadn't expected her to assist in this move, so she ended up flying toward me. As she collided with my chest, I wrapped my arms around her to steady us both.

Her hands had come up to keep her from face-planting into my sternum, and I instinctually gripped her lower back. I looked down at her and she looked up, and our gazes held for a long moment.

"If you wanted a hug, all you had to do was ask," she said, finally breaking the silence. Her voice was so low and husky, it shifted the air in the room to something more tense and heavy.

"I'll remember that for next time," I replied, my voice almost a whisper.

We continued looking at one another, and it was as if we were caught in a bubble we were both terrified of popping.

"You saying there'll be a next time?"

"Stranger things have happened."

She nodded. "Like having a guy pretending to be your gay brother quickly becoming one of your best friends?"

I inhaled sharply at her words. Granted, we'd gotten along well, but hearing her voice and how she felt about me filled me with affection for this drunk idiot in my arms.

"Yeah. Exactly like that."

She hummed in response, and the sound seemed to rumble down her body and radiate into my chest. Pinpricks of awareness popped out on my arms where I held on to her.

I should've let go minutes ago, but the thought of doing so held no appeal. And when I noticed her begin to move her face up to meet mine, I started to lean down to meet her halfway.

But just before our lips connected, I pulled back. She was drunk and vulnerable, and damn did I want to kiss her anyway. But I couldn't. Not like this. Honestly, not like anything.

Hooking up with Sophia would top the list of Worst Plans Drew Ever Had. And that list wasn't exactly a short one.

Her eyes were closed, and she swayed forward a bit more, clearly expecting my lips to be there. She startled a bit when she was met with only air. She opened her eyes slowly and looked up at me questioningly.

I stood there without saying anything, without moving closer.

Pulling out of my grasp, she stumbled a bit but quickly regained her balance.

"Guess I should go to bed."

"Are you . . . I mean, do you . . . can I do anything?"

She smiled at me, but it seemed a little forced. "I got it." She walked toward her room and turned just enough to look at me. "Thanks. For everything."

"Anytime," I replied.

As I watched her walk into her room and close the door, I hoped she knew I meant it.

SOPHIA

I woke up the next morning in rough shape. My head pounded, my stomach felt unsettled, and I wanted to sleep for at least ten more hours. When I rolled to my back, I threw my arm over my eyes to block out the sunlight streaming in through my windows while I thought back to last night.

I wished I'd have been drunk enough to forget what had happened. The way Drew had practically had to carry me into the apartment, plead with me to go to bed, and the way . . . oh God. I'd almost kissed Drew.

"Fuck my life."

Realistically, I knew no one could blame me. Drew was extremely kissable, and I'd already confessed my attraction to him. But *Jesus Christ*, could I not keep it in my pants when so much was riding on me not, well . . . riding him?

And it wasn't just Brody and me who were depending on us keeping our heads on straight. Drew needed this to work out too. He had an opportunity to better his life, and I was going to make that more difficult because I wanted to suck on his tongue. I was fucking unbelievable.

After cursing my drunken self a little more, I rolled out of bed so I could use the bathroom. Once I was finished showering and making myself feel slightly human again, I peeked down the hall and saw Drew still sacked out on the couch.

I wasn't sure how he did what he did. He worked until closing well past midnight and then went to classes during the day. All while still finding time to do his schoolwork. He deserved more than to be dragged into my mess. But since that decrepit ship had already sailed, I decided to pay him back with the only thing I had in my arsenal: breakfast.

As a rule, I avoided cooking. If it was touted as a recipe that couldn't be messed up, I messed it up. But breakfast was a different story. I attributed it to the fact that my mom and I had made breakfast for the family every Sunday when I was young.

It was one of the only bonding experiences with her I completely enjoyed because there'd been no ulterior motive behind it. She hadn't been trying to groom me into some kind of debutante or list all the ways I hadn't lived up to her standards. It had simply been a time for us to drop the pretenses and work together to not burn the house down. And we succeeded more times than not. Thankfully.

Those mornings were fun, and because there was no expectation to live up to—my mother was an even worse cook than I was—I was able to just figure things out. The result was a banging French toast recipe and a near-savant level of adequacy when it came to cooking bacon. Tools I used to make Drew the best breakfast I could.

After returning from the corner store with the items we hadn't had on hand, I set to work. I tried to be quiet, but between the clanging of bowls and the scent of bacon wafting through the apartment, he stirred before I was finished preparing everything. In my periphery, I saw him scrub his eyes as if he were looking at a mirage.

"What are you doing?"

"Tuning an engine," I responded dryly as I put the freshly dipped bread in the pan.

"Is that . . . do I smell bacon?"

"Yup."

"Where did we get bacon?"

"From a pig, same as everyone else."

"Not people who eat turkey bacon."

"That's *not* bacon." I pointed a spatula at him to punctuate my point.

He sat up and rubbed his hands over his face a few times before standing and walking toward the kitchen. "I'm not dreaming. You're really making breakfast."

"Don't get used to it," I mumbled. But bantering with him, while fun, wasn't supposed to be what this was about. I set the spatula down and turned to face him fully. "I wanted to thank you. For last night."

"You already thanked me for that."

"Yeah, but . . . " I shrugged and looked around at the mess I'd made. "Sometimes words aren't enough." I pointedly didn't mention that I'd already used the no-words approach when I'd tried to kiss him.

He looked at me for a moment. "You don't owe me anything, Soph. I'm happy to help you."

"Well, I'm happy to make you breakfast."

The crooked grin that never failed to make my insides flutter a bit spread across his face. "I like dinner too, in case that also makes you happy."

Laughing, I grabbed a nearby dish towel and threw it at

him. "Don't push your luck."

Sadly, he caught the towel before it could smack him in the face. "Do I have time to grab a shower?" he asked.

"A quick one, yeah."

"Okay, I'll be right back."

And he was. Ten minutes later, we were filling our plates and carrying them to the small kitchen table, where I'd already put two glasses of orange juice.

We ate for a bit in silence. Drew didn't seem like he was burning to discuss anything, namely our almost-kiss the previous night, and I hoped that was a sign that he was willing to pretend it never happened. But while the silence wasn't uncomfortable, I didn't want him grasping at things to fill it with.

"I got an email this morning from Macy, our sorority secretary," I said.

He finished chewing and took a sip of juice before replying. "Oh yeah? What was it about?"

"It outlined what I'd have to do if I wanted to move forward with my claim to run for president."

Drew gave me a *go on* motion with one hand as he heaped more bacon onto his plate with the other.

"First thing would be for me to send an email of intent to the dean of student affairs. Once I get the okay from her to proceed, Erin'll put together a meeting where Aamee and I'll both present why we're the best choice to be president. Then, everyone votes. Since Aamee is already president, I'd need a three-quarters vote to take the position from her."

Drew chewed for a second, his brow furrowed. Finally, he set his fork down and looked at me. "So what are you going to do?"

I'd been asking myself that question since I read Macy's email. Though I guess I'd really been asking it since I opened my big mouth during my appeal. I didn't want to pursue this for a petty reason. I wanted to be sure that I could be the president Zeta Eta Chi deserved, instead of the one they got when Aamee stepped into the role.

There was no mistaking the hopeful look on Drew's face. He wanted me to go for it. He had wanted that since he found the rule in the first place. But I couldn't do this just because I didn't want to disappoint him. The reason needed to be bigger than that. Bigger than him. Bigger than even me. It had to be for what was truly best for the sorority that I'd been pressured to join but loved nonetheless.

I leaned back in my chair and regarded him for a second. "I guess I'm going to draft a letter to the dean of student affairs."

Drew punched the air with his fists. "Yes!"

And while I watched him celebrate, I dared to let a tendril of excitement unfurl inside me. This could happen. I could become president of Zeta Eta Chi.

And for the first time, I truly wanted to be.

Chapter Thirteen

SOPHIA

I expected to have more than a few days to get ready for the next sorority meeting, but if I wanted to become president, I was going to need to perform under pressure. And preparing a written statement outlining my qualifications was my first test.

I'd had much of what I planned to say floating around in my head, but getting it down on paper proved much more difficult. How did I make myself seem fit for the position while showing Aamee's weaknesses without looking like a spiteful bitch? There was a gentle finesse to it that I hoped like hell I got right.

I glanced around the living room of the sorority house I hadn't been in for weeks and tried to mentally settle the acid moving around in my stomach. I hadn't had an appetite since the previous night, and it was almost five.

Aamee sat across from me, both of us in hard chairs brought in from the dining room table, while the rest of our sisters made themselves comfortable in furniture of their choosing sprinkled around the perimeter of the room. It made me a little happy that Aamee didn't have her throne tonight.

Emma and Gina gave me small smiles, and a few other girls nodded in my direction, probably in an attempt to give me confidence I didn't exactly feel. Since Aamee was going to be part of the meeting, the other officers suggested the vice president, Sam, run the agenda so as not to have a conflict of interest.

As Sam looked down at her iPad, it struck me that Aamee hadn't brought anything formal. She had no notebook or tablet in front of her, and I momentarily felt more adequately ready than she was. Maybe she'd underestimated me.

Even if she had an idea of what she was going to say, showing up empty-handed made her seem ill-prepared. At least to me. I could only hope the other girls would notice it and think the same.

Finally Sam spoke, breaking the tense silence and causing all of us to sit up a little straighter. She addressed the rest of the room first.

"The secretary has taken attendance, and as we are only missing three members, this meeting shall come to order and proceed as planned. Sophia Mason has prepared a statement of her intent. We'll let Sophia read her statement first, and then Aamee will have an opportunity to respond. We will continue with the meeting in a debate style to evaluate each candidate's presidential qualifications."

Then Sam's attention turned to Aamee and me. "You will both get sufficient time to respond to any questions asked by chapter members, as well as thirty seconds to rebut any comments made by each other. Other members may ask questions as they see fit, and you must answer them honestly. Do you both understand the rules as they've been outlined for you?"

Aamee and I nodded, both of us clearly eager to get started.

"Good," Sam said. "Do either of you have any questions?"

"Does this really need to be so formal?" Aamee asked. "We all know Sophia's only challenging my position in office as retaliation for a punishment."

Sam looked directly at Aamee, a sternness to her face that I hadn't expected to see. Sam and Aamee had always seemed to be friends, and they were, as far as I could tell. But I was thankful to see Sam was approaching this meeting seriously and with an unbiased attitude.

"While that may be true," said Sam, "it is a challenge nonetheless, and we'll hear Sophia out. She's still one of our sisters, and she's entitled to this meeting."

Aamee rolled her eyes but had nothing more to say. That was a first.

Sam turned her attention to me. "Sophia, you may begin whenever you're ready. Please address Aamee directly, as she is your opponent."

Clearing my voice, I glanced at my notes, which I'd spent most of the morning trying to memorize, and then looked up at Aamee. I wouldn't let her intimidate me.

"I'm here today to formally voice my intention to run for the office of president of Zeta Eta Chi," I said.

Aamee glared at me, her light eyes barely blinking.

"You're right that I originally sought this presidency because of retaliation, but I'm seeking it currently for reasons beyond that. I believe that I am better qualified to run this sorority than you, and I hope that after this meeting, the rest of the group will agree with me."

I looked back to Sam to signal that I was finished with my opening.

"Let the record indicate that Sophia Mason has formally identified her intent to run for president." Sam looked to Macy, who was transcribing the meeting on her laptop. "Aamee, what, if anything, do you have to say in response to this challenge?"

Aamee stood, her hair flipping around as she looked back and forth at the other girls. "This challenge is a joke, but if Sophia thinks she can prove her competence as president, let her. The burden of proof is on her to show she's better qualified to hold office."

"Actually," Sam said, "that's not entirely true. Even though you currently have the title, once she challenges you, it's as if you are both running for office. Everyone should vote based on who is a better fit for the position, not whether you have done anything worthy of being removed from your position. This isn't the same as a courtroom, where there is a 'burden of proof,' as you say. You are not innocent until proven guilty."

Aamee looked pissed and sat back down. I tried not to smile. Essentially, we were equal candidates running for the same position, and I hoped the other girls understood that.

Sam continued. "But since Sophia is the one challenging you, I think it's fitting that she be the first one to outline her qualifications." She looked to me. "Sophia."

I stood this time, though I really didn't know if I was supposed to. "After my removal from the house, I spent some time going through the sorority handbook." I looked down at Aamee. "Thank you for bringing that to my attention, by the way. I hadn't thought to read it closely until then." Aamee rolled her eyes again and crossed her arms in a huff. She was so mature. "The handbook highlights some of the qualifications and traits of an effective officer, and I'd like to quote from that section if I may."

Sam nodded. "Go ahead."

"According to page forty-two, 'Any position is a leadership role, and the officer should behave as such.' I don't think I need to point out that Aamee has not exhibited leadership in the sense that she's had members of the opposite sex in her room plenty of times."

"We've already been over this," Aamee said.

Sam held up a finger to silence her. "You'll get your time to speak in a moment."

"You're correct," I said. "We've been over that. I'm bringing it up now for another reason. Previously, I pointed out this fact as a way to show Aamee's bias against me and the hypocrisy of her choice to punish me harshly for something she's done herself. I'm pointing it out now for the purpose of proving that Aamee does not lead by example."

"Aamee? Would you like to address this?"

"Yes, I'd like to address it. Your accusation is worthless. You're just as hypocritical as me. You call yourself a leader, but you had a boy in your room too. How can you claim you're fit to hold office if you're saying I'm not for the exact same offense you're guilty of?"

I looked to Sam. "Since she asked me a direct question, may I answer?"

"You may."

"I wasn't an elected officer, though, and while ignorance isn't an excuse in any circumstance, I wasn't aware of the rule until you pointed it out to me. I can assure you that if I become president, I will abide by the rule, as arcane as it may be."

"So you're saying that previous to retaliating against me, you never read the handbook?"

"I'd skimmed it." I was aware of how the admission sounded. "Just as most of our sisters who aren't officers have done. Clearly, you knew the rule, yet you still chose to break it." Then I went out on a limb—took a chance I hoped was worth the risk. "Have you broken it since you evicted me?"

Aamee remained silent, but a few of the girls murmured to each other, effectively answering the question for her.

"That'll be enough of the back and forth," Sam said. "Sophia, do you have any other accomplishments or qualifications you'd like to add that you believe would make you an effective president?"

"Yes, the handbook also speaks of character and service to both the university and the community. I don't think I need to cite examples of Aamee's lack of integrity, but I will anyway. Last year she admitted to cheating on Dr. Lind's final."

"First of all, Sam asked about *your* accomplishments, not my sociology exam. Second, everyone cheated on that final. It was impossible."

"Not me," I said. "And I still managed to get a higher grade than you. I worked my ass off for that B-minus. As far as community and university service go, I volunteer with the writing center and have tutored another student since last year. I've also signed up to help out at the animal shelter and give kids swimming lessons."

This time it was Gina who asked a question. "Was that before or after you decided to run for president?"

"Before," I answered, knowing that Gina had asked the question because she'd already known the answer and knew it would make me look good. *Thank you, Gina.*

"Why don't you talk about your service record, Aamee?" Sam asked.

"I'd love to. Last year I coached a local cheerleading squad of eight- to eleven-year-old kids. This year I'm doing that as well as mentoring young girls as part of the Big Siblings program."

I wondered if the parents of these poor children knew who their kids' role model was, and I decided that they probably didn't. Aamee could project quite a clean image when she needed to. She was like a mute swan—beautiful and delicate on the outside, but if you encroached on her territory, you'd likely end up with a few bruises after she spread her wings.

"That's also impressive," Sam said. "Shall we talk about sorority events and fundraising now?"

"Sure," Aamee answered, a broad smile spreading across her deceitful face. "I've already been planning this year's fall festival. It'll be a costume party around Halloween, and all proceeds will go to the local women's shelter. Theme still to be determined. How about you?" she asked me, knowing I wouldn't have been in charge of anything of the sort.

"You know I've been helping with that, but it's not my place to plan something of that magnitude myself."

"It would be if you were president. How do we know you'll be able to keep up with previous years' events if we've never seen you plan one?"

"You got elected president without having to prove that."

"I was running unopposed, remember?" she asked with so much sarcasm in her tone that no one in the room could have missed it. "Since you feel you're so much more equipped to lead a sorority, I think it's only fair that you should be required to plan a large-scale event also."

The fact that Aamee had suggested it told me she was worried she might lose to me if the presidency came down to a vote today.

"Do I have a motion to extend the decision until Sophia can run her own event?" Sam asked.

A few hands raised in the air as the girls agreed that would be a good idea.

"I'll need more than two weeks to plan something. Aamee's been planning the party since the beginning of the school year, maybe even longer."

Sam looked to the other officers, who seemed to nod in agreement with me. "That only seems fair. Near the end of the semester would give you the same amount of time as Aamee had to plan hers."

"I think I'll be fine with a November event," I offered confidently. It was a daunting task, but I was sure I could find help, and I needed to prove I was more qualified than Aamee. Planning an event of the same caliber in less time would help with that.

"November it is, then," Sam said. "Let us know when you have an exact date for your event and what it will be. I would assume that the judging would mostly be based on the event's turnout, attendee opinions, and funds raised, but I'll let you know of the exact criteria when the other officers and I have had a chance to talk over the specifics."

Aamee and I muttered our okays, and Sam turned to the rest of the group. "I guess the voting is deferred until a later date after both events have been held and we've gotten an opportunity to review the feedback and fundraising efforts. Until then, good luck with your event planning, ladies. If you need your sisters' help, please don't hesitate to ask. And that includes calling on each other if needed. Remember, you're still both a part of this sorority, and we're all here for each other."

Aamee and I both looked at each other, a silent exchange that both of us understood perfectly. We'd rather be eaten alive by a rabid animal than request the help of the other.

This shit was on.

Chapter Fourteen

SOPHIA

Though Emma and Gina wanted me to hang out for a bit, I didn't spend time at the house after the meeting. I didn't have much of a desire to be there longer than I had to, which did cause me to become at least slightly concerned that I shouldn't be running for president. What type of leader doesn't want to be in their own sorority house?

But after analyzing it, I knew my hesitance wasn't indicative of my ability to be an effective president. I didn't want to be in the house. Aamee asserted a certain power over some of the girls, and that power caused fear, which then resulted in them treating me differently. It was like Aamee had spent the beginning of the school year creating little robots who followed her every command.

Sophia is the devil.
Yes, Master.
Don't talk to her.
Yes, Master.
I hoped if I became president, they would stop acting out

of fear and see Aamee for who she really was: a Barbie Doll with the personality of Annabelle. And I wasn't about to let that demon influence my sorority sisters if I could help it.

With a long huff, I walked through our apartment door. *When did it become our apartment, when it is neither mine nor Drew's?*

Drew and his group were spread out in the living room again, working on their project. He'd told me they were going to try to meet here once a week, but I'd forgotten until now because I'd been so preoccupied with the sorority meeting.

Carter was also there for his study session, and even early for once. His gaze darted from the TV to me when I tossed my bag onto the table by the door.

"How'd it go?" Drew looked up from where he'd been messing with Brody's laptop. "I'm hoping your sigh means you're just acclimating to your new role and you're disappointed you won't be living with me anymore."

Aniyah gave him a look like he'd just tried to explain quantum physics. "Why would she rather live with you than her sorority sisters?"

"Uh, because I'm awesome. And the life of the party."

"What party are we speaking about exactly?" Carter asked. "I have yet to see you at one."

Drew shrugged, and I recognized that he'd dug himself a little hole. He played the easygoing, happy-go-lucky senior well, but when it came down to it, he cared more about actually learning something than anyone else in the room.

"The semester's still early," he said. "I'm just gearing up. And besides, it's why I had to transfer here to begin with. No way my parents were paying for another year at Buckley with the way my grades were. I gotta focus and take this whole school thing seriously."

"I'm confused," Xander said. "So you *do* party, or you don't?"

"I party," Drew said confidently.

Xander reached into his bag. "Nice, 'cause I just got my hands on some good shi—"

"But not your kind of partying, I guess," Drew added quickly.

Xander shrugged and settled back against the couch cushions. "Suit yourself."

"Speaking of parties, I have to throw one," I said, plopping down next to Xander. "What do you have in that bag?"

Xander's eyes lit up, and I realized they were so dark, I couldn't tell whether his pupils were dilated or not.

"I'm kidding," I said.

Drew was leaning forward, his forearms on his legs, which were spread wide. "So did you win or not?"

"I didn't win, but neither did Aamee. They said it was too tough to decide with a vote right then because neither of us has really proved ourselves as president yet. We each have to throw an event at some point during the semester, and the other officers are going to gauge attendee opinion and the amount of money we raised and things like that before everyone votes."

After no one said anything, I looked away from Drew and around the room at everyone. "I hate that I have to wait another month or two before the vote, but I get why they're doing it. As long as I think of a good solid idea for the party, I'm hoping I can make the rest fall into place."

"Don't look at me," Toby said. "The only party I've ever been a part of is a political one."

"I already enlisted the help of my best friend from home. She's supposed to come Saturday and just stay for the night.

If anyone can help me figure out how to throw an event of the century, it's Taylor. When our high school chose a venue for our prom no one liked, Taylor threw her own at a better place. Most of our class went to hers." I looked to Drew. "I should've asked you if she could come first. Do you mind?"

"Of course not."

Carter stood. "You can tell Taylor she doesn't need to make the trip. I'm all over this. We can get a keg and some strippers. One of my buddies—"

"This isn't a bachelor party," Drew said.

"Parties are lame," Aniyah said, and her contribution began and ended with that.

We were all silent for a minute or so, all presumably thinking about what to plan, when Drew's phone rang.

He held it up so that everyone could see it was his mom calling. "I should probably take this."

Then he excused himself to the bedroom, leaving me alone with Lazarus University's motleyest crew.

DREW

My mom and I didn't make it a habit of talking. It wasn't that we didn't get along or didn't like each other. It was just that neither of us typically found a reason to call the other. Plus, we didn't share many things in common. While my mom and sisters were content to sit on the porch, gossiping about neighborhood drama over a carton of Newports, I'd wanted better for myself.

I always had. And while most parents should be happy their kids wanted better than they had, my mom and dad seemed to resent my drive in a way that highlighted just how insecure they were with their own lives. They'd settled, and they knew it.

Even in their marriage, they hadn't put forth the effort it deserved to raise five kids. For years, they'd gone through the motions rather than work hard to make their lives better. To most, they didn't appear to be more than friends who cohabitated for the sake of a budget and convenience. I wanted more than that for my life.

So when my mom called me, I answered. I always did. Because someone was either dead or dying or she needed something from me. And while the latter frequently annoyed me, I couldn't help but hope for it when the alternative involved someone's demise.

"Hey, what's up?" I asked, closing the door to Sophia's bedroom behind me.

"Hi, Andrew, it's Mom."

It always sounded strange to be called Andrew. Only my mom referred to me that way. I was Andrew Christopher Nolan III, and since my dad went by Drew, my mom had always called me by my given name to distinguish us from each other. If she'd had it her way, she would've named me Jesse, a *Full House* nod I was thankful I didn't receive.

When my younger brother was born seven years later, she tried Jesse for him too, but my dad wouldn't have it. The most he would allow it for was our bulldog, who we all called Uncle just to mess with my mom.

"What's new?" I asked, waiting to hear whose funeral I'd need to attend or what she wanted from me.

"I just called to see how you're doing. How's the bar?"

"Good. Same as it always is. What's up with you guys?"

"Not much," my mom said casually. "Dad started working at the car dealer up the street."

I was pretty sure he had worked there years ago, but I didn't ask. Management had probably changed since then, and they must have had no clue he'd ever been employed there. I tried to remember why he'd left, but my mom spoke again before I could.

"He hurt his back trying to lift a tire he had no business going near in the first place."

And there it was. The reason for her call. Undoubtedly, my dad's injury meant he was unable to do as much around the house, so she'd called me.

"He okay?" I asked.

"He'll be fine. Lying around on the couch, milking it every chance he gets."

I laughed softly. "I'm sure." Silence lingered on both ends of the phone for what felt like a long time. "Can I do anything to help?" If I waited long enough, she'd ask anyway, so I put it out there first.

"Yeah, if you have the time. Just some yard work and stuff. The grass is getting pretty long, and that branch finally fell off that tree in the backyard the other day. It can probably just be broken up and tossed into the woods."

"Okay, I'll get time at some point to come over this week. What's Cody up to? He should be doing some of it too."

My brother still lived at home, and there was no reason he shouldn't be helping if I could find time to.

"I could ask him if I ever saw him. He's never home."

Sounded like Cody. "I'll call him."

"Thanks, Andrew. The girls and I miss you around here." She said "girls" like they were all jumping rope and playing dress-up. Two of the three "girls" were older than me but still lived at home, mooching off my parents, who barely had anything to give.

"I miss you too." And it was true. I did miss them. I just didn't miss that life. It was why I'd moved out when I was old enough to get a job that paid for a small apartment and why I only talked to a couple of my buddies from high school.

I'd realized shortly after graduation that if I were going to go anywhere in life, be anything, I'd need to distance myself from the people and places that were holding me back. And then, when I'd agreed to "sub" for Brody, I'd all but cut them off completely.

I didn't know for sure, but I had a pretty good feeling they'd have opinions about my choices that I didn't care to hear. I knew damn well they thought college was a waste of time and money, and I didn't think their perspective would change just because I wasn't paying for it—especially since I wasn't even getting college credits for them. It wasn't something they'd be on board with, and I didn't need any more doubt infiltrating my mind. I already doubted myself enough.

It was the reason I'd always been so protective of Cody. I wanted better for him than he wanted for himself. He was a good kid with a sharp mind. I didn't tell him that enough. No one did. It'd be good for both of us to spend some time together, even if it was cleaning up our parents' yard.

"Have you guys thought about Cody's birthday?"

"What about it?" my mom asked. "It's not until December."

"Yeah, but it's his eighteenth. I thought we could do something special for him."

"What'd you have in mind? We never did anything special for the rest of you."

That was true, though her argument didn't do much to help her maternal image. She meant well. She and my dad both did, but there was no giving five kids anything more than they needed.

"I don't know. Just like a small party or something."

My mom was quiet for a few seconds. "You think we could have it at Rafferty's? Do you guys have a back room or something? Maybe the owner'd give us a deal."

My first choice would not have been to volunteer the bar as a place for my kid brother's birthday party, but my mom clearly wasn't offering their house as a venue, and something was better than nothing. There was no way they could afford to rent a place out.

"I can check."

"Okay, we can make it a surprise!" she said, suddenly enthusiastic. "Let me know if you need any help with the planning or anything. I'm sure the girls would be happy to help too."

"Sure, okay. And I'll let you know when Cody and I can help with the yard work."

We said our goodbyes, and as I hung up the phone, I wondered how I always seemed to bite off more than I could chew. I was currently taking higher-level college classes, working almost full-time, helping someone run for sorority president, and now I was planning a surprise party.

My life was almost unrecognizable. And it made me happier than I'd been in a while until I remembered much of it wasn't really my life.

By the time I made it back out to the living room, my group was packing up to leave.

"I think I just agreed to plan a party," I said, scratching my head as I let my conversation with my mom sink in.

Aniyah shook her head. "Does every member of the Mason family need a lesson on why parties are manufactured popularity contests?"

"Apparently," I said.

Aniyah just shook her head again and threw the last of her books into her enormous purse. We'd gotten a good amount accomplished, and once everyone knew what their individual responsibilities were, they headed out. Carter was still there, about to begin his study session with Sophia. He pointed to her room now that I wasn't in there and told her he was going to get set up.

Once he was out of earshot, Sophia said, "Everything okay? You seemed like you weren't expecting her to call."

"Yeah. Fine. She just needed me to help with some stuff around the house." I pressed my hands into my eyes before massaging my temples. "And then I somehow agreed to plan a surprise party for my brother."

"Yikes." She winced.

I'm sure my face showed just how daunting I found the whole process, even if it was only a birthday party for my little brother.

"I also think I somehow made it my idea, which means I can only blame myself for whatever work I have ahead of me."

She smiled widely, raising her eyebrows in a way that made me nervous for what she was about to say. "I'll help you plan your party if you help me plan mine."

It was an offer I couldn't refuse.

Chapter Fifteen

SOPHIA

I was straightening up my—well, *Brody's*—bedroom when I heard a distinct ringtone coming from my phone, which was charging on the bedside table. I took a deep breath before picking it up and answering.

"Hi, Mom."

"Sophia." Her tone was clipped as sharply as her chestnut bob. Everything about Kate Mason was severe and angular, and while she could, at times, be as warm as a bonfire, she could also ice someone out with a simple stare. It depended on her mood. And her mood right now sounded positively glacial.

"What's new?" I asked as I sank onto the side of the bed, trying to sound upbeat and sincere.

"Quite a bit, it would seem. I just got off the phone with Vivian. You do remember Mrs. Follett, don't you? Macy's mother? The conversation was . . . enlightening."

And here I thought things had already gotten as bad as they could get. What an idiot I was. Of course, I knew that it was a possibility that someone in my sorority would tell their parents about the house drama, but I hadn't really thought that my name would get back to my mom.

Usually the sisters were good about not snitching on one another, knowing that some of our mothers were part of the Zeta Eta Chi grapevine. But evidently Macy was a narc in sheep's clothing... or whatever.

"Oh yeah? Did she want to discuss Macy's botched plastic surgery?" No need to overplay my hand. Maybe she didn't know what I thought she did. Or maybe I could distract her with juicy gossip of a Mexican boob job gone awry.

"No, she did not. Though that is something I'd like to hear more about."

Score one for me.

"*After* we discuss why on earth you're threatening to run against Aamee for president."

And tied up again. "I wouldn't say 'threatening' so much as following through."

Her sigh, which she'd inherited from my grandmother, was deep and long. I always wondered if the women on her side of the family had a higher lung capacity than the average person.

"Do you have any idea how embarrassing it was to hear about this from Vivian? Why didn't you tell me?"

"First of all, I don't think Macy should be talking about house business anyway. So the fact that you heard it from her mom is an invasion of my privacy."

"Is it not public knowledge that you're running?"

"Well... yeah... I guess."

"So maybe 'invasion of privacy' is a bit overstated. Besides, Macy had no idea how to proceed in a situation like this. She reached out to her mother for *help*. A novel idea for you, I know." Her voice was dry and dripping with sarcasm, but I knew it for what it truly was: a mask covering up the hurt.

She felt betrayed that I hadn't come to her with this, and that made me feel even shittier than having her know in the first place.

"It's not … I'm sorry … that I didn't tell you. I wanted to show you I could handle it and not make you worry about me being kicked out of the house."

"You were kicked out of the house! Sophia Mason, what the hell is going on?"

I cringed. "So I guess Macy left that part out, huh?"

"Start talking."

So I did. I told her about what had happened with Carter and Aamee's subsequent punishment. I also threw in all the ways Aamee was a shit president for good measure.

"Are you telling me you've been out of the house for weeks? Where have you been staying?" My mom's voice was bordering on shrill, and part of me warmed at her concern. Not because I didn't think she worried about me but because it was good to have proof every now and then.

"At Brody's."

She was quiet for a moment, probably wondering if she'd heard correctly. "Your brother let you move in with him?" The disbelief in her tone conveyed all that needed to be said about my relationship with my brother.

"Yeah. He even let me have the bedroom." What the hell. Might as well give the guy some brownie points where I could.

"Oh. That's … well, that's very nice."

"Yeah, he's been great." The fact that I was referring to Drew was something I'd keep to myself. What she didn't— *couldn't*—know wouldn't hurt her. Until a loudmouth sorority mom blabbed to her, anyway. Hopefully that was one secret I'd be more successful in protecting.

"I have to say, I'm not overly pleased with how you've gone about dealing with this situation, including your decision to keep it from me. If you'd simply called me, I probably could've gotten you back in the house without all this ... drama."

That was probably true, but what would the cost have been? All my sisters thinking the rules didn't apply to me because my mommy had strings she could pull? No thanks.

"I'm sorry for not telling you," I said again, because even though I'd had my reasons, hurting her hadn't been one of them.

"Yes, well, what's done is done. And it does sound as if Aamee is ... ill-suited for the position. You're a much better choice, and I'm proud of you for stepping up."

I was silent for a second as my throat got tight, and a tear slipped down my cheek. My mom had said similar things before, but more like I owed it to her to follow in her footsteps than I actually deserved the honor. It was nice to have her support, not just because it was what she wanted but because she thought I'd be good at it. It was a boost to my confidence that I was in desperate need of.

"Hey, Soph. You in there?"

My eyes widened as I heard Drew's voice bellow through the door.

"Oh, is that Brody?" my mom asked. "Put him on. He hasn't been answering my calls recently. I was about to send out a search party."

Shit, shit, shit. I was going to kill my brother. What if Mom had shown up here because he couldn't answer his damn phone? He really was a fucking moron.

"Oh, no. It's my . . . study partner."

"The one who got you kicked out of your house?" she asked, clearly unimpressed with Carter's role in getting me evicted. "Is there more going on there that I should know about?"

"No," I replied on a laugh. Carter and me? Hilarious. The guy was definitely growing on me, but more like a happy-go-lucky weed than a romantic vine.

"All right." She sounded like she didn't necessarily believe it was all right, but she was willing to drop it in light of all the other fires threatening to burn down my life. "Can you tell Brody to call me when you see him, please? I would like to hear how he's doing every now and then."

"I will. And thanks, Mom. I feel better about everything after talking to you." The truth of the words was more than a little shocking. Probably to both of us.

"Maybe you can remember that for next time, hmm?"

I smiled, and I hoped she could hear it in my voice. "Definitely."

Chapter Sixteen

DREW

Fridays were by far the most tiring day of the week. I had class from eight until around eleven in the morning, a "break" until noon, which was barely enough time to walk back home, grab some lunch, and get back to my afternoon class, which didn't end until almost three since it was only one day a week.

If Brody wanted me to go to his classes second semester, he'd have to let me choose the times. And since I didn't get home from work until almost two in the morning, my Fridays never ended. They just rolled into Saturday without my noticing most of the time. Whoever came up with the phrase TGIF clearly hadn't ever gone to college full-time while bartending.

I was looking for a black button-down—a requirement at Rafferty's—that wasn't wrinkled, when I heard a knock at the door.

I wasn't expecting anyone, and since Sophia still wasn't home yet, I had no idea who it could be. I ignored it and hoped they went away so I wouldn't be late for work, but when the knocking continued after a few minutes, I figured I'd better answer it.

I was still working on buttoning my shirt when I pulled the door open to find a very tall blond-haired girl standing on the other side. I found her slightly intimidating, and it had nothing to do with her height.

"Hi, is Sophia here?" She looked a little confused as she peered around me and into the apartment.

"No, but she should be home any minute. Can I help you?"

There was no way I was letting this random in, especially when I was about to leave. For all I knew, she could be a spy sent by Aamee to scope out her competition. Or worse, to sabotage it. I wasn't about to let that happen, even if it meant boxing out this Jolly Blond Giant so she couldn't infiltrate enemy territory.

"Oh, okay, how about Brody? Is he here?"

"I'm Brody," I said. *And if you think you're getting into this apartment and going through my pretend sister's stuff, you'd better think again!*

The girl laughed, but when I didn't join her, she stopped.

"What's so funny?" I asked.

"You're not Brody."

Fuck, fuck, fuck.

How had I not anticipated this? I'd underestimated Aamee. We both had. She'd figured out who I really was, and now the charade was up. She'd sent her bodyguard or mercenary to take me out. I just hoped my death would be more figurative than literal.

Brody and Sophia's parents would find out what was really going on, they'd both get in a shit ton of trouble, and I'd have to find a new place to live. I had to keep this going as long as I could. Maybe Aamee didn't know for sure that I wasn't Brody. Maybe she'd just suspected it for some reason and was testing me.

"If I'm not Brody, and this is Brody's apartment, who am I, then?" I finished buttoning my shirt and grabbed my shoes from beside the door, sliding them on as I waited for her to answer.

"I don't know who you are," she said, pushing her eyebrows together in confusion. "A friend of Brody's, maybe?"

Good. She didn't know anything for certain. "Nope. I'm Brody," I said with a confidence I hoped would put to rest any doubt she had about my identity.

"Is this like a joke or something?" she asked. "Sophia," she called. "Are you in there somewhere?"

She tried moving to the side of me, but I stepped in front of her. "No way," I said. "You're not coming in. I'm about to leave for work, so you can go back to the sorority house and tell Aamee her little espionage mission was a failure—just like her presidential campaign will be."

"Why would I be on Aamee's side when I'm coming to help Sophia?"

Now she wasn't the only one who was confused. "I'm sorry," I said skeptically. "*Who* are you?"

"I'm Taylor," she said. "But I'm pretty sure I should be the one asking who *you* are, because I know Brody, and you're definitely not him."

I'm not sure how I'd managed to have nearly the exact same conversation twice since I'd moved in, but I knew one thing for sure: I was not making it to work on time.

SOPHIA

I didn't expect Drew to be home when I arrived at the

apartment, and even more surprising was that he was sitting with Taylor, who wasn't supposed to arrive until the next day.

"Oh my God," I screamed, causing her to jump up from the couch where she'd been sitting with Drew, scrolling through her phone. "When did you get here? You're early! You're never early." I didn't mean that last part as an insult, but it'd slipped, and since it was true, I didn't apologize for it.

"My night class got canceled, so I thought I'd surprise you."

"I'm so glad you did! When did you get here?" I asked, my smile wide with all the possibilities now that Taylor would be staying two nights. She was always a blast, and if anyone could help me plan a party, it was her, because she was the life of it.

"A half hour or so ago."

"Give me a hug."

We each ran in place with our arms outstretched. It was a strange dance that probably looked like a cross between an Irish dancer and a toddler who had to pee.

We'd performed this dance since we were young, every time we'd see each other after a long time. It was a ritual that was so old, neither of us could remember how it began.

We added a few squeals to our celebration before we wrapped each other up in a huge hug. I hadn't seen Taylor in six months because she'd stayed on campus over the summer for an internship. Our reunion was long overdue, and I was ecstatic she'd made it here almost a day earlier than she'd planned.

We were still hugging when she pulled far enough away to look at me and ask, "So are we gonna talk about the hot elephant in the room?"

I laughed loudly and looked to Drew, who was still sitting on the couch looking up at us, amused.

"I was planning to call you tonight and explain our... living situation, since I didn't have time to get into it when I asked you to come out here."

"What's going on? Where's Brody? Why is Drew living here?"

"You didn't explain anything?" I asked him.

He shrugged. "Didn't know if I could."

The "hot elephant" made a valid point. It wasn't really his place to share where Brody was or why he wasn't here, and that meant Drew couldn't explain why *he* was living here. It was considerate of him to keep the specifics under wraps until I could tell her myself.

Drew was quiet while I gave Taylor the details of Brody's overseas adventure, my hesitance to live with a complete stranger who I had to pretend was my brother, and Drew filled in the part about how the arrangement benefited him as well.

I apologized for not telling Taylor about all of it sooner, but she understood. Our lives were hectic enough without the added drama Brody had heaped on me.

"Okay, so let me get this straight," she said. "You're Brody, and I've known you since I was little. Shouldn't be too hard. I'm only here for two days. I'll just refer to you as Brody no matter what so I don't mess it up if I'm around anyone else."

"Okay, that's fine," I said. I'd been expecting her to at least act like all of this was a bigger deal than it was, but I guess to her it wasn't. Taylor had always been matter-of-fact and possessed an efficiency for getting things done that I'd envied since we were kids.

Other than the fact that she was my ho from long ago,

Taylor's determination and drive was much of the reason she was my first call after I'd realized what I'd need to do to become sorority president. If anyone could help me outline a plan for election, it was Taylor Peterson.

"That okay with you, Brody?" she asked Drew.

Clearly amused, Drew smiled and gave her a nod.

I looked between the two of them. "So if you didn't fill her in on all of this, what'd you guys talk about for a half hour?"

Drew smiled almost to the point of laughter, but he didn't let it fully erupt. "Taylor showed me pictures of the two of you from when you were kids."

I put a hand over my face, but I was sure it didn't do much to hide how red I could feel my cheeks getting. "You did not!"

"Don't kill me." Taylor was already backing away.

"Oh my God! What pictures did you have? They didn't even have iPhones when we were little."

"When I told my mom I was coming up here, she got so excited she started texting me all these pictures of us from the albums she has." Taylor looked at me apologetically. "Nine to fourteen weren't our best years."

"Aww," Drew said, glancing at me with a smile. "I thought you were cute."

"In like a three-legged dog kind of way where my cuteness is directly proportional to how sorry you feel for me?"

He laughed but didn't argue. "If I can find some old pictures of myself, I'll show them to you. I wasn't getting any modeling contracts either."

"Do you get them now?" Taylor asked sincerely, causing me to smack her.

"You're so embarrassing," I told her.

"Seriously, though," she continued. "What are you doing

taking classes for some idiot when you could be in a magazine or starring in a Netflix Original?"

Drew laughed loudly, but I could tell he was a little embarrassed by the comment. He'd received more than his share of superficial compliments since I'd moved in, and something told me he wasn't used to getting them. Damn college girls.

"I don't know," he said. "Acting's not really my thing."

Taylor let her gaze drift to me and then back to Drew, who was still showing off that sheepish grin that revealed just how modest he really was.

"Hmm, could've fooled me, Brody," she said.

I loved Taylor, but I also wanted to kill her sometimes.

Chapter Seventeen

DREW

"We're done!" Taylor announced as she and Sophia emerged from the party-planning headquarters of Sophia's room with an empty bottle of tequila.

They'd only retreated to Sophia's room an hour ago, when Aniyah, Xander, and Toby arrived for another group project session.

"An entire bottle of tequila?" I asked.

Sophia wasn't kidding. When Taylor put her mind to something, she got that shit accomplished.

Taylor looked at the empty bottle before tossing it into the recycling. It landed with a loud clang, and I tensed, unsure of whether I would hear the sound of glass breaking.

"Well, yeah," she said. "But there wasn't much in there to begin with when I brought it."

"We're done with the party planning," Sophia clarified.

"Jeez, that was fast," I said. Taylor really was an asset. Maybe I'd have to ask her to help me plan Cody's before she left.

"Is that for the sorority thing or for Brody's thing?" Xander asked.

"Sophia's. My thing's for my little brother, Cody, and it's not till December, so I haven't really started thinking much about it yet."

"Cody and Brody?" Aniyah asked before looking to Sophia. "Your parents should've named you Jodi."

"Ha!" Sophia laughed humorlessly. "I hear that a lot."

Xander nodded before saying, "So when you say *your* little brother, is that like . . . " He gestured between Sophia and me.

I suddenly realized if Cody were my brother, he should be hers too, a fact Sophia had clearly picked up on after Aniyah's comment. I was so slow on the uptake sometimes.

"How does that work that he's your brother but not Sophia's?" he asked.

My heart picked up its pace as my fight-or-flight instinct kicked in, and I felt adrenaline rush through my body. It was one of those moments where you feel your stomach tense instantly and you wonder if you're going to shit yourself.

I wasn't sure what I actually looked like in the moment, but when my eyes went to Sophia, I had a pretty good guess. She looked pale—well, as pale as her complexion would allow—and almost sick.

I hadn't been kidding about being a bad actor. The fact that we'd been able to keep all of this going for this long had been a miracle even Mother Teresa would have been impressed by.

Neither of us seemed able to speak, and I felt the light closing in around me like I was about to faint in front of a roomful of people I barely knew. Maybe if I did, they'd have to call for help and they'd forget about Xander's question completely.

How had we been so careless? How had *I* been so careless? I'd held up the phone so everyone could see it said *Mom* when she'd called. Had I said it was *my* mom? Had I said anything at all? My life—or rather Brody's life—was flashing before my eyes in a moment that seemed to drag on endlessly. Until suddenly from the depths of my mind, I pulled out an explanation that made complete sense.

"We have different moms," I said, feeling the color come back to my face and my breathing settle.

I looked to Sophia, and her shoulders seemed to relax a bit. I wondered if anyone in my group noticed the change in our appearance.

"Right, brothers from another mother," she said at the same time I told them, "Sophia and I share a dad."

Had she just said Cody and I had different moms? I felt like I was trying to solve a calculus question under water. Nothing made sense, time was running out, and I was in desperate need of rescue.

After a few more seconds, Toby was the first to speak. "Wait, you and Cody have different mothers, and you and Sophia have different mothers? So you two have the same dad, but it's not the same dad Cody has because he's not Sophia's brother."

His words were slow, deliberate, but that didn't change the fact that none of the pieces were going to fit into a complete puzzle.

"But wasn't it your mom who called about Cody's party?" he continued. "Why does she care about Cody's party if he's not her son?" He seemed to be talking out loud as he pointed between us, as if hearing the words would cause them to make more sense.

Prepare to be disappointed, Toby.

I looked to Sophia, hoping like hell she could fabricate some sort of explanation that would magically make all of this believable. Unfortunately, she was staring at me with a look that said the same.

I'd nearly gotten us out of this mess when she'd thrown us back into it. There was no way I was capable of delivering *two* plausible explanations when I'd barely come up with one. We muttered some "yeahs" and then a few "nos," trying to buy ourselves more time, but it only made the story more convoluted.

"It's a funny story, actually."

It was Taylor who'd spoken. I looked to her with hope. She was coming to save us—running down the beach in her red swimsuit, her blond hair waving in the breeze as she jogged in slow motion.

"When we were all kids," she continued, "Brody used to tell people Sophia was his little brother because he'd always wanted one, and Soph was a huge tomboy."

There it was. The rescue tube we'd been waiting for.

"I was?" Sophia said as more of a question, and I looked over to the kitchen counter to see if there was any tape around so I could put it over her mouth.

"I mean I was," she said, more confidently this time. "Short hair, polo shirts, baseball caps, these really saggy pants with boxers showing. It wasn't a good look."

I was tempted to shift my focus from Sophia to the others, but I was scared if I looked away from Sophia, she might blurt out something we wouldn't be able to get ourselves out of. She'd already confessed to wearing boxers.

"She always shortened my name to Bro," I cut in, just so

Sophia wouldn't keep talking. "So then I started calling her bro because she looked like a dude." I turned to Sophia. "Right, bro?"

"Yeah, Bro," she said slowly.

"How old were you guys?" Xander asked, appearing truly interested.

This time Sophia and I made eye contact so we wouldn't say something different than the other. "Uh, what were we, Soph, like . . . five and seven or so?"

"Something like that," she agreed.

"So whose idea was it for you to get your hair cut short?" Aniyah asked.

"And did your parents buy you the boy clothes on their own?" Xander added. "Or did you ask for them?"

Sophia hesitated before saying, "I can't remember. Does it matter?"

"It does through a sociological lens. This would've been before assigning a gender to your child would've been considered taboo to some of our society, so the details seem important to your development as a young woman."

Toby was studying us like we were guinea pigs in an experiment he was conducting. "This is all so interesting. I'd like to know the specifics as well."

"You know," Taylor said, clapping her hands together once. "It was an awkward phase. Sophia doesn't really like to talk about it."

"Right on," Xander said. "Whatever you're comfortable with."

Toby and Aniyah nodded and muttered their agreement. "We can drop it."

And thank fuck they did. If it wouldn't have made an

already strange situation even stranger, I would've kissed Taylor right then and there. She'd saved our dumb asses.

"But if you need any help planning Cody's party," Aniyah offered, "I'm happy to help." It was a clear effort to ease the tension and transition to a subject Sophia was comfortable with. She probably didn't actually have any intention of helping with Cody's party, but she'd offered, and it'd be rude of me to decline.

"Thanks," I said. "That'd be great."

SOPHIA

Drew and his group got back to work pretty quickly after that, and I was happy to have things go back to normal. Or as normal as they could be anymore.

Taylor looked at me wide-eyed as we headed to the kitchen to grab some snacks. I wasn't sure if it was the tequila or the conversation I'd just been a part of that had me feeling queasy, but something told me it was probably a combination.

Taylor started opening up cabinets like she was raiding a house in some sort of apocalyptic society. Apparently, people there survived on Wheat Thins and peanut butter, because she currently had both in her hands, and she was clutching them to her chest like she was afraid someone might tear them from her grasp.

I didn't want to tell her that person would be Drew. The food was his. She probably wouldn't give it up even if she'd known, so I'd just have to replace the items later. I couldn't blame him for being possessive over his Wheat Thins.

Taylor opened the box and dug into the bag, pulling out

a handful of the crackers and tossing a few into her mouth. Planning on getting something of my own, I managed to restrain myself for only a few seconds before I caved and realized I couldn't resist them. I'd be replacing them anyway, so what the hell.

We each poured ourselves a glass of wine—at least *that* was mine—as we ate and chatted some more about the party I'd be throwing in November. Aamee was doing a costume party for Halloween—a musical couples' theme. So I'd opted for a black-and-white theme with the twist of allowing green and silver accents, which were the school colors.

We were just deciding whether we'd encourage any shade of green or if it had to be the Lazarus University hunter green when Xander spoke up from his spot on the couch.

"So you're just having people follow a dress code like we're in some kind of elitist private school?" He laughed, making his comment seem less insulting than it originally came across.

I spun the barstool I was sitting on so I could face him. "It shows school spirit, which is important since I'm running for president of a *school*-sanctioned group."

"It's cute," Taylor added.

"It's lame," Aniyah said. "You need something innovative and trendy that'll make you stand out."

While she did have a point, I hesitated to admit it. It would not only mean going back to the drawing board, but I also had no idea what was considered trendy and innovative. Pretty much every theme had been done at one point or another. All you had to do was Google it. Which we'd already done for forty-five minutes before deciding on the black, white, and green theme.

"Okay, did you have an idea?" I asked, careful not to sound

rude. I was honestly curious.

If Aniyah had anything good to offer, I'd be more than happy to entertain the option. I'd go with whatever would result in the best turnout and most funds raised. And unlike Aamee, who valued her own opinion more than any other, I thought it was important to gather a mix of perspectives. Even if a few of them would never step foot in a sorority event.

Aniyah thought for a minute, putting her pen to her lips before looking back up at me. "I don't, actually. But I bet if we all thought about it, we could come up with something better."

"Okay," I said, looking to each person in the room to gauge if they seemed like they were on board to brainstorm.

Toby was on the edge of his seat. Literally. He'd probably never been involved in something social at school, let alone a party with so many females. He looked ready to explode with excitement.

Xander, on the other hand, appeared less thrilled. He pulled his beanie down lower so it almost covered his eyes and settled back against the couch cushions. I wasn't sure if he was preparing to tune us out or take a nap.

"Do you guys really want to help?" I asked.

"Of course we do," Xander said slowly and with so much sarcasm, it practically bled from his pores. Then he looked to his other group members out of low eyelids. "We're never finishing this project, are we?"

"Relax," Drew said. "We're almost done. I can type the rest of it up tomorrow and share it with you guys to edit." He looked to me at the mention of typing, which almost made me laugh. But I'd be happy to help him, especially since he'd been so helpful to me.

"Okay," Xander said. "Let's think about this logically.

Most of the same people who attend Aamee's party will be the ones attending yours, right?"

"Yeah, I'd assume so. Why?"

"I'm just thinking they aren't gonna want to go to two parties that close together."

Taylor looked at him like his head had just fallen off his neck and she was trying to figure out how he was still able to speak. "Do you know anything about college kids?"

"Uh, yeah. I am one. I get that they like parties, but there are a million of them. Sophia should do something different. Something that will raise a lot of money and still have a ton of participation."

"Obviously," Taylor said. "That's the whole goal."

"Yeah, but I get what Xander's saying," I said. "If they pay to get into Aamee's party and they're bidding on things or whatever she's planning to do to raise money, they aren't going to want to do that again, especially right before Christmas break when people have to put out money for other things, like flights home and presents and stuff. We have to make it something they feel like they're missing out on if they don't attend. Something they *get* something out of if they're paying."

"A Quidditch tournament!" Toby said with a level of excitement that directly mirrored everyone else's level of *No fucking way!* "Teams could pay to participate. People could even place bets."

"I don't think the school would like us gambling to make money," I said.

"And I don't think anyone likes Quidditch," Taylor added, causing everyone else to agree.

Drew looked at Toby. "I don't even know what that is."

Toby opened his mouth to speak, but thankfully Aniyah

spoke up before he could explain the rules and regulations.

"Maybe not Quidditch," she said, "but the idea isn't bad. We could do like a Powder Puff football game or something. Maybe Carter could get the team on board, and each girl could be matched with a different football player or something. Girls could pay to play. I don't know all the ins and outs, but we could work out the details, I'm sure."

Drew looked skeptical. "I think that would get an okay turnout, but would we raise enough money? I mean, we could charge people to get in, but how much would people pay to play or pay to watch?"

I shrugged. "No idea. I think paying *for* something is key though. So let's run with that for a minute. What do people pay for?"

Answers came from all areas of the room: alcohol, food, entertainment, sex. The last suggestion had come from Toby, causing everyone to stare quizzically at him.

"I mean, I wasn't talking about *myself*," he clarified. "I was speaking in general terms."

"Maybe he's on to something," I said.

Drew laughed. "I don't think turning the sorority house into a brothel is the best way to get you elected as president when you got evicted for letting a guy study in your room."

I got up to smack him on the arm and then sat down on the floor next to the comfy chair he was in. "I was actually thinking of a bachelor auction."

Xander rolled his eyes. "Of course you'd want guys to be the fresh meat. Flipping gender roles doesn't make it any less sexist."

"Worried no one will bid on you?" I teased.

He balled up a piece of paper and threw it at me, but it

soared over my head, even though I was only about three feet from him. Suspicions confirmed: Xander had no athletic ability.

"I'm serious, though," he continued. "Just because people are bidding on guys doesn't mean people won't be offended. What if the situation were reversed, and a frat was auctioning off women?"

"That's a good point," Aniyah agreed.

"But people are offended by anything these days," I said. "You'll have people claim the black-and-white theme is racist or something. And I was thinking of auctioning guys off so they could do things for people. It can be simple things like carrying books to class or bringing someone lunch. But we could have them outline their strengths when they volunteer, like if they can repair things around the house or cook or tutor or something."

The more I spoke, the more excited I got about the idea. I hoped everyone would see the potential in it, but even if they didn't, I might have to consider doing it anyway.

"Maybe it could even have to do with their majors," I continued. "I bet some of the guys in the fitness and nutrition programs would love to create workouts or meal plans for people. They can use it as volunteer work, so it's a win-win. We could open up the bidding to the sorority legacies if we wanted."

"We'd have to create some pretty strict rules," Drew said. "You don't want some elderly woman making an eighteen-year-old freshman mow her lawn in nothing but a Speedo."

"Um, that's exactly what I'd want if I were an elderly woman," Taylor said.

"Let's worry about the specifics later," I suggested. "Do

you guys all think this could work?"

Aniyah was the first to speak. "I do."

Drew agreed. "You'd probably get a pretty big turnout, and people might pay a lot of money for someone depending on what their skills are."

I looked to Toby, who nodded, and then to Xander, because even though their opinions didn't *really* matter in the sense that it wasn't a formal vote, they mattered to me.

"You better not expect me to be in the auction," Xander said.

"I'd never dream of it," I said with a smile.

I finally had something I could be truly excited about. Something that was "trendy and innovative," as Aniyah had suggested. Something that could raise a shit ton of money for a charity of my choice. And something that would hopefully show Aamee and the rest of the sorority who was the best fit for president.

I just prayed I was right.

Chapter Eighteen

DREW

We'd all gotten sidetracked talking, and by the time we realized we were starving, it was almost eight. I felt bad I hadn't thought to have more snacks on hand for my group, but whatever. Hindsight was twenty-twenty.

"We should go out," Aniyah stated after poking around in the kitchen and coming up empty.

"There's a sandwich place down the street that's pretty good," Toby offered.

"No, I mean *out* out," Aniyah corrected. "We should go somewhere that has greasy food and dancing."

Xander looked at her cautiously. "You want to go somewhere people congregate to dance?"

The look she gave him would've made the balls fall off a lesser man. "Are you implying I'm not a people person?"

Xander simply smirked. "Not implying it so much as indirectly stating it."

She crossed her arms over her chest and popped a hip out. "I go out all the time."

Nodding slowly, Xander said, "I totally believe that," in a tone that showed he didn't believe it at all.

The rest of us watched the two of them as if they were partaking in the world's most violent tennis match. There was a weird tension that radiated between them. Something that was close to hate but narrowly missed the mark and jettisoned them toward something even more incendiary. Which for Xander was probably a bad thing.

Aniyah narrowed her eyes at him. "I'm more fun than you could even contemplate trying to handle."

Xander rose slowly, never taking his eyes off her. "Then I guess it's a good thing we're going out so you can prove it."

The stare-down continued until Toby spoke up. "Um, should we . . . I mean, are we dressed okay? Should we change?"

I gave him a quick once-over. He was at least wearing jeans, so that was a step in the right direction.

"You can borrow one of my shirts," I told him. The idea of launching Operation Get Toby Laid was becoming increasingly appealing. Not to mention the fact that I couldn't wait to watch Aniyah and Xander rage-grind all over a dance floor—not in a perverted way, but because I wanted to see how much angry friction they could create before they combusted.

"Oh, I don't think . . . Are we the same size?" Toby asked.

We weren't, but I'd fucking hand-knit him something to wear to make this happen.

"We'll figure it out."

And we did. Fifteen minutes later, I was dressed in a white button-down and a pair of dark jeans, and Toby was in a polo of mine that was so tight on me, it bordered on obscene. I usually reserved it for nights when I had an itch that needed to be scratched and wanted to be noticed quickly. It fit Toby well enough, and he seemed to like it even if he was a bit uncomfortable in peach.

"Are you sure it looks okay?" he asked for at least the sixth time.

I put my hand on his shoulder and squeezed. "It takes a certain kind of guy to pull off that color, and you, my man, are pulling it off."

His smile was wide and happy. Fuck did I like this kid.

The girls had all disappeared into the bedroom to do whatever girls did in order to get ready for a night out. Xander continued to recline on the couch and play on his phone, seemingly unbothered by the fact that he was in sweatpants and a plain black Henley.

It thankfully wasn't much longer before the girls joined us. Aniyah was still wearing the tight red shirt and dark-rinse jeans she'd had on when she arrived, but she'd definitely added some makeup to her eyes.

Taylor was also in jeans but had on a light-blue tank top that she was pulling a soft-looking white jacket over. Both girls looked good—great, really—but I only had eyes for Sophia, who was wearing a beige sweater-dress thing that came to mid-thigh and fell off one shoulder. She'd paired it with boots that came up to her knees.

She stopped beside me, and my tongue felt numb when I said, "You look nice."

"Thanks," she replied. "Figured if I was going to run for president, I needed to look the part."

I wasn't sure how what she wore to a club would impact her role as president, but I also sure as shit wasn't going to complain.

"We ready?" Sophia asked everyone.

Everyone murmured assent as we followed her and Taylor out of the apartment. I locked the door behind us, and we were on our way.

The bar Aniyah had chosen was only three blocks from the apartment, so despite it being a bit chilly out, we decided walking was our best bet. Our hodgepodge of a group moved like a chatty blob down the sidewalk, causing people to walk around us as we made our way down the street.

We hadn't gotten far from the apartment when I felt my phone buzz in my pocket. I fished it out and saw a text from Carter.

Hey, man. Did you know football
players who can hold their liquor
are a dying breed?

I stared at the phone in confusion for a second, unsure what the hell he was talking about. Not that I should've been surprised. Carter had taken to texting me random things in the couple of weeks we'd known each other. I typed a response.

I did not. I also find that surprising.
Aren't you guys all huge?

His reply came quickly.

The bigger they are the
harder they fall, dude.

I didn't think you guys would
drink much during the season.

*Ha! Half of these guys will be in AA
by the time they're seniors. But it's
worse than usual tonight because
we have a bye this weekend.*

Ah. Gotcha.

What are you doing?

*Heading to some bar with my study
group and Sophia and her friend.
Aniyah said it was called Tonic.*

*I know that place. Total meat
market. I'll meet you there!*

I couldn't help but laugh at his last text. Sophia must've heard me because she turned and looked at me quizzically.

"It's Carter," I explained. "He's gonna meet us at the bar."

"Cool" was all she said in reply, but her smile showed she meant it.

I texted Carter that we'd meet him inside and then put my phone back into my pocket.

We arrived at the bar soon after and paid a five-dollar cover to get in. I hadn't thought to ask and make sure everyone in our group was twenty-one—some bartender I was—but everyone produced an ID, so I guessed we were set.

Aniyah led us to a corner of the bar where there were two open tables. I paused to take the place in. The bar was huge and set in the center of the room, with leather-upholstered chairs surrounding it. Three bartenders shared the space, filling orders, while servers floated among the tables that lined the walls. The floor was wood, and the space had a kind of rustic vibe. Definitely not what I was expecting from a place called Tonic.

"This place is nice," I said.

"There's a second floor that's more like a club," Aniyah explained when we sat down. "I figured we could eat down here before heading upstairs. Have any of you been here before?"

"I have," Sophia answered, but everyone else stayed quiet.

I was surprised there was a club overhead. They must have excellent soundproofing.

We looked through the menus and decided to order a bunch of apps to share. The server was just returning with our drinks when Carter showed up.

"Hey, can I get a Corona?" he asked her. "Thanks." Then he plopped down into an open chair next to Toby and almost immediately leaned over him and extended his hand toward Taylor. "Hey, how's it going? I'm Carter."

Taylor didn't hesitate to grab his hand and introduce herself.

Carter relaxed into his seat and turned to Toby. "Nice to see ya, man. Love that shirt. Very suave."

"Oh, uh, thanks. Brody lent it to me."

Carter sat back in his seat and regarded me. "That's what my life has been missing. A gay friend to give me fashion advice."

I saw Taylor's head whip toward Sophia, to which Sophia subtly shook her head. Taylor schooled her features, but I was sure there'd be a discussion happening there as soon as they were alone.

"You're gay?" Xander asked.

"Oh, uh, yeah. Yup. Definitely." Pretending to be gay gave

me new appreciation for LGBTQ people. Coming out over and over again was exhausting.

"Huh," he said. "Never would've guessed."

Aniyah scoffed. "Why would you? What, you think all gay people look and act a certain way or something?"

"Simmer down, Cujo," he replied dryly. "I usually have great gaydar is all."

Aniyah opened her mouth to no doubt yell at Xander some more, but Carter cut in before she could.

"Not me. A dude could basically blow me, and I'd have no idea."

Jesus Christ, I needed out of this conversation stat.

"How come you're out tonight, Carter?" Sophia, bless her, asked. "Doesn't the team usually hang together after games?"

"Nah, we have this week off," he answered as the server dropped off his drink. He thanked her before taking a long pull.

"Oh, that's right," Sophia said. "I forgot."

"You're a wide receiver, right?" Toby asked. He hadn't done much conversing with Carter on the few occasions they'd been in the same proximity. Maybe the shirt was giving him confidence.

Carter's face lit up like the sun. "Yeah. You like football?"

"I, yes, I do. There's a lot of strategy involved that's intriguing."

Carter wrapped an arm around Toby's shoulder. "Where have you been all my life?"

Toby's smile was wide, and as he and Carter began talking about all things football, I suspected I wasn't the only one who'd be taking Toby under his wing from here on out.

SOPHIA

Dinner went well. Carter announced proudly that he had the perfect costume for Aamee's party, but he'd been having trouble finding a date to agree to be the other half. He refused to tell us who he was going to be, but since a good-looking football player was having trouble finding a date, I could only assume he wanted someone to be something like Wardrobe Malfunction Janet Jackson.

"How 'bout you guys?" he asked. "Who are you going as?"

"Someone who thinks Greek life is a way to make money and steal people's individuality," Aniyah said.

Carter looked around like he had no idea what she was talking about. "The theme's musical couples, so you might wanna rethink that."

"I'm not going, Ochocinco."

He eyed her like he wasn't sure what to make of that before saying, "You will," as if it were his decision. "And I'll choose to take the Ochocinco comment as a compliment." Then he looked around at the rest of us. "What about all of you? Who are you going as?"

"I haven't thought much about it," Drew admitted, and I said the same. If I were going to put my focus into a sorority event, it was going to be my own.

After some peer pressure from the rest of the group, Xander said he'd consider going but couldn't make any promises, and Toby was just shocked he was invited. I didn't want to pop his pseudo-popularity bubble by telling him it was open to anyone who wanted to attend.

It surprised me how much our odd little group got along,

but there was no denying that we meshed well.

Carter drained his second beer before putting it down loudly on the table. "We heading upstairs?"

Everyone agreed, so we settled our tab and made our way up to the club. I'd been here a couple of times before—once for an eighteen-and-over night and another with a fake ID. It wasn't normally my scene, especially since Greek life came with a built-in social calendar, but I was looking forward to blowing off some steam with Taylor.

The club was much more crowded than I would've guessed, considering how laid-back it was downstairs. Music pulsed through the room as strobe lights flashed to a DJ's beat.

"Come dance with me," Taylor yelled over the noise, and she began dragging me behind her before I could reply. Not that I would've refused, but I might have at least tried to make sure the others were following us. We were quickly swallowed by gyrating bodies, and I lost sight of the others.

It didn't take long for me to lose myself to the music. Sweat began to slick my skin as we moved to the beat. On the dance floor with Taylor, I let it all go: the bullshit with Aamee, the fundraiser I'd have to throw, the complicated mess with Drew, the stress of school, all of it.

It was like the perspiration pushed it from my body and it dissipated into the air as we danced. Guys came and went, but Taylor and I paid them little to no attention, so they quickly moved on.

Eventually, though, I began feeling my body getting sluggish. I leaned close to Taylor and said into her ear, "Wanna get a drink?"

She nodded instead of responding verbally. I grabbed her hand so we wouldn't be separated and led us to the bar. There was a throng of people—at least two deep—around the bar.

"This is intense," I yelled to her.

"Maybe we should go to the bar downstairs?" Taylor asked.

I was contemplating it when I felt a presence at my shoulder. "Need a drink?" a deep, raspy voice asked.

I whirled around and locked on to a set of dark eyes. I didn't know the man who'd spoken, but I was interested in rectifying that. He was gorgeous, with curly dark hair, a wide smile full of perfect teeth, and there might have even been a dimple. It was tough to tell in the dark. It could've been a shadow from his stubbled jaw.

"Yeah," I replied, motioning to the people in front of me. "But it's probably going to be a while."

"I think I can help you out with that." He gestured for us to follow him before making his way to the end of the bar, where there was a large assortment of glasses waiting to be put away. "Wyatt!" he yelled.

I leaned in and saw a guy look over at him, hold up a finger to say he'd be over in a minute, and then finish the drink he was making.

"He'll be right over. I'm TJ, by the way." He shook my hand and then Taylor's as we each told him our names. "It's nice to meet you," he said to us, though he looked at me.

"Jesus, it's fucking packed in here," Wyatt said, slightly out of breath. "What can I get ya?"

"I'll take a fresh one," TJ said as he held up his glass. "And then whatever they're drinking."

I didn't want to order something that was a hassle to make so I asked for a Malibu and Sprite.

"I'll have the same," Taylor said.

Wyatt nodded and set off to make our drinks.

TJ turned his attention back to us. Well, to *me*.

"You guys from around here?"

I always hated questions like that, because while it could be harmless small talk, it was also exactly the kind of thing a creep would want to know.

"Not originally," I replied, being intentionally vague.

"Me neither. But I came here for college, stayed for a Master's, and now I work downtown, so I guess I'm here to stay." TJ's smile was charming and endearing—the kind of smile I couldn't help but return.

Wyatt returned with our drinks, and TJ said, "Add them to my tab."

"Oh, you don't need to do that," Taylor said.

TJ waved her off. "No worries. It'll save Wyatt time if he doesn't have to open a new tab."

That was likely bullshit, but there wasn't much point in arguing.

"Thank you," I said.

"So, what do you two do for a living?" he asked.

"We're students," Taylor replied before I had a chance to.

"Oh, what are you studying?"

"Criminal Justice," Taylor said, the words thrown out almost like they were a warning. Though I couldn't decide if it was because she usually had to deal with dudes who expected her to say something like Supermodel Training or because she was warning him that she wouldn't hesitate to turn the law against him if he stepped out of line.

"Nice. Going to go into law enforcement?"

"Law School."

TJ nodded before turning his attention to me.

"I'm a little more boring," I said. "Marketing, with a minor in psychology." I felt dumb after I added the last bit, but marketing wasn't the most interesting field, while psychology was. Not that I was trying to impress this guy. Even if he was movie-star handsome and bought me drinks and looked at me like he wanted to devour me.

Shit, I'm trying to impress him.

Though, what was so wrong with that? I was single and therefore totally available to mingle. Sure, there was the awkward attraction to my pseudo–gay brother niggling in the back of my mind, like an annoying student raising her hand despite the teacher obviously ignoring her.

But his eyes brightened, and he stood up a bit straighter. "Marketing, huh? I'm in advertising."

"Oh, wow," I replied, because what else did one say to something that wasn't at all fascinating while trying to pretend it was?

"Yeah," he said as he swayed a bit closer to me.

I could feel Taylor burning a hole in the side of my head with her eyes, but I didn't look back at her. This could be good. TJ had nothing to do with any of the drama in my life. He could be an uncomplicated side note in an otherwise chaotic narrative.

"Do you want to dance?" he asked me, his voice as low as it could be while still allowing me to hear him.

"Sure," I replied, though I kind of didn't want to join him. I felt like I *should* want to, but . . . I wasn't sure. The connection was missing. That desire to actually get to know a person wasn't there, but it could get there. After all, it was only a dance. And maybe spending more time with him would make me feel . . . something.

"Hey, TJ!" We all turned to see Wyatt motioning TJ over.

"I'll be right back," TJ said with a vehemence that made me think he was worried I was going to pull a Cinderella on him.

"I'll be here," I replied with a smile.

As soon as he walked away, Taylor rounded on me. "He's cute. Oh, and, what the fuck are you doing?"

I felt my brow furrow in confusion. "What do you mean?"

"Why are you dancing with him?"

"Because he asked," I responded slowly.

"What about Drew?"

"What about him?" My voice sounded too casual and dismissive, even to my own ears.

She glared at me, an effective strategy that always made me cave and fill the silence.

"There's nothing going on between Drew and me. You know that."

I'd spilled all the details regarding Drew, even about the almost-kiss. I had maybe skimmed over my feelings surrounding the kiss, allowing it to be written off as a drunken mistake, but did that really matter? I couldn't act on my attraction to Drew, so acknowledging my feelings out loud wouldn't change anything.

"Nothing physical is going on, but . . . " Taylor trailed off, casting a glance to where TJ was still talking to Wyatt.

"But what?"

She sighed. "You look at him. A lot. And he does the same thing."

"Of course I look at him. I live with him. I see him every day."

"Don't be intentionally stupid."

I rolled my eyes. "Okay, fine, I like looking at him. Can you blame me?"

She hesitated a moment before saying, "I like Drew."

I reared back a little because hearing her say she liked Drew was like a smack to the face, even though I had no right to feel that way.

Her eyes widened suddenly. "No, no, not like that. I mean I like him for *you*."

We stared at one another for a beat before I sighed. "What do you want me to do? Hook up with the guy who's pretending to be my brother? Sure, we've gotten close, and I maybe wish that there could be something there, but there can't."

My voice was laced with frustration because I *didn't* want to get into this. Especially not in the middle of a crowded club with the subject of the conversation lingering somewhere nearby.

Taylor opened her mouth to reply, but TJ's return cut her off.

"Sorry about that. You ready?" he asked me, gesturing toward the dance floor.

I forced a smile. "Yeah. Will you be okay?" I asked Taylor.

Nodding, she said, "I'll go find everyone else. Just . . . don't do one thing to avoid doing another."

The words were vague, but I got the message. I wasn't going to heed it, but I'd heard it. Instead of replying, I followed TJ into the throng of dancers.

When we began dancing, there was a respectable distance between us, our bodies lightly grazing when our movements were in sync enough to cause contact. But as time passed, TJ began to press closer, wrapping an arm around my back to pull me toward him as he ground against me. I shifted back a bit, but his grip on me didn't let me get far.

A red flag went up, but I dismissed it because I'd danced more provocatively in my own sorority house on a Thursday night. The talk with Taylor was clearly throwing me off my game. So I gave into the beat of the music and let my body run the show.

Until a rigid part of his body pressed into my stomach. Instead of shifting away, he ground into me harder, his lips moving to trail kisses down my neck. The red flag had become a flare gun.

If circumstances had been different, I might have basked in the attention. But as it was, this felt all kinds of wrong for a whole host of reasons—the principal one among them being Drew. The frantically waving student in my head wasn't raising her hand anymore. She was sitting smugly at her desk, knowing it was about damn time I acknowledged the truth.

I liked Drew. And whether we could act on it or not was irrelevant because the feelings remained. Which meant I needed to extricate myself from the Hoover attached to my neck.

I managed to work both hands between us and shimmy them to his shoulders so I could apply enough pressure to push him away. But the move only caused him to wrap me up tighter, his body pressed up against mine so firmly, I doubted there was a shred of space separating us.

"I'm going to go find my friends," I said loudly into his ear.

"Mmm, later," he said before sucking my earlobe into his mouth.

"No, right now," I said, using my forearms to shove him back more firmly. He went, but as I whirled around to walk away from him, I felt his hand latch on to my forearm, tugging me back toward him.

"Where do you think you're going?"

I squirmed as I tried to free my arm from his grasp. "Let go," I ordered.

"Or what?"

I glanced around. There were some people watching our exchange, but no one made a move to intervene. And everyone else was so caught up in their own experience, they didn't even notice.

"TJ," I ordered. "Let. Go."

He smiled, but it wasn't the charming one from before. There was a hint of the predator in this one.

"No." He yanked me back so that my body was flush against his again.

The move startled me, so I didn't react immediately. Just as my brain had come back online and told me to kick this asshole in the balls, he was wrenched away from me, and then Drew's big body stepped around him in order to block him from me.

"What the fuck?" I heard TJ yell.

I moved closer to Drew's back, wishing I could burrow into him. Even though the situation was still precarious, there was a sense of calm that washed through me with Drew close by. He'd keep me safe—there wasn't an ounce of me that doubted it.

"Time for you to go," Drew said, his voice harsh and steady. Usually Drew's voice was like warm honey, but now it sounded like a block of ice: cold and unbending.

I heard TJ laugh over the music and knew that he'd moved closer to Drew. "Oh yeah? You gonna make me, tough guy?"

The thought of Drew getting into a fight because of me

scared me even more than what had happened when I'd been dancing with TJ. I fisted my hands in the back of Drew's shirt, afraid that if I didn't hang on to him, we'd get separated.

"You really wanna do this?" Drew asked as he took a step forward, pulling me along with him. "Because I don't have a hell of a lot to lose. Can the same be said for you?" Drew's tone was scarily calm, a hint of danger underneath. It was the sound of someone who knew how to handle himself and was likely not someone to trifle with.

TJ must have sensed the same thing, because when I released Drew's shirt so I could peek through the gap between Drew's arm and his ribs, I saw TJ take a step back.

"Whatever, man. I'm just looking to get laid. And she's not hot enough to be worth the drama."

I felt Drew's body tense. He took a step toward TJ, but I grabbed at his shirt again and he stopped immediately.

TJ walked away smirking, and Drew stood in front of me until he was out of sight. Then he turned and put his arms gently on my biceps.

"Are you okay?" he asked, the smooth honey back in his voice, though it was sprinkled with concern. His thumbs rubbed soothing circles on my skin as he looked me over.

"Yeah, yeah, I'm fine." My voice was shaky. I looked around. "Where's everybody else?"

"They went downstairs a little bit ago. Too crowded at the bar up here."

I looked up into his eyes. "You didn't go?"

He shook his head.

Our gazes stayed locked on each other's, as if we were trying to see all the things neither of us was comfortable saying.

"Why?" I asked.

He took a deep breath and then released it harshly. "I promised Taylor I'd keep an eye on you."

I felt my body sag with disappointment. I looked down at the floor. "Oh. Yeah, she's good like that."

Drew released my arms, and I glanced back at him.

He dragged a hand through his hair. "We should probably get the hell out of here."

"Yeah." I began walking, knowing he was close behind me, the sensation still comforting even though he hadn't said what I'd wanted to hear.

Once we were off the dance floor, in a spot that was slightly quieter as we neared the steps that would lead us downstairs, he called my name.

I turned to find him looking tense as hell, his hands fisted at his sides.

"What?" I asked, wondering if he saw TJ lurking around somewhere. The thought caused me to instinctively step closer to Drew, seeking the safety of his proximity.

I didn't realize how close I'd gotten until his arms wrapped around my shoulders, and I sagged into the hug he was giving me.

His cheek grazed my ear as he said, "I didn't...I didn't like seeing his hands on you. So...so I stayed. Not because Taylor asked me to but because I just...I had to."

I squeezed him tighter, not entirely sure what his words meant—if it was a brotherly protectiveness or a romantic possessiveness behind them—but right now, I didn't care. I'd needed him, and he'd been there, just like he'd been since we'd met.

There'd be time to figure everything else out later.

Chapter Nineteen

SOPHIA

On the way out of the bar, Drew stopped to let the rest of our group know we were headed out. I figured Taylor would want to hang there for a while, but when I saw the state she was in, I didn't plan on giving her much of a choice.

She'd either had about five too many drinks while I was upstairs, or someone had laced one with a drug that made her giggle uncontrollably while trying to speak in a fictional language she insisted was real.

"You're coming with us," I told her.

"Ratcha Borey Unosis," she replied.

"I'm assuming that means you'd love to accompany us home."

"It means 'Why you leavin'?'" she slurred from her seat at the bar.

Drew looked to Carter, who stood behind her like he was the Alpha and a member of his pack had gone astray. "How much did she have to drink?"

Carter shrugged but seemed more concerned than he'd

been when we'd come over.

"I wasn't counting," he said. "I was busy trying to convince that blonde over there to be my plus one to Aamee's party."

I squeezed my forehead before running a hand down the side of my face in frustration. Fucking Carter. I wrapped an arm around Taylor's chest and gave her a hug.

"Come on. Time to call it a night."

"Bachsa orpham!" she snapped, pushing my hand off her but standing with some help from Drew. She was a mess, and I knew there was little chance she'd remember any of this tomorrow. I'd have to film it.

Since Taylor was in such rough shape, Drew called for an Uber to take us the few blocks home, and he helped her up the stairs and into bed.

"She's sleeping," he said when he came out of my room. "I took her shoes off, but you might wanna take her jacket or jeans off so she's more comfortable."

I nodded, unsure of whether to go deal with Taylor or stay with Drew. The latter definitely seemed more appealing, but the friend in me overruled that urge.

"I guess I'll go make sure she's okay and then get ready for bed," I said.

We were standing a few feet apart, and I wanted to close the distance completely, wanted to be as close to him as possible. Even closer than when I'd been wrapped around him at the club. But things felt different back in the apartment. In the darkness of the club, we'd been honest. Vulnerable even. But in the apartment, the spell was broken, and I had no idea how to get it back.

The harsh lights in the living room shone around us, and I suddenly wished we could go back to the darkness of the club, where we were just two souls who could count on each other instead of two people who needed something from each other.

"You going to sleep soon?" I asked.

Drew looked at the couch for a second before turning his attention back to me. "I'm going to try, though I'm kind of wired."

"Yeah. It was a crazy night."

"That's one way to describe it."

We stood there awkwardly for a second, both of us fidgeting restlessly, before I decided to put us out of our misery. "I guess I'll go check on Taylor."

He nodded, and I flashed him a small smile before hightailing it to my room. Once I was inside the bedroom, I closed the door behind me and sank back against it. My brain was a jumble of emotions, and I wasn't sure how I was ever going to parse through any of them.

The night had been intense. What I needed to do was go to bed and think about all this shit when I had a clearer head. Nothing good would come out of obsessing over things tonight.

I moved away from the door, did the best I could to make Taylor comfortable, and then got myself ready for bed. All that was left was to go into the bathroom so I could wash my face and brush my teeth.

When I reached the bedroom door, I leaned forward and rested my head against it. Closing the door had been like sealing Drew off—separating him from me figuratively as well as physically. Opening it felt . . . overwhelming.

This was ridiculous. I'd go out there, use the bathroom, and then go right to bed. I'd wake up tomorrow ready to move forward and forget all about tonight. My hand gripped the doorknob and turned.

As soon as I was out in the hall, my chest grew heavy, as if I were harboring thousands of butterflies in there. It was then that I wondered how I was supposed to move forward when every fiber of my being wanted to rewind to an hour ago when I'd been in Drew's arms.

DREW

When Sophia had gone into the bedroom, I'd plopped down on the couch with my head in my hands. The night had been draining, but it had somehow been energizing too. I wasn't sure whether I wanted to sleep for days or scale a building. It probably didn't help that my body was used to being up late on Saturdays because of work.

I told myself to get up and get ready for bed, but I still hadn't moved when I heard the bedroom door creak open and another one close. Sophia was probably using the bathroom. I promised myself I'd get my ass in there as soon as she was done. But then I heard feet padding softly down the hall, which caused me to look up.

She was standing just inside the room in a black tank top and white-and-black striped sleep shorts. Sophia all dolled up to go out was a sight, but there was something infinitely more appealing about her when she was comfortable and unguarded like this.

Sometimes I felt like she used her clothes and makeup and countless products as a kind of shield that accompanied the persona she projected to people on campus. But like this, she was sweet, a little shy, and absolutely breathtaking.

"You okay?" I asked, my voice a little hoarse from talking over the music all night.

"Yeah." She looked down as her fingers nervously danced together. "Yeah, I'm fine. I just . . . ." She let her gaze flit up to me as she motioned over her shoulder. "Thank you. For helping me take care of Taylor."

"Sure. No worries."

She looked like she was gearing up for something, and I felt my eyes narrow as I tried to figure out what was wrong and how I could help her. Was she still worried about the guy in the bar? I'd kill that fucker if he ever came near her again. I was just about to say something to that effect, when she looked up from her hands and locked eyes with me.

"Thank you for taking care of me too."

The words were soft, but I heard the way her voice wobbled on the last word.

I was on my feet before the first tear fell, darting over to her so I could sweep her up into my arms. "You don't ever have to thank me for that." I rested my cheek on top of her head.

"I do," she said after sniffling. "I should honestly say it every hour on the hour."

"Promises, promises," I mumbled, causing her to giggle, though it sounded wet.

She clung to me for another few seconds before drawing back and wiping her hand over her face. "God, crying all over you is not the way I wanted to show my gratitude."

"It's fine. I needed a shower anyway."

She laughed again as she playfully smacked me in the chest. "You're gross."

I smiled down at her as I tucked an errant strand of hair behind her ear. But as our eyes stayed locked on one another's, the smiles slid off our faces.

"That guy tonight . . . " I trailed off because I wasn't sure how to say what I wanted to without scaring her. My attitude toward that asshole wasn't exactly conciliatory.

"TJ," she supplied, maybe thinking I was searching for an identifier. Dickhead was a good enough one for me.

"TJ?" I asked, my voice relaying my disgust. "What the hell kind of name is that for a grown man?"

She looked confused by what I'd said but also amused. "A normal one?"

"No way. I've never met an adult TJ."

She shrugged. "I'd never met an adult Drew, but . . ." She gestured to me instead of finishing her sentence.

"Drew is a very mature and manly name." My face was serious, but inside I was lighting up. I loved bantering with her like this, and I liked it even more that we could get back to this place after the crazy evening.

"Totally. Like Nancy Drew. Very manly."

"You did *not* just say that."

"If the teen mystery fits."

I looked at her quizzically. "I'm not sure what that means."

She shrugged. "Me neither. It's all that popped into my mind, so I went with it."

We laughed again, and it was looser than it was before—more genuine, like the more we did it, the more we meant it.

I didn't want to lose the lightness we'd managed to uncover, but I also wanted to get back to the point I'd been trying to make.

"That guy—*TJ.*" I said his name like he was a pretentious toddler. "I wanted to plant my fist in his mouth." That maybe hadn't come out as tactfully as I'd intended, but it was the truth.

Her face softened as if I'd just complimented her skin-care regimen. "I'm glad you didn't."

"I'm...less glad. But I'm telling you this because... Jesus, this is hard to say the right way. I didn't only want to hit him when he wouldn't let you go."

"You didn't?" She looked thoroughly confused, and I inwardly cursed myself for not being better with words.

"No. I wanted to hit him from the beginning."

"The beginning of the night? You saw him earlier?"

I shook my head, getting frustrated with myself and a little with her. Why couldn't she be a mind reader so I didn't have to verbalize all of this?

"I wanted to hit him as soon as he approached you. As soon as he bought you the drink and started flirting with you. And definitely when he started dancing with you. And then I felt like shit, because there I was, wishing the guy would give me a reason to get between the two of you, and then he did. I'm so sorry. Having someone hurt you...I'd never want that. But at the same time, I feel like I almost willed it to happen."

"So you, what...think you can control situations with your mind now?" Her lips twitched like she was fighting a smile, and my entire body sighed in relief that she didn't hate me. "And people call Aamee a narcissist."

I straightened in mock outrage. "Hey now. No need to be hurtful. I said I was sorry."

She smiled then and took a step closer to me. "You were watching me? The whole time?"

"That's what you want to focus on?" The timbre of my voice dropped at her proximity.

She nodded as her hand came up to lightly trace the buttons on my shirt.

I watched her hand slide down my shirt for a second before I put my fingers around hers, stilling her descent. Then

I looked up so I could see her gorgeous face.

"It probably makes me sound like a creeper, but it's hard for me to look away from you. Whenever you're in the room, my eyes are drawn to you. Even when you're dancing with assholes, I can't seem to look away."

"Drew," she said on a whisper.

"I'm sorry if that's weird or wrong or whatever. I can try to—"

"Drew." My name came out more forcefully this time, and I shut up and gave her my attention. "I like your eyes on me."

"Yeah?" I asked as a smile I couldn't possibly have repressed spread across my face.

"Yeah."

I'm not sure which of us moved first, but in the next instant, we were kissing. Maybe we both moved at the same time, our bodies in such sync that the timing couldn't help but be fluid and exact.

Her lips were soft and pliant under mine as we teased one another's lips with light kisses. Needing her closer, I brought my hand up to cup her jaw, my fingers gently weaving into her hair and bringing her more firmly to me.

Her lips opened on a gasp, and I deepened the kiss, allowing my tongue to tangle with hers. Her hands fisted the front of my shirt much like they'd fisted the back earlier, but I was glad that the cause was due to passion this time.

Kissing her like this was a gift I never thought I'd receive. So much between us was complicated, but this ... this was simple.

My body tingled with the sensation of sharing breath with her as our lips danced together. It felt as though we'd been building to this moment since we met, and we'd finally gotten out of our own way.

Neither of us pushed to take things further. Hands didn't wander, and bodies didn't gyrate. We seemed to agree that this was enough. At least for now.

There was no need to push anyway. We had time if we decided we wanted it. I already knew I did, but it was a discussion that needed to be had. Later. I was too busy memorizing the feel of the delicate bow of her lips as they pressed against mine to get too far ahead of myself.

Eventually, the kiss slowed, and after a few light pecks, we both drew back. Her eyes remained closed for a bit longer, and she didn't release her hold on my shirt. We stayed close, breathing one another in, perhaps both a little afraid of breaking the spell between us in case we never found the right means to bring it about again.

When her eyes did slide open, a smile accompanied. "That was . . . wow."

"Definitely 'wow.'"

"I wanna do it again," she whispered as her forehead rested against mine.

"Me too."

"Really?" She sounded surprised, which was baffling.

"I basically admitted to stalker-like behavior earlier. You really thought I was going to say no?"

"I just . . . things between us are—"

"Weird? Fucked up?"

"I was going to go with complicated, but it's those things too."

There was so much that could be said—*needed* to be said—but maybe all that could wait. The circumstances were messy, but the truth behind them didn't need to be. "Now that I've had a taste of you, I'm not going to be able to stop unless you tell me to."

She searched my face for a second, and I prayed she found whatever she was looking for. When she smiled widely, I guessed she had. "I don't want to stop."

Using the hand I still had resting against her jaw, I pulled her to me. "Good," I said against her lips before I took her mouth again.

This kiss was as unhurried as the one that preceded it, but there was something more to it. Maybe it was the promise behind it—that we were in this together for however long we both wanted to be here.

Our lips slid together in a rhythm that showed how good we were together. There was none of the clumsiness of typical first kisses. Well, *second* kisses. Sophia and I had found our groove weeks ago, so it shouldn't have surprised me that the expression of that was seamless.

Our tongues flicked over and over as we tried to devour each other. And when we pulled apart for good a short while later, my lips sore but tingling, we remained standing as we swayed to music only our bodies could hear. But exhaustion finally pulled us under, and we broke apart, neither of us saying anything because words would only ruin things.

And this night was too special to ruin.

Chapter Twenty

DREW

"You sure I look okay?"

I ran my fingers through my now blond hair. Sophia had straightened it for me so I could part it over completely to one side. How any woman found Justin Bieber hot remained a mystery to me. Especially because I was now convinced he looked like a butch Miley Cyrus.

"Yeah."

Sophia was busy playing with her own hair in the mirror by our apartment door, adjusting the strands of her wig until she found what seemed to be an ideal spot on her shoulder or back. She didn't look like Beyoncé necessarily, but she did look hot as hell.

"You don't sound sure."

"Will you please let me draw some tattoos on you or something before we go? Justin has both sleeves done."

"I am *not* letting you come near me with any markers. I've seen you doodle a few times, and it looks like something a preschooler did while tripping on acid."

She was still facing the mirror, but she turned to face me after my comment, giving me one of those tight-lipped grins that made me wonder if she was getting ready to burst out laughing or deciding how to dispose of my body.

"You love my drawings," she said.

I saw my eyebrows raise in the mirror. "I love many things about you. Your art isn't one of them." As soon as I'd spoken, I knew the question was coming, and I searched my brain for an appropriate way to respond.

"So what are these things you love about me?" she asked.

Her question had been asked casually, though I had a feeling the answer meant more to her than she was letting on. She walked over to the chair and grabbed the jean jacket she'd tossed over the arm, but she never looked away from me. Maybe she was scared I'd escape out the window if she took her eyes off me. I'd thought about it.

Though Sophia and I no doubt liked each other more than friends or pretend siblings, we hadn't exactly vocalized our feelings for each other any more than we had last week after we'd come home from Tonic.

Since then, the tension between us had built gradually. We'd sit next to each other on the couch, close enough to put a hand on the other's leg but ultimately holding back.

I'd come out of the bathroom the other day, towel around my waist, and I could see Sophia's eyes dart toward the laptop on her lap as I walked by to grab clothes because I'd forgotten to bring them in when I'd showered.

We'd both steal glances at the other however we could or the occasional touch to an arm or back, but neither of us took anything further.

Sophia pulled on her jean jacket—unfortunately covering

her exposed back where her tight black leather dress dipped down almost to her ass—and stared at me expectantly. I'd been so lost in admiring her, I'd almost forgotten I was supposed to answer the question.

Say something. Anything. Well, maybe not any*thing. Don't say boobs.*

"Your sense of humor." *Good boy. Totally innocent.*

She cocked her head to the side like I'd just told her my dog ate my homework. "You're saying that because you think it's what I want to hear." She slipped her bright yellow stilettos on, and I wondered if she'd be taller than me in them.

"Am not," I replied, sounding like a second grader.

"Bullshit, Bieber. Tell me what you really like about me."

"Those heels, for starters," I joked, but I wasn't really kidding. I'd probably jerk off to them later. *There's a first for everything.* Though it was more how they looked on the legs they were attached to that made me wish I wasn't wearing fucking skinny jeans.

I hoped Sophia couldn't tell how turned on I suddenly was. Or maybe I hoped she could.

"Fine," I said, rolling my eyes as if revealing my thoughts was more of an inconvenience than it actually was. "Like… pretty much everything about you. How beautiful you are… and smart…how resilient." I knew she didn't think these things about herself, so it was suddenly extremely important to me that I said them. "You *are* funny," I said. "I swear. But sometimes you don't mean to be, which only makes it cuter."

When I'd finished speaking, both of us were quiet for a bit before Sophia let out a soft, "Thank you."

"Sure," I replied. I moved toward the door, opening it for her so we could head downstairs to meet up with everyone before walking to the party. "There's a lot to like about you."

She walked toward the door, grabbing her small bag on her way and giving me an appreciative smile that spoke more than words could.

And because I was a sarcastic asshole whose superpower was ruining a moment, I added, "Except your art. No one could like that."

She shook her head and smiled, and we headed toward the stairs until Sophia stopped to check her phone.

"Taylor just texted. She said she'll meet us downstairs in a few minutes."

"I'm surprised she made it in time." I was surprised she was coming at all.

"Me too. Guess it worked out better that she got ready before she drove up. I can't wait to see what she looks like. I told her to send me a pic, but she never did."

Driving four hours dressed as Michelle Williams after a day of classes wasn't something that seemed particularly comfortable to me. Granted, I'd never actually been in an outfit like that before—a fact I was thankful for—so I couldn't say for sure.

When we got to the bottom of the stairs, I pulled the door open and held it so Sophia could walk out.

She turned toward me. "You know, you could always say Taylor's your date. We'll just say she's one of Justin's musical exes, like Selena Gomez or something."

"It's all right. You and Aniyah need a third member of Destiny's Child, right?"

She shrugged. "Not really. Girl groups drop members all the time."

"It's fine. I don't mind not having a date." Especially if

that date couldn't be Sophia. We stood near the wall of the building, and I put my arm around Sophia because it was colder than I expected. It was a good thing she'd brought a jacket.

She leaned against me, snuggling up to me as best she could while standing on a public street, and I wrapped my arms around her.

The moment was perfect until...

"Are you Brody?"

I let go of Sophia so abruptly, she nearly fell over. Once I made sure she was standing straight, I looked up to see a tall, thin man wearing a brown wig he'd pulled into a high ponytail.

I looked him up and down as I tried to figure out why this guy wearing ripped skinny jeans and an oversized white sweatshirt would be asking me if I was Brody.

"Depends who's asking," I said, sounding more curious than anything else.

He did a little curtsy type of gesture and smiled widely. "I'm your plus one."

"I'm sorry, you're my what?"

"Carter sent me," he clarified, clearly assuming Carter had told me he was sending a date for me.

"Oh, um... I didn't realize..." *Carter has a death wish*, but I managed to stop myself from finishing my thought.

"Sorry to surprise you like this. Carter's in one of my classes, and he told me he had a friend who needed a date to a costume party tonight, and I was free, so..." He held out his arms. "Here I am."

I glanced at Sophia, who was fighting back a smile.

"That's great." I tried my best to sound excited, but it

came out flat. "We're just waiting for a few others before we head over. I'll have to text Carter a thank-you." Or stab him in a dark alley and leave him for dead.

"Yeah, Carter's a great guy. We talk all the time in class. It's a shame he's straight."

He probably wanted me to agree, but I had limits.

"Oh, this is my sister, Sophia," I said instead. "Sorry, I should've introduced her."

"Great to meet you," he said with a wave. "And I haven't even told you my name, so I'm the one who should be sorry. I'm Joey." Then he turned to me. "But tonight I'm your Selena Gomez."

SOPHIA

Getting into Aamee's party was proving more difficult than I'd expected.

"Destiny's Child is a trio, not a duo or couple," she told us. "If you can't follow a theme, you can't come in." She looked to either side of her at two of our sorority sisters for confirmation. They both folded their arms in solidarity with Aamee, whose smile looked like Hannibal Lecter's before he sat down to a dinner of human flesh.

I hated that Aamee was so petty, but there wasn't much I could do. It was her event, and she enforced the rules. And much like at the sorority house, the rules she chose to enforce were fucking stupid ones.

"What do you wanna do?" I asked the others as I tried to think of the simplest solution.

As much as I didn't want to attend any event that Aamee

was in charge of, the competitor in me felt differently. I was still planning the bachelor auction, and knowing what Aamee got wrong and right would benefit me in the long run.

"I can leave," Aniyah said. "That makes the most sense. Taylor drove all the way here."

"You look fab," Taylor told her. "No way you're leaving."

Aamee was still looking at us as we decided what to do, but after a line began to form behind us, she said, "You're gonna have to get out of the way so other people can get in."

When we did, people flooded past us. Aamee didn't even question who they were as she let them in, bucket in hand as she asked for donations like she was a subway musician without the talent.

Some people tossed in a five or a ten, but most, it seemed, just threw in a dollar or two as their entry fee. Then they headed over to the Halloween backdrop to get their picture taken with their date.

We watched from the front lawn in silence.

"Let's text Xander," Aniyah suggested.

"And say what?" Drew asked. "He said he didn't want to go."

Aniyah was already pulling out her phone. "He said he'd think about it."

"He did," Drew said. "The fact that he's not here should tell you what his decision was."

"We can tell him we *need* him to come. I think if he knows we need his help, he'll do it. He can always leave after we're in." She texted rapidly, and when she was finished, we all stared expectantly at her phone for a response.

It came quicker than we'd anticipated.

Fine. Who do you need me to be?

I hadn't thought that far ahead, but evidently Aniyah had a plan that didn't require an actual costume.

Toby appeared with his date a few minutes later, and he seemed happier than I'd ever seen him.

His date had long dark hair and was dressed in a top that came just below her breasts, displaying abs only a celebrity should have. She looked like she should be walking a runway instead of attending some college party.

I'd have to ask Drew where he'd found her.

"Who are you guys supposed to be?" I asked Toby after we'd introduced him to Joey. Toby also introduced everyone to his date, Anna, who Toby made sure to tell us pronounced her name like the character from *Frozen*.

"Sonny and Cher," he said proudly. He was dressed in bell-bottom jeans and a yellow button-down shirt with polka dots and a pointy collar. I could totally see Anna's resemblance to a young Cher, but Toby, with his thick faux mustache, looked more like a dude who offered kids candy out of his van than he did the famous singer.

"You guys look exactly like them," I told him.

We all chatted for a few more minutes before Toby asked why we hadn't gone in yet.

"You can go," Drew told him. "We'll be in soon. We're just waiting for Xander to come so we can all be duos. Aamee gave the girls a hard time for coming as a trio."

Toby deferred his decision to Anna, who said, "Yeah, let's go in. We'll have some fun." She took his hand and practically pulled him toward the entrance.

We milled around the yard for a while longer until Xander

finally showed up. He was wearing jeans and a black T-shirt, which was probably what made Aniyah ask what took him so long.

"I was researching how to interact with cool kids," he said dryly as we walked toward the front doors.

"We're back," I announced to Aamee, who looked absolutely livid that we now had an even number of people.

"And who are you?" Aamee asked Xander.

"Jay-Z," Xander said. "I'm with Beyoncé."

"You're not even in a costume."

Xander put his hand in his back pocket and pulled out his wallet. "Are you actually debating whether Jay-Z owns jeans and a black T-shirt?" He tossed a fifty-dollar bill into the bucket Aamee was holding.

Aamee breathed deeply and sighed loudly before saying, "Have fun. Don't forget to get your pictures taken before you head in."

Not wanting to give Aamee anything extra since Xander had already paid so much, I dropped a few dollars in the bucket before heading toward the person taking pictures. We posed for a few different ones, each with our respective "dates" as Aamee requested, as well as a few group shots. Then we headed inside.

I spent the first twenty minutes or so doing some reconnaissance—studying the decorations, food and beverage offerings, and talking to a few of the people outside of the sorority to get a feel for their thoughts on the party so far. Generally, people seemed to be having a good time.

The DJ played a mix of songs that got everyone up and dancing, and there was even a cash bar with a few signature drinks that were clever puns on musical names and songs— like a John Lemon, which was basically a lemon drop with a frozen strawberry. She'd probably found most of the names and recipes on Pinterest, but still.

I was sipping on a Juice Springsteen and talking to Drew and Joey when Emma came running up to us. She gave us each a big hug before immediately relaying a story about one of the frat guys falling into the hot tub out back.

"Now the water's black because of his temporary hair dye," she said.

Emma continued to tell us a few other stories about things we'd missed while we'd been waiting for Aamee to let us in. I could tell when she seemed to realize that Joey might be with us.

"Sorry, I should've introduced myself. I'm Emma."

Joey introduced himself as well, both as Joey and Selena.

"Are you guys together?" Emma asked, gesturing between Drew and Joey.

Joey said "yes" as Drew said "no," and they both fumbled awkwardly before clarifying that yes, they were at the party together, but they weren't actually "together-together" as Drew so eloquently put it.

Thankfully, Emma seemed appropriately satisfied with that explanation. She nodded like it made complete sense.

"Who else came with you?"

"Some people I know from a class I'm in," Drew said. "And Sophia's old friend Taylor."

Emma's eyes moved back and forth between Drew and me. "Old like late twenties or like our moms' age?" She asked the second part like she was worried it'd kill the party on impact.

"Old like I've known her since we were little," I said. "She's our age. She goes to school in Jersey and went out with a bunch of us a few weeks ago when Carter was talking about the party, and she wanted to go."

I looked around to see where Taylor had even ended up, and here came Aamee.

"Are any of you planning to enter?"

"Enter what?" I asked.

"God, you're oblivious to life. I've been posting about it all week. I'm having a lip-sync competition. It's twenty dollars a person to enter. I'm taking last-minute entries."

Aamee asking us to participate meant one of two things. Either she wanted us to embarrass ourselves or she was desperate for people. Maybe a little of both. But something told me she was asking us because she needed the money. Asking us if we wanted to compete in the contest was a last resort. Aamee's version of being lost in a desert and realizing she'd have to drink her own urine to survive.

"Are there a lot of people competing?" I wanted to know even though I had no plans of entering.

Aamee craned her neck to wave to someone behind us. Even though she'd approached us, her expression was one of complete disinterest, as if she couldn't be bothered to speak to us.

"Depends how you'd define 'a lot,'" she muttered absently, her attention on some person she was waving to. "You in or not?"

I pretended to think about it. "Not."

"Not a chance," Drew said when Aamee looked to him. I thought Joey looked slightly disappointed, but he didn't say anything.

Aamee left without speaking, instead pulling Emma with her like a mother dragging an uncooperative toddler around a grocery store.

"Guess she didn't like that answer," Drew said with an amused shrug.

The three of us chatted for a few more minutes until Drew saw Carter.

Carter had just ambled in, obviously having been able to convince his plus one to be Nala from *The Lion King*. He'd also convinced the entrance guards that Simba and Nala were a musical couple.

Carter was going to get an earful from Drew.

Once I was by myself, I took the opportunity to move around the party and take in the effort that went into planning something like this. I'd helped my mom with events from the time I was a child, but heading one seemed so much more daunting.

Not that Aamee didn't have help, though. The event was co-run by a frat, which was the sole reason Aamee could serve alcohol. It was another ancient rule that prevented sororities from hosting events with alcohol. Some schools had already done away with that regulation, but Lazarus wasn't one of them.

So much for modern-day feminism.

If I won the presidency, maybe that would be one of the changes I'd make.

I talked to a few other sorority sisters as well as some other people I ran into whom I knew from classes. People seemed to be having a good time dancing, drinking, and lip-syncing...

But all I could think about was Drew. Here and there we'd locked eyes for a moment, just long enough to catch each other's attention, but other than when we'd first arrived, we hadn't seen much of each other.

Drew was busy talking to some other guys he must've

known, and I hung out with Aniyah and Taylor for a bit, throwing back a few shots that Taylor had gotten us. We danced drunkenly to "Say My Name" and a few other Destiny's Child songs, which Aniyah had requested the DJ play.

We laughed and flipped our hair around and tried to look sexy—a feat that always seemed easier for others than it did for me.

By the time the three of us were tired, I was sweating, even in my short dress without the jacket I'd brought.

"I'm gonna go outside to get some air," I told them as they headed back to the bar.

"You want anything?" Taylor asked.

"I'll grab some water when I come back in."

Taylor yelled an "Okay" over the noise, and I headed for the back door.

There was a hot tub sitting on the small back lawn of the frat house, and it held way too many bodies, some of which looked completely naked, even though it was a costume party. A few other groups of people milled around, tossing footballs or chugging beers.

I moved away from everyone and around to the side of the house, leaning against the cold stone and enjoying some peace and relative quiet. My heart began to slow from the dancing, but the second I heard Drew's voice, it picked right up again.

"There you are," he said.

I wished it was a little lighter so I could see him better, but even in the dark I knew the shape of him—his height, his broad shoulders, his posture as he stood in front of me. I hadn't realized I'd paid that much attention to any of those things until now.

"I saw you go outside," he said, "but I didn't see you out back."

"I'm out*side*. Get it? Out*side*," I said slowly in case Drew suddenly morphed into someone who couldn't understand my corny jokes.

"I get it." He moved into the haze of light that was shining from around the corner until I saw him smile. "Clever."

"Really?"

"I was just being nice."

I smacked him on the arm. "Where's Joey?"

"I'm not sure. He isn't who I want to focus on." Moving a little closer to me, he said, "I saw you dancing."

I was sure my cheeks blushed as I thought about Drew watching me gyrate drunkenly to nineties girl jams.

"And you came out here to tease me about my moves?"

He shook his head slowly as he brought a hand to the back of my neck to play with my hair.

"I came out here to tell you how hot they were. Especially since there wasn't some creep grinding all over you this time."

"I think you need glasses," I said, my voice quiet and serious.

Gradually, our mouths inched closer to one another until our lips touched. And once they did, I knew I couldn't stay away from him. His mouth was warm, and as he brought me closer to him, I moaned.

The kiss started slow, but the pace picked up quickly. Both of us hungry for the other, we let our hands roam wherever they wanted to go—over each other's backs and lower.

When he grabbed my ass and pulled me harder against him, I became a puddle of want. I wanted him to lift me up so I could wrap my legs around him, wanted to feel the taut sinews of his chest and back as he held me.

But mainly I just wanted him to fuck me against the side of this house.

Is that too much to ask?

Apparently it was, because Drew pulled away.

"We probably shouldn't do this here," he whispered, his voice low and gritty.

The fact that he'd said *here* and not that we simply shouldn't do this made me hopeful that we could pick up where we'd leave off, though probably not tonight since Taylor was staying over.

"Okay, yeah. I should get back inside anyway. Taylor and Aniyah are probably wondering where I am." As I walked away, I tried to think of anything other than Drew Nolan and how incredibly turned on he just made me.

Once inside, I found Xander and the girls pretty quickly. We still hadn't seen much of Toby, which hopefully meant he and his date were hitting it off. Drew found us a few minutes later, and I was just getting ready to suggest we all call it a night when the music cut off and Aamee's voice boomed over the DJ's microphone.

"Sorry to interrupt everyone's fun." Her smile was wide and borderline psychotic. "But I thought I should let all of you know that there is a short video posted of tonight's party on my Insta. Or more specifically, a video of Zeta Eta Chi's presidential candidate Sophia Mason making out with her brother."

A low murmur carried through the crowd. People were already taking out their phones, including Drew.

I was incapable of retrieving my phone because I was stuck in a catatonic trance that didn't allow for any movement except my heart pounding out of my chest. I wondered if people could hear it.

"I don't know about you," Aamee continued. "But I don't

think someone involved in this type of thing... Incestuous relationships," she clarified proudly for anyone who was too stupid to infer her meaning, "should be leading a sorority. I'd say her judgment is clouded and her morals are slightly skewed, wouldn't you?"

Enraged and embarrassed, I hadn't taken my eyes off Aamee.

It was only when Drew showed me the video—shot from a window above us—that I managed to look away from her.

It was dark, but anyone could tell it was us. I wondered who'd filmed it, because something told me Aamee hadn't. If she'd been watching, there would've been no way she could've kept her mouth shut. Drew and I would have no choice but to admit we weren't related and that Brody wasn't Brody after all.

The real Brody would be nothing less than pissed, but right now, my reputation was on the line. And I wasn't about to let my brother continue to wander around Europe without a care in the world while people thought I was some sort of incestuous deviant.

The video couldn't have been more than ten seconds long, but whoever had taken it had gotten the good stuff. At the time, I was disappointed Drew had pulled away when he had, but now I was glad he had. Who knows what would've been captured.

Both of us stared at the screen. Drew, no doubt, was searching for any excuse, any solution that might fix this situation.

Maybe I could say I thought he was someone else and he could say the same. It was dark. We were both wearing costumes. We were drunk or could at least pretend we were. All those things would be believable, but they still didn't let us off the hook completely. Making out with a sibling was making out with a sibling whether you realized it or not.

"Are you sure that's Sophia?" came a voice from behind us.

I recognized it as Gina's, and I'd never been so thankful for any question in my entire life. Hopefully it would put doubt in the minds of others. Whether she believed it was me or not didn't matter right now. I just needed people to *think* it might not be so I could deny it.

"Please," Aamee said. "It's obviously her."

"Obvious to who?" I asked. "You can see the tops of two people's heads in the dark. You can't even make out what clothes they have on. It was a good try, Aamee, but you'll have to do better than that. Destroying your opponent's image just to get a few votes is pretty dirty."

I watched her lip twitch up into an evil grin. "I bet you and Brody like it dirty."

"You're disgusting."

I couldn't help but cringe at the idea that Brody and I would ever make out with each other, even though she'd actually been talking about Drew.

"You're calling *me* disgusting after I caught you sucking on your brother's tongue?"

She laughed, directing it at her audience, who now seemed captivated by the show.

"I told you it wasn't me," I responded.

"Well, if it wasn't you, who was it?" She looked around the room for anyone who might step up to say they were the one on the video.

"It was me."

The words had come from Taylor. So anxious about what

to do, I'd forgotten she was even here. And in basically the same outfit as me. Had I been first to think of it, I would've tossed Taylor's name out there from the start, knowing she would have my back.

She held up her hand from across the room, and Aamee looked over.

It took her a few seconds to place who Taylor was, but when she did, she said, "That's convenient. Your friend just happens to be the one who's kissing Brody? I think it's more likely she's covering for you."

"Is it?" I asked, now talking more loudly so others could hear me. "Is it more likely I made out with my brother or that my friend did?"

"If it was you in the video," Aamee said to Taylor, "why didn't you say that right away?"

It was a valid question and one I hoped Taylor had an answer to because I sure as hell didn't.

"Because she didn't wanna out me," Drew said. Aamee looked completely confused. "As straight. Or bi. Or… whatever." Drew waved a hand around as he explained. "I don't really know what I am. That's what I'm trying to figure out."

"So you were worried people would find out you might be straight?" Aamee asked skeptically.

"Yeah. I've known Taylor since we were kids, and we've always been close. I figured she was a safe person to experiment with. You know…to see if I felt anything…sexually. Or emotionally."

"And did you?" I wasn't sure why Aamee asked the question because she had no way of verifying if Drew's answer was true or not, but I found myself wanting to know the answer too.

"I did. I felt a lot, actually." His eyes darted briefly to mine as he said it. "I think it's time I'm honest with myself and admit I like women."

"I knew it!" Emma called from across the room.

"Prove it," Aamee said to him, and then she looked at Taylor to let her know the directive was aimed at both of them.

"How am I supposed to prove it's me in the video?" Taylor asked.

"Kiss him," said Aamee.

This bitch was crazier than I thought.

Drew and Taylor looked at each other, and I hoped it was only me who could sense their hesitance.

"This is ridiculous," Drew said. "We're not gonna make out in front of all these people just to prove to you it was us in the video. It doesn't even prove anything."

It was a solid try. It really was. But I knew they weren't getting out of this even if none of us wanted it to happen.

Aamee crossed her arms and looked between Taylor and Drew, like she was directing some sort of fucked-up amateur porn and was deciding how she wanted the scene to play out.

"No. I guess it doesn't prove anything. But it can't hurt."

Taylor and Drew both looked at me before they moved toward each other, the crowd parting for them. Once they were close enough, they closed their eyes and locked lips. Their mouths stayed closed for a moment before they both seemed to realize that wasn't going to fool anyone, so they turned up the heat a little.

It was painfully awkward to watch. It was more orchestrated than natural, but maybe that was because I knew what others didn't—there were no romantic feelings between Taylor and Drew.

I, on the other hand, felt things for Drew that I hadn't wanted to admit until now. Even to myself.

Watching him kiss someone else, put his *hands* on someone else, made my skin feel like it was on fire from the inside out.

They gave it a few more seconds before they broke contact and looked back at Aamee.

"Happy now?" Drew asked.

"Yup," she answered.

That made one of us.

Chapter Twenty-One

DREW

"Remember when no one knew you made out with your sister?"

Carter was referring to my living hell since the party. He slung an arm around me as we walked toward the stone building that housed the library. I was pretty sure he had no intention of actually using the library, so I could only assume he was tagging along because he wanted to bust my balls a little more.

I removed a hand from one of my pockets just enough to elbow him in the ribs, which made him reflexively pull his arm from my shoulder. Once he was off me, I gave him a shove.

"I didn't make out with my sister, you dick."

Carter ignored my lie. "Whatever you say, bro. I gotta admit, though, the gay thing was a good cover."

I stopped walking and glared at him.

Either he knew I'd been lying about being gay, or he was fucking with me. I wanted to punch him either way.

"You think I *pretended* to be gay so I could fuck my sister?"

Carter raised his hands in the air innocently and jerked his head back. "Whoa, whoa, no one said anything about fucking her. Jesus, dude, that's some seriously messed-up shit right there. Kissing your sister is one thing. Fucking her is, well... Fucking her is... fucked up."

"With your speaking skills, majoring in communications is clearly your calling." Adjusting my backpack from where it'd slipped a little when I'd shoved Carter, I turned toward the library again and continued walking.

"Don't change the subject. I'm just concerned for your future children if you forget to pull out. Look at all those old royal families whose children had all sorts of deformities because they didn't want the bloodlines to thin. You don't want your son slash nephew to have three ears or something, do you?"

I ignored his comment, hoping that if I sped up, he'd finally realize I absolutely did not want to talk about this. It was bad enough I'd been hit on four times since Friday night. Two guys, two girls. Evidently the jury was still out on my sexual orientation.

"Okay, maybe that was a little too far," he said.

"You think?" I wondered when the novelty of all this would wear off. At some point, the student population would have something else that captured their attention, and Sophia and I would drift into the backs of their minds until they forgot about it completely. Or at least I hoped so.

How long did we have to wait until someone got a video of Brenden Willis letting his dog blow him? Everyone knew Dr. Hayes's TA put peanut butter on that shit and let his corgi have an afternoon snack when no one was looking.

"You know that was Taylor, right?" I said. If someone who

was supposed to be my buddy didn't believe it, there wasn't a chance in hell any of these other people did.

"I don't know, dude. I wanna believe it, but it looked a lot like Sophia."

"It was dark." We'd used the excuse every time anyone mentioned it because it was all we had.

Carter let out a sigh that sounded too serious to have come from him, and then he said, "I've known Sophia for two years. I've seen her in different light, wearing different clothes, with makeup and without." He shrugged. "Looked like her to me. And listen, whatever you guys are into isn't really for me to judge. I wish you'd both just tell me the truth about it."

"I'm telling you the *truth*. I would never have an intimate relationship with my sister." At least I was being honest about that.

It was easy to tell when Carter was thinking hard about something. He was like a cartoon character with a thought bubble that he looked to for suggestions of what to say. He was quiet for a few seconds. "Okay, then kiss me."

"I'm sorry, what the fuck did you just say?"

"Kiss me."

"I'm not gonna keep kissing people to show that I didn't kiss my sister. That proves even less than kissing Taylor did."

"It proves you're gay. Or bi, or whatever you claim you are. Or *were*. And then I'll at least know you weren't pretending to be gay so you could sleep with your sister without worrying about other girls hitting on you."

"That theory makes no sense."

"Makes sense to me. Now kiss me." He said it loud enough that people passing by probably heard him, but he didn't seem to care.

"You want me to kiss you in the middle of our college campus with people all around?"

"Sure, why not?"

"Because it's weird, that's why." What the fuck was wrong with this guy? What heterosexual male athlete in their early twenties would be comfortable kissing another man, let alone in the presence of others?

"Maybe a little for me, but not for you. Unless you're totally straight. Then we'd just be two dudes putting our mouths on each other for no reason."

"We're that either way!"

I struggled with the reality that I might actually have to kiss another guy. Though there were worse things, I supposed. Like having someone you consider your good friend think you made out with your sister.

I breathed in deeply, and without making eye contact, I asked, "Tongue?"

I was sure he'd say no.

"Whatever you feel like."

Carter looked like he was preparing himself to face a firing squad and wanted to die with honor. He seemed composed and eerily calm considering what was about to happen. Though maybe he was trying to call my bluff and was banking on me backing out.

But I wouldn't back out. If kissing Carter to prove I was bi would make him believe that the girl I'd kissed wasn't Sophia, then the few seconds with my lips on his would be worth it. Carter would, no doubt, speak on our behalf, and he had influence over others. Girls wanted to be with him, and guys wanted to *be* him.

"Okay," I said. "You're sure about this?"

Carter glued his eyes shut. "Just do it."

Not wanting to witness what was about to happen, I closed my eyes too. But as I inched closer to his face, having my eyes shut made the action feel more intimate. So I opened them wide.

My lips paused just before they reached his, and I was sure the two of us looked like middle school kids playing spin the bottle for the first time. This would be the least hot public display of affection anyone had ever witnessed. I was sure of it.

And as my lips finally met his, the comedy of the moment hit me. Our Poster Children for Awkward moment lasted way too long. I was hoping he'd pull away because he wasn't expecting me to go through with it, but he didn't move. And there we stayed, lips touching and our bodies still.

To avoid anything below my waist touching him, I contorted myself into a position where my ass was sticking out, which only made the situation stranger.

My arms hung loosely at my sides as I debated where to put them. Eventually, I placed them on Carter's hips, sure that I looked like a twelve-year-old boy having his first dance with his crush.

If only a chaperone were here to tell us to break it up, because neither of us was pulling away. This was like a fucked-up version of the game Chicken where both teams lost. One of us was going to have to do something to end this.

A few more seconds passed... and then Carter's lips parted unexpectedly, and the tip of his wet tongue touched my lips.

I couldn't have moved faster if it had been a Komodo dragon that had licked me. I quickly wiped my mouth on the sleeve of my jacket.

"What the fuck was that?"

Carter looked pleased with himself. "That," he said, "was me proving you're definitely not attracted to men and therefore *are* attracted to your sister."

It took me a minute or so, but I managed to calm myself down enough to respond. "I'm not attracted to my sister," I said firmly.

"It's cool, man," Carter replied casually. "If anyone asks what I think happened between you guys, I'll say nothing and that I knew you and Taylor had been talkin' for a while. I love you and Soph. Your secret's safe with me."

Damn it.

Why did this moron have to be such a good fucking friend to Sophia *and* to me, especially when he'd only known me less than two months? He was like a loyal goddamn mutt we'd rescued from the pound, and I was like Michael fucking Vick using him for my own agenda.

I hoped like hell Sophia trusted Carter like I did, because what I was about to do would be pretty much unforgivable otherwise.

"I'm glad you can keep a secret," I said. "But that's not the one I need you to keep."

SOPHIA

It had been a day that felt longer than usual. I'd gotten up at six to go for a run, had three classes nearly back to back, and then had made some phone calls and other preparations for the bachelor auction.

I'd been home for an hour but was still finishing up a

paper that was due tomorrow. I only had to read it over. When Drew got home, we could grab something to eat and watch a movie since he didn't have to work tonight.

The idea of cuddling up next to Drew put a smile on my face. Things had undoubtedly been strange between us after the party, but it didn't take us long to realize there shouldn't have been any reason for us to feel weird around each other. It wasn't like we were actually siblings.

But Sunday night we'd both kind of agreed to let whatever this was play out without trying to steer it in one direction or another. Whether we had a long, leisurely drive or went a hundred miles an hour before crashing into a tree and bursting into flames remained to be seen. But we both figured we'd enjoy the ride while it lasted. We hadn't taken things any further than we had already, but I was hoping that would change soon.

I was shutting down my laptop when I heard the lock turn on the apartment door. I looked up to see Drew enter, his backpack already sliding off his arm.

He let it drop near the door before heading over to the couch and plopping himself down next to me. His body seemed heavier than usual, and I guessed he was probably just as worn out as I was.

"I'm glad you're home," I said, already snuggling against him. I moved my hand to his chest and began tracing imaginary designs over his pecs and down the center of his stomach.

He let his head drop back against the top of the couch, and he closed his eyes gently. "I'm glad I'm home too." He moved his fingertips over the exposed skin of my arm as I continued to rub his torso lightly.

Both of us had goose bumps now, and I couldn't take my eyes off Drew's lap, where a bulge was forming inside his jeans. How long would it be before I got to touch it? Or even better...

I'd imagined plenty of times what that would feel like alone in my room with the door shut. I'd imagined my fingers were his, and I'd brought myself over the top with such intensity, I knew the real thing would be nothing short of amazing.

I'm not sure when my inhibitions left me, but before I could stop myself, I was kissing his neck, feeling his abs tense at my touch as I moved my hand toward that magical area, and when I reached it, I grazed my hand over it lightly.

He flexed his hips up and stifled a groan.

I loved seeing him like this, all vulnerable and needy. And I was just as turned on.

When he moved his fingers to the waistband of my thin cotton joggers and tugged them down enough to let his fingertips flutter over the sensitive skin just above the edge of my thong, I wanted to beg him for more. I needed him to rid me of the emptiness.

We roamed our hands over each other's bodies enough to thoroughly turn each other on but not nearly enough to push us over the edge. It was some sort of sexual game that I simultaneously loved and hated.

When I couldn't take it anymore, I moved to straddle him, letting my weight settle directly on his lap where he was straining against his pants.

As I moved over him, he worked his hands over my hips to create a rhythm that worked for both of us, I knew this would get me there. I'd want more eventually, but for right now, this was enough.

Wrapped up in this new sensation between us, neither of us said anything. We were all heavy breaths and low moans.

I nestled my head into the crook of his neck as I felt myself climb steadily toward what I hoped would be the most satisfying orgasm I'd had in a long time.

But I didn't quite get there before Drew held me in place. I tried to squirm, feeling the female version of blue balls start to creep up on me.

"I gotta tell you something," he said.

It sounded serious, but so was my need, which felt more urgent than whatever Drew was going to talk about.

"Can we talk after we finish?" I hadn't been that forward with a guy before, but Drew was different. Living together had forced us to get closer than we would have otherwise. The emotional connection was there. We were only missing the physical. And God, was I missing it.

"I'm not sure you'll want anything to do with me after I tell you this."

The seriousness of his voice had me climbing off him and settling in on the couch for whatever it was he had to tell me.

Drew sat up taller, rubbing his hands over his thighs nervously before finally looking at me.

"Just come out with it," I said.

A few more seconds passed, and I wondered what it was that was such a big deal he had to tell me at such an inconvenient time but also couldn't bear to reveal it. I honestly couldn't come up with anything.

"I told Carter."

"Told Carter what?"

"About us," he answered quickly.

Did he mean what I thought he meant? His expression said yes, but I prayed he must've meant something else because why the hell would Drew tell anyone that we aren't siblings? That meant he wasn't who he said he was either. It was detrimental to both of our goals.

"What *about* us exactly?"

"That we have a thing going on." He gestured between us. "Whatever this is. And that you're not my sister. I'm not Brody Mason. Everything."

He looked like he was physically afraid of what I might do to him after he said it. His expression made me more conscious of my own, because while there was absolutely some anger in every bone of my body right now, the predominant emotion I felt was disappointment. At what, I wasn't exactly certain.

Sure, I was disappointed that our secret was out, and if Carter leaked it to anyone, it would jeopardize any chance I'd have at becoming president, but Drew's big mouth also meant it wouldn't be long before his college boy gig was up.

Brody would have to come back to the States—my parents would hire an international hitman if he didn't—and they'd probably force me to move back home and attend a college I could easily commute to. And that was how Drew's and my journey would end—crash and burn it would be.

Maybe that was the crux of my emotion. I knew this thing with Drew had a shelf life, but I didn't think it would expire before we'd even gotten a chance to taste it.

"I'm sorry, Soph," he said quietly. "He seemed sure that it was us kissing that night."

"But he didn't *know* it was us. The only other person who knew for sure was Taylor."

"I know I fucked up, but I felt bad lying to him. Carter's been a good friend, and I started to feel guilty—"

"Do you feel better *now*?" We both knew what his answer was going to be, so I didn't wait for him to respond. "Ugh, this is so messed up." Rubbing my hands over my face, I tried to think of the best possible outcome. I'd already considered the worst.

But maybe Carter wouldn't tell anyone. I didn't think he would share what he learned intentionally with anyone, but it was Carter, for Christ's sake. He wasn't exactly the most cautious person I'd ever met. And this was college. He'd get drunk and tell one person he trusted or slip up and tell a roomful of people without thinking.

And now I was back to thinking the worst.

"There's no way Carter can keep this secret. He's *going* to tell someone. It's just a matter of when."

I hoped it would at least be after the auction when I'd had a chance to prove my ability as sorority president and Drew had an opportunity to finish out the semester.

"I don't know. He swore he wouldn't. I trust him."

"It's not that I don't trust him. But it's Carter," I said, as if that were an explanation in and of itself. It really should've been. "He's so impulsive. There's no telling what he'll do."

Shaking his head, Drew barked out a sharp laugh. "You're right about that. I definitely didn't expect him to kiss me in front of the library earlier."

What the... "I'm sorry?" I said, my attention shifting from one subject to a much more interesting one. "Carter kissed you? Like kissed you kissed you?"

Drew nodded slowly, like the memory of it caused him some sort of lasting trauma. "If we're being technical, I actually kissed him."

"Can you rewind to the beginning, please?" I tried to picture a scenario where two completely straight men just decided to kiss each other in public, and I was stuck for ideas.

Drew settled back against the couch and put his feet on the coffee table. I envied how relaxed he seemed, all things considered. But then, he'd had time to process everything hours ago, and I was just hearing about all of it now.

"Carter came up to me and was teasing me about the good old days when no one knew I liked to make out with my sister. Then he started telling me that I was pretending to be gay so no girls hit on me."

"So you kissed him to prove otherwise?"

"Well, I didn't just do it. He kind of asked me to. It was like a dare, I guess." Drew's face transformed into a sort of unexpected pride. "I'm sure he thought I'd chicken out and he wouldn't have to kiss me."

"Soooo you kissed him to prove you weren't lying about being gay, but then you told him the truth about everything anyway?"

"When you say it like that, it sounds crazy."

"That's because it *is* crazy. And so are you and Carter. Jesus, what did he do when you kissed him?"

"Nothing really. We both kind of just stood there with our lips on each other." He shivered as he thought about it. "Eventually he slipped me the tongue, and I freaked out, which I'm sure was his plan. That convinced him even further that me being gay was a sham, and I couldn't have him thinking I had a sister-fetish, so I just came clean.

"Of course, as soon as I did, he shouted that he knew it and applauded me for holding out so long despite his teasing me. Turns out he didn't think I was actually making out with my sister, but he *definitely* thought I was making out with you. He's brighter than he looks."

"So you kissed a guy for nothing?"

"Basically," he answered, smiling. And I couldn't help but smile too when he said, "Would it help if I said you're a way better kisser than Carter?"

"A little." I wanted to hang on to my irritation, but my arousal from earlier was still thrumming through my body, and this was *Drew*. Staying angry at him was like staying angry at a puppy who just ate your flip-flop. "But it would help more if you reminded me what a good kisser *you* are."

So he did.

Chapter Twenty-Two

SOPHIA

Volunteering at an animal shelter always sounded like a great idea. It conjured up images of frolicking around with cute puppies who smothered your face with kisses. The reality was far less glamorous.

"Why do we do this every year?" Gina asked. "It's always a disaster."

I had no adequate response as I rinsed the soap out of the coat of the terrier I'd been assigned to clean. Evidently Bethany and Emma didn't either, since they also stayed silent. The dog looked at me for a second, and I would've sworn he smirked at me.

"Don't do it," I warned.

But he didn't listen. He shook his entire body, spraying water everywhere. The shelter had rubber aprons for us to wear to protect our clothes, but I'd have needed a hazmat suit to be completely safe from the dog's aggressive drying methods.

"Oh no. Your hair," Emma said plaintively.

My arms were outstretched to either side as I dangled

them in the air, letting droplets roll off me and onto the floor.

"Why don't these rubber suits have sleeves? And hoods?"

"That can be your contribution to society," Gina exclaimed. "You can make ones that cover your whole body."

I gaped at her for a second, wondering if I should be offended that she thought so little of my offerings to humankind or touched she thought I had entrepreneurial potential.

In the end, I shook my head and grabbed a towel, though its purpose was slightly defunct by this point. I rubbed the dog's coarse coat. When I leaned down to reach his back legs, the dog seized on the opportunity to lick me.

Reeling back, I wiped a hand over my mouth. I pointed a finger at the dog. "The last guy who tried that almost got a knee to the balls."

I unhooked the dog I'd been washing, lifted him out of the tub, and crated him before moving on to the next dog. I opened the door to see a cute black-and-white puffball. The dog looked sweet, with its tongue lolling out.

When I reached in to grab him, he growled and lunged at me. I sprang back, slamming the crate door closed before Cujo could take a bite out of me. I looked around to see the other girls staring at me.

"I think I'm going to save this one for the staff."

There were no other dogs there for us to wash, so I took off my apron and hung it up before settling back against one of the unused basins.

Gina cleared her throat. "Bethany, how does Aamee feel her fundraiser went?"

Bethany looked surprised to be spoken to. As one of Aamee's closest friends in the house, things had been frosty between us at best. But she'd signed up for this service opportunity at the beginning of the semester and, for whatever reason, hadn't found a different one. Maybe Aamee had sent her as a spy.

Once Bethany recovered from her surprise, she said, "It went well."

"Oh good," Gina replied in a voice that was dripping with false enthusiasm. "I'd heard Aamee was nervous because she thought she didn't raise much. I'm glad to hear that's not the case."

Bethany's eyes managed to both flit in Gina's direction and roll at the same time. "Why would Aamee be nervous? The party was packed."

I wanted to point out that since Aamee hadn't charged admission, a packed party meant nothing, but I managed to hold my tongue.

"Sophia's auction will probably be packed too," said Emma. "I can't believe you got some of the football team to participate." She looked like a kid who'd been promised a lollipop.

I was surprised too. Carter had come through big-time for me. When I'd explained my idea to him, he'd told me he'd get a few of the guys from the team, and he'd certainly kept his word.

He'd not only convinced the quarterback to participate but also one of the defensive linemen, Tim Long, who was scorching hot. He'd probably be able to beat Aamee's fundraising total all on his own.

"Is your brother going to be in it?" Bethany asked.

"What?"

It hadn't ever occurred to me to ask Drew to be one of the bachelors. The thought of some other girl touching him made my heart beat faster. The auction wasn't intended for people to bid on guys they wanted to hook up with, but I wasn't stupid.

Most of the girls bidding would be doing so because they had some level of interest in the guy they were trying to buy. And even though I'd explained the auction was for men to do small chores for the people who "won" them—and not some elaborate escort scheme—people were still going to bid with their libidos.

"Your brother," Bethany repeated slowly, like I was intellectually impaired. "Is he going to be in the auction?"

"No. Why would he be?"

Bethany shrugged, but it looked too cavalier. This had been her mission, and she'd chosen to accept it. That Aamee would ask one of her lackeys to try to get intel on my event didn't surprise me, but Bethany's focus on Brody did. Or Drew. Whatever. I couldn't figure out what her angle could possibly be.

"He's obviously attractive," Bethany stated as she finished drying her dog. "He'd probably bring in a good amount of money. I've heard quite a few girls talk about how hot he is."

"He doesn't want to."

"So you asked him?"

Jesus Christ, is this chick majoring in interrogation techniques or something?

"No, I just know he wouldn't want to."

Bethany looked skeptical. "Even if it would help you with the fundraiser?" She turned her back for a second while she put the dog in his crate and then turned back to face me. "Unless, of course, there's another reason you don't want him to participate."

I crossed my arms over my chest. "And what reason would that be?"

She looked down and examined her nails. "A few of us were just wondering if you were maybe a little too . . . interested in your brother."

"What the hell does that mean?"

She looked right at me. "You just seem . . . close."

I was really getting tired of this shit. "How many times do I have to tell you guys? That was *not* me in that video."

"So you've said," she said dismissively.

"But you don't believe me." It was a statement because I already knew the answer. I hated that she wasn't technically wrong.

She gave me a look that let me know she most certainly did *not* believe me. Which meant Aamee didn't believe me either, and wasn't that just a shitstorm sandwich on what-the-fuck bread?

Aamee was clearly hoping to get something to discredit me with, and I couldn't give it to her. Not when this was so close to being over. Not when I was so close to defeating the big, bad bitch. So I did the only thing I could think of.

"I'm sure Brody would participate if it's that important to you."

Bethany simply smirked in reply as she took off her apron, hung it on the hook, and left the room.

I wasn't sure if I'd called her bluff or played into her hands, but I had a feeling—no matter how I'd reacted to her accusations—that the cards had been stacked against me from the start.

"What the hell just happened?" Emma asked.

I wished I knew.

DREW

"How's everything been going, man?" Brody asked me, his voice sounding slightly tinny over the long-distance connection.

I relaxed back into the couch and propped my feet on the coffee table. "Not too bad. Classes are going well. I'm carrying all As."

"Oh. Um, hey, I'm happy you're doing well and all, but maybe you're doing a little too well for . . . me. Like maybe some of those can come down to at least Bs? Cs would be better, but I could compromise with Bs."

My brow furrowed. "I thought you wanted good grades so your parents saw that you were following through on your promise to do better."

"Yeah, definitely. But better for me is passing anything. Acing every class will raise every red flag that's ever been made."

"Oh. Okay." There was no hiding the disappointment in my voice. This was likely the only chance I'd get to go to college. I wanted to prove to myself how good I could be at it, not purposely fuck up my grades.

Brody hesitated a second before saying, "You know what? Ignore me. Get whatever grade you can earn. My dad'll probably applaud whatever nefarious means he'll think went into me acing the semester."

"No, it's fine. You're the boss here. I'll do whatever you need me to."

"I need you to do your best."

"That's obviously not—"

"Drew?"

"Yeah?"

"Shut up and do your best."

His voice managed to be stern and encouraging. It sounded very different from the exuberant frat-boy tone he'd always had when we'd spoken before. For the first time, I got a glimpse of what the grown-up Brody could be if he ever let himself grow up.

"Okay. Thanks."

"Don't mention it." The statement sounded more like a directive than an acceptance of my gratitude. "How's living with my sister been?"

I allowed him to divert the conversation like he so clearly wanted to, even though this was a more uncomfortable topic for me. Brody might have backed down on the grades, but I doubted he'd be so magnanimous about me hooking up with his little sister.

"Fine."

"Really? She hasn't been a pain in the ass? I couldn't imagine living with her."

"Didn't you grow up with her?"

"Yeah, but not in such tight quarters. We didn't interact much, especially once we were both teenagers."

The dynamic between Brody and Sophia baffled me. Granted, I wasn't very close with my own sisters, but they were soul-sucking. Sophia and Brody were both good people. Both a bit reckless and impulsive in their own ways, but solid human beings. I wondered if they saw how alike they were. Brody obviously took his antics to much higher levels, but they were both wild cards with good hearts. But it wasn't my place to get into that.

"It's gone smoothly. No problems."

"You must be a spoiled-brat whisperer," he said, a smile obvious in his voice.

Despite the teasing tone, though, I couldn't let the dig at Sophia lie. "Must be, since I'm talking to a guy currently gallivanting around Europe."

Thankfully he laughed. "Touché."

The snick of a lock sounded before the door swung open, and Sophia clomped in, looking a little damp and a lot exhausted.

"Speak of the devil," I said into the phone.

She looked at me quizzically as she settled onto the couch beside me.

"Is she home? Put me on speaker," Brody said.

I clicked the button and then said, "Okay, go ahead."

"Hey, squirt."

Her nose scrunched up as she rested her head on the back of the couch. "Ugh, what do you want?"

"I called Mom, so you can stop texting me reminders about doing it. I told her I was settling in well with classes and I just *loved* having you living with me."

"Way to screw up the whole thing. She's never going to believe you like having me around."

He gasped in what I interpreted as mock outrage. "I am completely convincing. Hell, they still think I'm in college when I'm not even in the country."

"This is true," she conceded.

"How's everything going with getting back onto so-*whority* row?"

"You think you're really clever, don't you? How long have you been waiting to use that one?"

The only response was Brody's cackling.

"Ugh, I don't have the mental energy for you. Have fun fucking your way through Italy or wherever the hell you are."

"You really overestimate my stamina. I'm almost flattered."

"I'm hanging up now," she said.

"No, wait. Seriously. How is everything going with getting back into the house?"

Sophia looked perplexed, like she wasn't sure if he was actually asking or making fun of her somehow.

"It's going okay. I think I have a good shot at making it back in for next semester."

"That's awesome."

Sophia's face softened at his words.

"Because I was going to see if Drew wanted to stay for the rest of the year, and I figured I'd have a better shot at getting him to agree if he didn't have to share the apartment."

"And there it is," Sophia said, her voice strong as if she'd been expecting his reasoning, but there was no missing the disappointment on her face. She got up and wandered into the kitchen.

"I haven't made any definite plans," Brody continued. "But are you interested in staying for another semester, Drew?"

I watched Sophia remove a bottle of water from the refrigerator and take a drink. I wanted to go to her, both because the sight of her head thrown back and her throat working was hot as fuck and because she looked like she needed a hug, but I also wanted to focus. What Brody was asking was important.

"Yeah, maybe. Just let me know, and I'll see what I can work out." I didn't want to waste a ton of mental energy on the pros and cons of staying another semester until Brody told me what his plans were for sure.

"Okay, great. I'll give you a call soon and let you know."

"Sounds good."

"Later, man. Bye, Sophia."

She didn't bother replying, but it didn't matter. Brody hung up before either of us could've gotten a word out anyway.

I dropped my phone onto the table as I stood up so I could make my way to Sophia. She was setting the bottle on the counter when I reached her and slid my hands around her waist. I liked how she leaned back into me, allowing me to support some of her weight.

I pressed a soft kiss into her hair. "You okay?"

"Yeah, just sorority drama."

"Anything I can do?"

She turned around and wrapped her arms around my shoulders. "First, you can kiss me."

That was something I would gladly do. I lowered my face to hers so I could press our lips together. The kiss was soft and sweet at first, but as it typically went with us, our hands started to roam and our tongues tangled.

She ground her pelvis into my erection as I moved a hand up to cup her face so I could deepen the kiss. Christ, this woman did it for me.

Needing to catch my breath, I began trailing kisses along her jaw. When I'd made my way to her neck, I asked, "Was there a second thing you needed?"

"Yeah," she replied, her voice breathless and turned on.

"Gonna tell me what it is?" I asked right before claiming her mouth again.

We hadn't gone much further than kissing yet, but it felt like we were quickly approaching the next step...whatever that might be. I was definitely excited to find out.

She was the one to pull away this time, and I dropped down so I could suck on her neck.

"God, that feels good," she moaned. "I . . . I need . . ."

I pulled back so I could look deeply into her eyes. "What do you need?"

She took a deep breath. "I need you to be in my bachelor auction."

Chapter Twenty-Three

DREW

It had been a long night at Rafferty's. Well, truthfully, every night felt long when my day was filled with classes and helping Sophia with last-minute tasks for the auction. Wasn't it enough that I'd agreed to participate? Did she really need my help choosing fonts for the signs she was planning to display? She could put them in Wingdings, and I probably wouldn't have even noticed.

My commitment to it was there. It really was. I'd just never been the type to concern myself with small details. At least when it came to event planning. Which suddenly reminded me that I was supposed to be planning Cody's birthday party, which was in about a month and a half. Maybe after the auction dust settled, I could rope Sophia into helping me. She'd offered, but too caught up in all the sorority stuff, we hadn't talked about it further.

"What's up?"

Max's words stilled my wiping of the bar. He'd been sitting there for over an hour, so I knew better than to think his question was a casual inquiry about what I've been up to since I last saw him. He was asking me what was wrong because, clearly, I wore my feelings on my face like a gigantic banner advertising my most recent concern.

How I'd ever managed to maintain a lie as huge as my identity for a few months had been a sort of magic even Houdini would've been impressed by. Though as Sophia had pointed out, our imaginary family might be coming to an end as soon as Carter slipped up.

I looked up from the spot on the bar I'd been scrubbing at even though I knew the stain was permanent. Sighing heavily, I left the rag on the bar and leaned against the steel fridge behind me. Crossing my arms, I wondered what part of everything would be easiest to fill Max in on.

"Well, I've been pretending to be gay, the majority of the student population thinks I'm fucking my sister, and I agreed to prostitute myself this weekend for Sophia's bachelor auction." That about covered it.

Max's eyes had grown a little wider with every detail I'd revealed, and now he looked almost sorry he'd asked anything. He knew a little about my relationship with Sophia, but I'd left all the peripheral details out.

"Okay," he said slowly. "That's definitely a lot to deal with." He was quiet for a moment while I guessed he was processing everything. "So is the auction really for people to bid on sex?"

"No," I said with a laugh. Then I added seriously, "And no, you can't come."

Max laughed, his big belly jiggling with the sound of it. "Well, let me know if she opens it up to the public."

"Even if it were open to the public, it wouldn't be open to you," I joked. "Seriously though, Max, I don't know how

I got myself into this mess." I moved to the register to begin closing everything down for the night.

"I do. You wanted to better your life."

Max's statement was true, but so many things had changed since I'd initially agreed to play Brody Mason, it made me wonder if, when all of this was done, I'd have accomplished what I'd set out to. Right now, it just felt hectic and complicated.

Max slid off the barstool stiffly and pulled on his coat. "I'm sure you'll figure it all out." He smiled before putting some money on the bar and heading toward the door.

He'd said it with confidence, like he was in on some secret I wasn't privy to. That or he had no idea how any of this would play out but wanted to assure me it'd be okay anyway.

I decided Max was a better actor than I was.

The remaining couple at the end of the bar closed out their tab, and I managed to close the place down in less than half an hour and couldn't wait to get to bed. Or couch. Whatever.

I wasn't sure if it was the low temperature, but the ride home felt painfully long. By the time I parked and climbed off my bike, I could barely feel my fingers. I didn't typically like to ride when it was this cold out, but Brody's apartment wasn't exactly within walking distance of the bar. At least I'd found a spot out front this time so I didn't have to walk far.

Shoving one hand into my pocket, I tucked my helmet under my other arm as I walked toward the apartment. As I approached the steps, I noticed Sophia sitting outside, a big jacket on. She had the fur-lined hood pulled over her head, and she was fumbling with something in her hand. I jogged toward her, causing her to startle slightly.

"Sorry," I said. "I didn't mean to scare you. What are you doing out here? It's two in the morning and freezing."

"Smoking," she answered, a white cloud coming out of her mouth as she spoke.

"You don't smoke."

"I know. I've been stressed out. Carter brought me this when he stopped by earlier." She held up something that definitely wasn't a cigarette.

"You're not smoking. You're vaping," I said with a soft laugh. "You realize that has no smell, so you can just do it inside, right?" Her silence told me that she absolutely had not realized that. "What's even in that, anyway?"

"What do you mean?" She brought it closer to her face, holding it up in the dim ray of light that shone from our building.

"You can't tell what it is by looking at it," I told her, laughing. "Carter didn't say?"

She shrugged. "I figured they were all the same. I don't smoke, remember?"

I nodded toward the door. "Come on. Let's go inside. We can text Carter and ask if you're high right now." She let me help her up, and I pulled the door open for her. Warmth spread through my bones immediately upon entering. "I can't believe you were out there in the middle of the night like that."

Not only was it cold, but I didn't love the idea of Sophia alone in the dark. I tried not to think about what could've happened to her.

"I can't believe you still ride that death trap" was her reply.

It wasn't the first time she'd mentioned the old motorcycle and its lack of safety features. But it was the first time I'd realized she was probably as concerned with *my* well-being as I was with hers.

SOPHIA

Carter had texted back pretty quickly that I wasn't smoking marijuana. Apparently it was some sort of CBD oil that was supposed to give you the calming effect without the high and paranoia that was often associated with the drug. I think it had its desired effect. I felt more relaxed than I had in weeks. Or maybe I was just tired.

I shrugged off my coat and hung it on the hook by the door, wondering how long it would take me to crawl to my bed. "I think I'm gonna try to get some sleep."

"Me too," Drew said. "After I take a shower and scrub the Rafferty's grime off my body."

"See you tomorrow, then?"

He ran a hand through his hair, which was messy from his helmet, and nodded.

I turned toward my room, but something didn't let me move. "Unless..." I knew what I planned to say but wasn't actually sure how I planned to say it. "Unless... That couch can't be very comfortable, and you're probably exhausted."

Drew's eyebrows narrowed a bit before the implication of what I'd said seemed to wash over him. His lips parted, and for a moment I thought he was going to make an awkward suggestion less awkward by making it himself, but he remained silent as he waited for me to continue. Why did he have to be such a goddamn gentleman?

I tried to think of the best way to go about inviting him to stay in my bed, but all I could come up with was, "Do you want to sleep with me?"

That was so not it.

If this conversation had been through text, I would've immediately sent one of those emojis with the girl's hand covering her face. Instead I did nothing as I watched his mouth open wider.

"I mean ... That's not what I meant. I mean do you want to sleep with me in my bed? Sleep. Like actually sleep. My bed's gotta be more comfortable than that couch."

"Technically it's Brody's bed."

"Whatever," I said with an eye roll. "Don't make this even weirder than it already is."

"Where's the fun in that?" He moved toward me, a goofy smile threatening to spread across his face. "I'd love to sleep with you, Sophia."

I wish I could've figured out how to trap those words in a little box that I could open whenever I needed to smile.

Chapter Twenty-Four

SOPHIA

I was going to throw up. Or my head was going to explode. Or both. The auction had finally arrived, everything was set up in the sorority house, and people were starting to arrive. This was a great time to start having a panic attack.

"Hey, Soph, where did you want these flowers?" Gina asked. "Oh God, are you okay?" she added when she got a better look at me.

"Yeah," I wheezed. "Great. And anywhere."

"Are you having an asthma attack? Do you have an inhaler or something?"

"No. I'm just feeling a little ..." I flailed my arms around, hoping that would convey my breakdown without alarming her.

"Do you want some water?"

"Yes. Water ... great."

"Okay, I'll be right back." She practically sprinted away from me.

Bending over, I put my hands on my knees. I was behind

the curtain of the small stage I'd rented for tonight that fit perfectly. I'd never been more thankful for our enormous main room.

I tried to focus on taking deep breaths in through my nose and out through my mouth. My heart had barely started to feel like it wouldn't pop out of my chest like one of those creatures from *Alien* when I felt a large hand on my back.

"Hey, you okay? Gina said you were freaking out."

Drew.

I stood up and turned toward him, wanting to fold myself into him but knowing I couldn't. My sorority sisters were milling around in an effort to help with the finishing touches, and I didn't want them to intrude on any more intimate moments. Instead, I looked up at him and used the look of concern he had in his eyes to ground me.

"I'm fine," I said. "Just a little overwhelmed. And a little scared."

Drew put his hands on my shoulders and squeezed. "Everything is going to be fine. There's already a line outside, and you've planned this thing down to the smallest detail. It's going to be great."

I wished I could share his enthusiasm. Maybe when it was all over. But now, my prevalent feeling was panic laced with terror. Instead of saying that though, I gave him a once-over.

"Damn, you clean up nice."

We'd asked the guys participating to wear a suit if they had one and, if not, to get as dressed up as they could. Drew had borrowed a charcoal-gray suit Brody had in his closet, and it fit him remarkably well.

"Yeah?" His hand shook a bit as he ran it down the lapel of the jacket, as if he were insecure wearing it, which made guilt slam into me. He shouldn't have to do this. He should be at home hanging out or getting caught up on schoolwork or whatever the hell he felt like doing. Participating in a bachelor auction simply because I'd asked him to was really going a little above and beyond.

"Yeah," I croaked out instead of confessing my adoration and gratitude for him. I'd already barely managed to stave off a panic attack—this night didn't need to get any more embarrassing.

"Soph?" I looked around Drew to see Emma standing there. "It's eight. We good to open the doors?"

I took a deep breath before nodding. "Let's do this."

Drew and I moved closer to the entrance so I could greet people coming in and oversee that everyone paid the cover to get in. I wasn't going to make Aamee's mistake and count on the kindness of people's hearts for donations. I also wasn't going to count on the auction being a success. We'd decided that charging three dollars to get in was reasonable enough for people to willingly pay it.

My mouth dropped open as the line of people entering was still steady nearly five minutes after we'd opened the door.

"So many people came," I whispered.

Drew put his arm around my shoulders and squeezed. "You did good, Sis."

I elbowed him lightly as a smile pulled at my lips.

Eventually the line thinned, and I managed to resist the urge to run over to where Macy and Kyla, our house treasurer, were collecting the money and ask them how much we'd raised so far. Instead, I busied myself making sure the party was running smoothly and we had enough food and drinks to accommodate the crowd.

I also checked on the two lacrosse player frat boys I'd hired to make sure only people over twenty-one came to the table where the alcohol was. I hadn't wanted to limit the party to people legally able to drink, but I also didn't want to get busted for serving people underage. So I'd decided parting with a hundred bucks for the two guys to guard the liquor table was a small price to pay. Macy and Kyla had been checking IDs at the door, and putting brightly colored bracelets on people twenty-one and over helped the process.

After looking everything over, Gina and I began herding all the bachelors backstage to get ready. Once they were situated, I did another lap to make sure the party was still running smoothly. Which ended up being a mistake because it caused me to run into Aamee.

She stepped into my path, looking around haughtily. "Your event seems to be going well. Hopefully your auction idea works out."

Her voice was dubious, as if she doubted it would. Not that I expected otherwise. And since I'd hoped her party would be a monumental flop, I couldn't fault her for it.

"Thanks," I replied brusquely as I moved around her.

"I'm excited your brother is participating."

Her words stilled me, and I slowly turned my head so I was looking at her. "Why?"

She shrugged innocently. "Since he's on the market for men *and* women, he'll probably be pretty popular. There may even be a bidding war. I'm looking forward to seeing the action."

She couldn't know how much her words bothered me. Couldn't know that I'd been dreading having to watch people bid on my secret boyfriend. Could she?

"Good," I replied with conviction I didn't feel. "Whatever helps us raise more money for charity." I hoped the words hit her where it hurt. There was a very real chance she was going to lose this fight, and whatever games she was playing weren't going to change that.

Her eyes flashed for a second, but she didn't otherwise react. Which was a real shame. "Good luck." The words would've sounded more heartfelt coming from the villain in *Taken*.

I watched as she flounced away for a moment before mentally shaking myself, and then I made my way to where the bachelors were. I'd almost made it when I heard a booming voice.

"Sophia!"

I whirled around to see Carter striding toward me with Joey trailing behind him. I felt my eyes narrow as I took them in. Were they friends now?

When Carter reached me, he stepped close, his face jutting over my shoulder as he spoke lowly. "I'm here to save the day."

Oh God.

"It's nighttime," I replied, my smartass remark cloaking the worry over what Carter thought needed saving.

"Then I'm here to save the night."

"Whose night?"

"Everyone's."

Pinching the bridge of my nose, I took a deep breath. "Okay. Against my better judgment, I'm going to ask you to explain."

"Well, I know *Brody* is worried about who might bid on him. So I figured we could just have Joey do it."

I glanced over at Joey to see if he'd heard any of what Carter said, but he'd stayed a bit away from us.

"You told him?" I asked, my voice low but still harsh and accusing. I knew Carter wouldn't be able to keep his damn mouth shut.

"Who?"

"Joey."

Carter looked over his shoulder as if he'd forgotten the other man was with him.

"Oh. No. He still thinks Drew's Brody. And gay. That's why he's willing to bid on him. He wants a second date something fierce." Carter hesitated. "I'm starting to see the flaws in this plan."

"Jesus Christ," I muttered.

"No, listen, it's still good. Having a dude win will help get the gay plot line back."

"Plot line?"

"Yeah. Before you two made shit all complicated by sucking each other's faces off in public, everyone thought Drew was gay. This will help us get back to that."

This was insanity. Absolute Carter-induced insanity.

Unfortunately, it was a better plan than having some chick bidding on Drew. We'd made it clear when we'd promoted the party that there was no sexual element to this auction—no one was buying a sex slave. But these were still horny college kids.

At least if Joey won, I wouldn't have to worry about Joey hitting on him. Not because Joey *wouldn't,* but I felt better knowing Drew wouldn't be tempted by his advances.

And then I felt like shit for thinking Drew would be tempted by anyone's advances, but I quickly set that aside. I could only deal with one crisis at a time.

"This is a horrible idea," I said, but the words lacked any conviction.

"You have a better one?" Carter asked.

"Is Joey bidding with his own money?" I asked instead of answering.

"Hell no. I gave him two hundred bucks and told him he could keep whatever was left over. I didn't think people would be willing to bid too much for a guy of ambiguous sexual interests."

"Ambiguous interests?"

"Yeah. Guys, girls, sisters. He's fucking complicated."

Why did I ask?

"Okay, I'll pay you back."

"No worries. You've been tutoring me for free for months. We'll just call it even."

I gave him a small smile. "Thanks. Hopefully this works."

"My plans always work."

Rather than stay and debate that fact, I hightailed it backstage to fill Drew in on the plan. I found him standing with two other guys.

"Hey," I interrupted. Drew turned his attention to me and smiled. I let myself sink into it for a second before I said, "Can I talk to you for a sec?"

"Sure." He waved to the guys as we walked away. "What's up?" he asked when we were out of earshot.

"Carter's here."

"Yeah, he told me he'd come by after he finished with his conditioning coach."

"He brought Joey."

Drew's brow furrowed. "As a date or ... ?"

"Yes, but not for him. For you. He's going to have Joey bid

so no one else wins you."

Worry was clear on his face. "Did he tell Joey the truth?"

"No, which I'm not sure makes me relieved or more nervous. Joey's evidently actually interested in winning you, which is a bit unfair to him, I suppose. But I figured we can cross that bridge when we come to it. And we're funding his bid, so technically he's not actually paying for you."

Drew pulled at his tie. "This feels a little like being pimped out."

I grimaced. "I'm sorry. Want me to pull you from the auction?"

At this point, I didn't even give a fuck anymore. I shouldn't have let my sorority sisters' gossip get us into this mess in the first place. So everyone thought I was fucking my brother. It wasn't like they had proof. Well, proof beyond a dark, grainy video on Aamee's phone.

He looked at me for a second before offering me a sweet smile. "Nah. It'll be fine."

I wanted to believe that, but there was mounting evidence proving the opposite. He must've seen the doubt on my face, because he stepped closer and wrapped a hand around my wrist, giving it a slight squeeze.

"Stop worrying."

We kept our eyes locked on one another for a second, and bit by bit I felt myself relaxing. I wouldn't be able to stop worrying until this was all over, but I could maybe get through this without having a mental breakdown.

His smile grew wider as he clearly noticed that I'd taken a few steps back from the proverbial ledge. "That's it. We got this."

DREW

I don't "got" this.

As happy as I was that I could help Sophia calm down, inside I was a nervous wreck. Waiting to walk onto that stage so people could bid on me was not something I was looking forward to. The rumors swirling around us didn't make the prospect of being thrust into the limelight any more palatable.

I watched the other men who'd agreed to participate march out, most of them at least appearing confident. People threw up the cardstock Sophia and I had spent the week gluing to popsicle sticks to serve as bidding paddles. Most of the guys brought in about a hundred bucks—not too shabby considering it was college kids bidding.

Sophia and I had agreed that I'd go out in the middle of the auction so as to not make a big production of myself. The hope was that I wouldn't stand out in any way. So as the seventh guy was called to the stage, I prepped myself to go on next.

Sophia's friend Gina had agreed to be the MC. Originally Sophia had planned to do it, but she thought it might be better to stay behind the scenes and make sure everything ran smoothly than be stuck up on stage. I tried to sneak a peek around the curtain to see if I could lay eyes on her, but the lights shining down on the stage were too bright.

I'd never considered the lengths sorority girls would go to to throw a successful party, but color me impressed. The company Sophia had hired to bring in the stage had also set up lights and sent a guy in to run them. Definitely impressive.

I moved back slightly as the guy who'd gone on before me waved to the crowd and came back behind the curtain.

"One fifty," he said. "Not too bad."

It wasn't bad at all, and I was torn between wanting to outdo him and wanting no one to bid so I could be done with this nightmare. But before I could solidly decide which I wanted, Gina was calling me to the stage.

Stepping into the spotlight—literally—was jarring, and I stumbled a bit before I got my shit together and stood up taller, striding down the stage with confidence I hoped looked believable, because it definitely didn't feel that way.

"Brody Mason, brother of Zeta Eta Chi's very own Sophia Mason, is a six-two, two-hundred-and-ten-pound ball of charisma and charm. He's not necessarily used to hard labor, but he's agreed to perform some moderate tasks for charity. We'll start the bidding at thirty dollars."

It felt like a slap to my ego to start the bidding so low, even though that was where all the guys had started. Sophia had explained that she thought she would get more people to participate if the bidding started out at a reasonable price. I just hoped I made it up to at least a hundred by the time this was over. Or not. I was still conflicted.

But the choice to walk out of here free and clear was squashed when a female voice rang out. "I bid thirty."

A male voice replied, "Thirty-five."

I shot my eyes toward the voice, and I saw Carter standing beside a smirking Joey, whose paddle was high in the air.

Even though Joey had been nothing but nice at the costume party, the way he was eyeing me up was a little unnerving. Maybe I didn't want him to win after all.

Another voice called out, "Forty dollars," but I didn't get a chance to see who had said it before a "forty-five" was yelled through the air. It turned into a bit of a bidding war after that, and I stopped trying to figure out who was calling out.

The lights made it difficult to see most people unless they were standing off to the side of the stage, like Joey and Carter were. And Joey, bless his heart, hung in there with the rest of them. I wasn't sure how much Carter and Sophia had given him to bid with, but I hoped it was a lot, because these chicks were insane.

When the bidding got to two hundred dollars, I noticed Joey look over at Carter, who looked a little worried. Then, when it *passed* two hundred and Joey stopped raising his paddle, *I* started getting worried.

I tried to tell myself that it didn't matter. The most I'd probably have to do was carry a girl's books around to class and hang out with her for a day. I didn't *want* to do it, but it wouldn't kill me.

The money kept climbing, and it began to feel ridiculous. The only reason anyone was interested in me was because I was the "gay" guy who was maybe bi and maybe fucking my sister. Just the thought of having to spend the day with someone attempting to pump me for information was exhausting. But as the total approached three hundred dollars, I resigned myself to exactly that fate.

Gina, on the other hand, seemed to be having the time of her life. "I've got two-eighty; can we get three hundred? Come on, everyone. It's for a good cause."

I heard murmurs in the crowd, and I saw a paddle begin to be raised but stopped midair as another voice rang out.

"I bid five hundred."

Everyone's head, including mine, swung toward the voice. I squinted into the crowd and held a hand over my eyebrows to block some of the glare. It took me a moment to find exactly where the person who had bid on me was, but the fact that a wide berth had begun to form around her was clue enough.

Sophia?

I felt my brow furrow as my hand dropped back to my side. What the hell was she doing? We'd had a plan ... didn't we?

"Uh, sold to ... Sophia Mason. Congratulations." Poor Gina sounded as confused as the rest of us, but there was also concern in her voice. This wasn't going to look good to anyone, and I couldn't for the life of me figure out why Sophia would bid on me, let alone bid so much.

Though I had to admit, part of me warmed at the action. That crazy lunatic had bid on me even though doing so was a horrible, horrible idea. The ramifications would likely be huge, but she'd done it anyway for some bizarre, poorly thought-out reason, and it made my chest flutter just thinking about it.

I was either falling for her or she was giving me a heart attack.

Eventually I realized I was standing on stage gaping like a dead fish, so I hurried off. Everyone backstage was either smirking at me or staring at me like they were contemplating calling campus security.

I could just imagine how that call would go. *"Um, yes, I'd like to report a possible case of incest. Please send every available officer to help clean up this train wreck."*

Unable to get the fuck out of here fast enough, I flew around the curtain to try to hunt down Sophia. But instead, I practically ran into Carter ... and Joey.

"Bro! What. The. Fuck? Why did Sophia do that?" Carter asked.

"I honestly have no idea," I replied distractedly as I tried to peer around him to find Sophia.

"She sounded jealous to me," Joey said, snark evident in his voice.

I fixed a hard gaze on him. "Really? She said, like, three words. You were able to pull jealousy from that? Get real."

He crossed his arms over his chest. "And you sound defensive. There's no need to get snippy."

I gave Carter a look that I hoped said, "Get this kid the fuck away from me," and it must've been relatively on point.

Carter gripped Joey's arm. "Come on, man. I'll buy you a drink and be your wingman for the night."

Joey seemed happy with this development, because he let Carter tug him away without any protest.

I scanned the room for Sophia again, and I was just about to brave the crowd to look for her when Emma hurried over to me.

"She's waiting for you up in my room," she said. "Take the back stairs through the kitchen so no one sees you going up. I'm the third door from the left."

I nodded at her before walking, as casually as I could muster, through the kitchen and into a small foyer that had stairs off to one side. When I got to the door Emma had directed me to, I tapped on it lightly. When I heard the door unlock, I turned the knob and went inside, relocking it behind me.

Sophia was standing in the middle of the room, two twin beds on either side of her. She was backlit by a small lamp, which was providing the only light in the room. She looked almost angelic, and it was all I could do to not kiss her. But the worried look on her face told me it wasn't the time for that.

"Taking men into *other* people's rooms now? Will you never learn?"

She stared at me blankly for a second, causing me to belatedly think it was maybe not the time for jokes. But then her shoulders dropped, and she gusted out a laugh. "Evidently not."

I'm not sure which of us moved first, but a millisecond later we were wrapped around each other. "You okay?" I whispered against her hair.

"Probably not," she murmured. "I think I just committed social suicide."

"It was probably a homicide slash suicide, since I'm pretty sure I was also a casualty."

She groaned loudly and burrowed into me.

I couldn't help but laugh. "I'm just teasing. It'll be fine."

"It really won't." Her words were muffled against my chest, but I could hear the genuine fear behind them.

Unsure of what to say to make things better, I continued to hold her and hope that was enough. We swayed gently together, the movement calming and almost meditative. After a few minutes, she pulled back enough that I could see her face.

"I'm sorry," she said.

"For what?"

"Continually messing everything up."

"You haven't messed anything up."

"You're just saying that."

"I know."

She smacked me, but it also got a smile out of her, so I considered it a win.

"Not that I'm not thrilled to have to be at your beck and call for a day, but why did you do it?" I didn't want to seem accusatory, but I was curious as hell. We'd had a plan. Not a great plan, but a plan all the same. And then she'd gone rogue, and I was dying to know why.

"I'm stupid," she replied.

I hesitated. "I feel like there's no good way for me to respond to that."

She rolled her eyes but smiled again before rubbing a hand over her face. "Joey wanted to win you."

"Well, yes, that would be a reason to bid."

"So did all those other girls."

"You did know what an auction was before you held one, right?"

She sighed loudly. "Can you shut up for a second? Jesus, I'm about to march you downstairs and sell you myself."

"I don't think Jesus is available for that." The menacing look she gave me had me quickly saying, "Sorry," and I mimed closing a zipper over my lips.

Her hand flailed around a little as if she were searching the air around her for the words she wanted to say. "I don't want someone else thinking they can have you."

When she looked at me, I nodded since I'd promised to be quiet.

"They can't," she continued. When I again didn't say anything, she stepped closer. "No one else is allowed to have you because you're already mine."

I slid my arms around her waist and pulled her close.

"I've never been good at sharing," she said quietly as she looked up at me, her face full of vulnerability.

"No matter who the highest bidder was, I still would've been yours." Maybe those words weren't the most reassuring that she'd done the right thing, but I needed her to know. Despite the crazy situation we found ourselves in, I wouldn't have traded a second of it, because it gave me her. And I wasn't going to lose that for some scantily clad coed who thought it was a turn-on to buy someone like a prized steed at a county fair.

"I know. But I needed them to know it too. Even though it complicates everything even more. I needed them to know, even if we'll have to figure out a way to spin it. At least for a minute, we weren't hiding."

I pulled her closer to me so I could rest my cheek against her forehead. "We won't have to hide it forever. This is a temporary situation."

"Are *we*?" she asked, her voice the smallest I'd ever heard it.

"Are we what?"

"Temporary."

I looked down at her so she could see the honesty in my response. "Fuck no." And then I kissed her like I never had before. I owned her mouth, demonstrating every ounce of possessiveness I could.

She met every bit of that kiss with an urgency of her own. There was no denying what this was: a claiming—just like what she'd done downstairs. We'd have to spin what happened at the auction somehow, but for a short time, we thrust our feelings into the spotlight.

And even though we'd have to lie about it afterward, I couldn't deny that I'd needed the proverbial moment in the sun. It was easy to tell someone what they wanted to hear behind closed doors. But declaring it in front of over a hundred people? No one had ever done something like that for me before. I didn't realize how much I needed it done until Sophia had found the balls to do it.

We broke apart before the kiss got away from us and we

ended up naked on Emma's bed. It was going to be hard—pun intended—enough to face everyone after that kiss, but if we'd actually gotten off, there'd have been no way of facing everyone.

Thankfully, when we got ourselves sorted and went back downstairs, the party was in full swing and people didn't pay much attention to us. We decided it would be best to mingle separately, so Sophia went off to keep tabs on how things were going, and I went in search of anyone who'd get drunk with me. It didn't take me long to find Aniyah, Toby, Xander, and Carter hanging out by the makeshift bar.

Xander saw me coming and turned and said something to the bartender. When I reached them, Xander was accepting a drink from the guy and handing it to me. "Don't ask what's in it. Just drink."

I knew there was a reason I liked this guy.

After slamming the drink back, I handed the glass back to him and he ordered me another. Once I'd knocked that back too, the burn making its way down my esophagus and into my belly, I felt better. They were all quiet, looking at me as if I were a ticking time bomb getting close to detonation.

"Where's Joey?" I asked because I wasn't sure what else to say.

"I'm not sure," Carter said with a shrug. "He was here one second and gone the next."

"Hmm." I glanced around the room.

"So that was an interesting turn of events this evening," Aniyah said.

"Yup," I replied.

"Are we talking about it?" she asked.

"Nope."

And . . . that was it. Xander asked Toby who in the room

was his type, and Aniyah began dissecting every woman he pointed out, explaining why she wasn't good enough for him and that he could do better.

Carter, who actually knew some of these people, clarified which girls should still be contenders, despite Aniyah's analysis. He'd described one particular girl as "open-minded," prompting Xander to immediately escort Toby in her direction.

The three of us shot the shit for a while until I felt a tap on my shoulder. I whirled around to see a girl holding a camera.

"We need a picture of all the bachelors and winning bidders."

"Oh, um, sure, okay." I handed Carter my beer, which I'd been nursing much more slowly than the drinks Xander had given me. After telling them I'd see them later, I followed the girl to where a group congregated. Sophia was already there, and the girl with the camera organized us so she could snap our picture.

Most of the bachelors stood close to the people who'd bid on them, some even slinging their arms around them, but I made sure to maintain a respectable distance from Sophia.

Once the girl, who Sophia had called Bethany, had fiddled with her camera for a bit, she yelled, "Say auction!"

Just as we all said the word to the camera, I heard someone yell my name and turned my head. Carter was motioning toward the door, where Toby was leaving with the girl Xander had taken him to talk to. I smiled widely as I turned back to the camera, but everyone was already moving, so I guessed I'd botched my photo op. Oh well.

"What time does the party end?" I asked Sophia.

She groaned. "Not soon enough. And I'll have to help clean up after."

Looking around, I made sure no one was watching us as I leaned down to whisper in her ear. "I hope what they say is true." She looked up at me quizzically, so I clarified. "That good things come to those who wait. I feel that we're both entitled to some very good things when this party is over."

A smile slowly overtook her face. "And just who will be delivering these good things?"

I locked my eyes on hers as I said, "I think we both deserve some solid delivery service after all this."

The heat in her gaze was all the affirmation I needed.

Chapter Twenty-Five

SOPHIA

We practically sprinted back to the apartment, and once inside, Drew pinned me to the back of the door with his hips. He looked at me for a moment, his eyes fixed on mine in a way that made my heart thump loudly in my chest. I felt blood spreading to every part of my body, specifically the parts below my waist, and my stomach tightened in anticipation.

It was one of those moments I wish I could've kept tucked away deep inside me. A moment to come back to when I needed to remember what it was like to feel wanted. Or what it felt like to *want*. Because God, did I want Drew Nolan.

Even this, I loved—sharing his space, breathing his air. All of it had me both wanting more and wanting whatever we had to never end. No guy had ever looked at me like Drew did, like he couldn't decide whether he wanted to hold me or fuck me. I hoped he did both.

His hands went to where mine had been scratching lightly under the back of his shirt, and he laced his fingers between mine. The backs of my hands pressed against the glossy paint of the door, and I was suddenly aware of how turned on I was. Drew slid my hands up the door and held them above my head, finally bringing his lips to mine.

And just like that we were on each other, the still moment replaced with a heated, rushed one. Drew's tongue moved over mine, teasing me in a way I didn't know was possible with only a kiss.

I felt him against me but needed him lower, against my abdomen. If this time didn't result in an orgasm, I might have to give up completely and commit myself to a nunnery.

He brought a hand up to the back of my neck and tangled his fingers in my hair, massaging me as he deepened the kiss.

He pulled away just long enough to say, "You have no idea how long I've wanted to do this."

I smiled. I definitely had some idea. As much as I'd tried not to focus on what I felt about Drew or what he felt about me, because it would only complicate things, the reality was a part of me always knew we'd end up here—our lips searching for anything they could make contact with, our hands fumbling frantically with articles of clothing like two hurried teenagers worried they might get caught.

Zippers unzipped, buttons unbuttoned, and clasps unclasped until both of us had nothing left to take off. But once both of us were naked, our rushed moment slowed to one that allowed us to savor every kiss and brush our skin against each other's.

Drew led me to my bedroom, guiding me backward so slowly it was almost painful. But as much as I wanted to consummate everything we'd experienced over the past few months, I wanted this moment too. The one where I was lost in the anticipation of it all, lost in Drew's scent of soap laced with salt from the little bit of sweat on his skin.

He was intoxicating, and I decided Drew-drunk was the best kind of drunk.

Arriving in the bedroom, he lowered me to the mattress and lay beside me as he traced his fingers in a line from my jaw to my breast, over my hip bone, down my thigh, and everywhere in between. Then his lips were on my chest, ears, anywhere he could reach.

I think we both knew our mouths had done enough talking.

It was time we finished what we'd started.

Chapter Twenty-Six

SOPHIA

The sun streamed into the bedroom through a gap in the curtains, leaving a bright streak of light across Drew's chest. I rubbed my fingers over it lightly, feeling the rhythmic way his chest rose and fell as he slept.

We'd spent the entire weekend in bed, and it had been glorious. Sharing space with Drew—not just living together but actually occupying the same physical space—for a prolonged period was novel, and I wasn't looking forward to bursting the little bubble we'd created.

There'd been a few texts from my sorority sisters digging for information about my bidding on "Brody," but I'd ignored them. My parents had called too, but I'd sent them directly to voicemail. Nothing could lift a sexual haze like my parents, and since I was perfectly content in my fog, I had no choice but to refuse their calls.

"Why are you tracing me?" Drew's voice was sleep-rough, and the low gravel tone of it rumbled through me.

"I'm trying to braid your chest hair."

His eyes popped open, and he actually looked down at where my fingers were caressing him.

"Really?" I said. "You don't even have enough hair to braid."

"Sorry I'm not up on the hair-length standards for braiding. What time is it?"

"Time for you to go get us breakfast."

"Me? You're the one who's been up for hours petting me like a creeper."

I withdrew my hand from him and propped it on my hip, which probably looked ridiculous since I was lying on my side. "Be sure to remember how creepy it was when you're begging me to *pet* you later."

"Mmm, I'll beg now if you want," he replied as he made his eyebrows dance.

Flopping backward, I sighed dramatically. "I would, but I'm afraid I haven't been adequately fed in order to keep my energy up."

He rolled on top of me, his weight pressing down on me in the best way.

Maybe I'm not hungry after all.

I shimmied a little, and a sexy smirk appeared on his face. "What time is your first class?"

"Ten," I replied, a little breathless as I allowed myself to get lost in the feel of him. "Please." My voice was a low whine, but I didn't have it in me to care about how needy I sounded.

But Drew didn't make me wait long. He was the consummate lover, knowing when to tease and when to make me see stars. Even after we fell over the edge together, it took a while to come back to myself. But when I did, I couldn't help but be a bit of a brat.

"I believe I was promised breakfast," I reminded him.

His eyes slid slowly open. "You're going to hold me to that?"

"I'm just trying to help you out. I wouldn't want you to fail a challenge you set for yourself."

"How helpful of you," he muttered dryly.

"What can I say? I'm a giver."

He burst out laughing. "You certainly are."

I smacked him as I joined in his laughter. "Perv."

When he settled down, he took a breath. "Bagels okay? I think we still have a couple."

Sighing, I replied, "I suppose." I didn't anticipate the tickling, though I should've. His fingers dug into my ribs, and he didn't quit until I was a squealing mess.

"All right, I'll make food while you get ready," he said when he finally crawled out of bed.

"Sounds like a plan."

I rushed through a shower and getting ready. When I made it out to the kitchen, a bagel was toasted and smothered in cream cheese waiting for me. He'd even made coffee.

"How did I ever survive without you?" I asked before taking a large bite.

"Beats me."

There was a prolonged silence after that, as if we both knew there were things that needed to be discussed, but neither of us wanted to be the one who initiated the conversation. Or maybe that was all me and I was projecting. Either way, I was suddenly glad I had to hurry to get to class on time.

It wasn't that I didn't want to talk more about the future, but I was also afraid I might find out we weren't on the same page. We had a lot working against us, and part of me couldn't blame him if he decided the hassle wasn't worth it. The other parts were all figuring out where I could dump his body if he didn't agree to be my boyfriend immediately.

But rather than voice any of that, I said, "I better go." After gathering my things, I walked over to where he was leaning on the counter and pressed into him. "See you later?"

"Absolutely. I work tonight, but I'll be home from class by four thirty. We can at least have dinner together."

"Good." I lifted up on my toes so I could press a kiss to his lips—a kiss he willingly met, and I almost bagged school so I could drag him back to bed. But instead, I broke the kiss and mentally lauded myself for my restraint.

We said our goodbyes, and I burst out into the chilly morning, ready to confront the day. Until I ran into Sam and Macy when I entered the liberal arts building.

"Oh my God, Sophia, where have you been?" Macy asked as she dragged me into a hug.

"At home," I replied haltingly, unsure why they seemed like they'd been ready to search local morgues for me.

"Everyone's been trying to reach you," Sam said.

I thought *everyone* was a bit of a stretch, but I couldn't deny that I'd been dodging quite a few of them all weekend. It probably hadn't been my wisest move if I wanted to beat Aamee, but I hadn't exactly been thinking about the presidency over the previous couple of days.

"Sorry," I said lamely. "I needed a couple days to… decompress." *That's one way to say it.* "The auction took a lot out of me."

"I bet," Sam said.

It wasn't snide. If I had to guess, I'd say she was concerned, which I couldn't deny made me feel warm and fuzzy inside.

But she continued, voice hushed and eyes darting around furtively. "What was the deal with you buying Brody?"

I should have prepared an answer to this question.

I probably looked like a deer in headlights as I stammered out an explanation. "I, um, well, I kind of . . . " I took a breath and told myself to chill the fuck out. And in doing so, I had a moment of clarity. "I had a suspicion that Aamee had put someone up to bidding on Brody as a way of messing with me." I forced out a laugh. "Which I guess worked since I blew a shit ton of money on him. But since he was only in the auction as a favor to me, I didn't want to chance him ending up in a bad situation. So I just bid on him myself."

They shared a quick look with one another, as if trying to telepathically figure out whether they believed me or not. After another couple seconds, their postures relaxed, and they seemed more at ease.

"We figured it was something like that," Sam said.

I managed to quash the urge to call her a liar, knowing she'd probably at least half believed whatever sordid rumors were flying around the sorority house. Not that I could blame her. I was sure what I'd actually been up to was much more X-rated than anything they'd managed to come up with. Minus the fact that they thought I'd been with my brother. That definitely elevated the MPAA rating.

"Your auction was great," Macy said. "I'm glad it went so well for you."

I smiled at them. Her words sounded genuine, so I let myself believe they were.

Other than Macy narcing on me to her mother, I'd never had issues with either of these women. I'd pulled away a bit recently in light of everything going on, but I'd need to do better by them going forward, whether I won the presidency or not.

If I couldn't give them a better leader, I could at least be a better friend.

"I need to get to class," I said softly. "But I'll stop being such a stranger. I'm sorry I didn't answer your calls."

"No worries," Sam assured me. "We get it. It all gets a little…*much* sometimes, having so many girls in your business."

It sure did.

XO

I don't remember a thing about my classes. All I could think about was what had happened since the beginning of the school year. Some of my thoughts were about the situation with my sorority. Most of them were of Drew.

By the time I headed home, I was mentally exhausted from thinking about my relationship with Drew.

Were we in a relationship?

I knew *I* wanted to be in a relationship, but I didn't know where he stood. I had a feeling he was in this as deeply as I was, but it was easy to second-guess. When I finally got back to the apartment, I was done with wondering.

We'd have a nice dinner, and then we'd talk about where we stood. It'd be good to clear the air and get everything out in the open. With this new resolve, I nestled into the couch to do some homework until he got home.

It wasn't long before I heard the door unlock and creak open. And before I knew it, I was off the couch and launching myself at him.

We could talk later.

Chapter Twenty-Seven

DREW

I woke up to Sophia snuggled against me, my face buried in her dark hair. It was a familiar and welcome way to start the morning. Definitely beat tossing around on Brody's couch while I hit snooze for the third time. Enjoying the moment, I breathed in deeply, and it wasn't long before Sophia stirred.

She wiggled against me and said, "Are you huffing me again?"

"Something like that," I whispered against her neck. "I would've said 'inhaling' though. 'Huffing' sounds so... dangerous."

"I'm dangerous."

She flipped over so we were facing each other, and I had to agree. She *was* dangerous. "Dangerously sexy maybe."

That made her smile. "Why is being sexy dangerous?"

Adjusting my arm so I could prop my head up on my hand, I stroked her hair before moving my hand down her back and up again. "I guess all of it's dangerous."

Her eyebrows pushed together, and she seemed more

253

alert at my comment. Like the implications of it brought about a feeling inside her that I couldn't quite identify. But it also brought up a whole slew of questions I was pretty sure neither of us was prepared to answer.

"I mean..." What *did* I mean? "I mean I like what we're doing. I like *you*, Sophia."

"I like you too." She smiled, but there was a caution to it. "You're making me nervous, though. I feel like you're breaking up with me or something."

I didn't realize how much a comment like that could mean until she'd said it, and judging by her expression, she hadn't thought it through fully.

"You think of me as your boyfriend?" I couldn't disguise the stupid grin that slid over my face because, as much as this was all so new, it also felt like it was long overdue.

Shrugging as much as she could while still lying down, she covered her face with her hands. But I could still see her cheeks flushing between her fingers.

"I don't know. Maybe? Is that weird?"

I pulled her hands down one at a time until she couldn't help but make eye contact with me. Then I leaned over to kiss her. Innocent and simple, it lacked the passion our other kisses had, but somehow that made it more intimate.

"It's not weird at all. I'll be your boyfriend if you'll be my girlfriend."

"I feel like we're in middle school," she said on a laugh. "This feels weird."

"Does it?" It felt so right to me.

"I don't know. What are we gonna do? You're supposed to be my brother."

Groaning, I rubbed my hands over my face. "Don't remind

me. I'm not sure how we should play this."

"Me neither."

We were quiet for a while, both of us staring at the ceiling like some sort of answer was magically going to scribe itself across the dull white of the paint.

When neither of us had come up with a new idea, I said, "Maybe we can just keep it a secret."

"For how long?" she asked.

It was a great question.

I was reminded of how this entire setup was doomed from the start. Eventually Brody would come back and have to return to his classes, letting everyone in on the fact that I wasn't him. Which I guess wasn't all bad since that meant Sophia and I wouldn't have to sneak around any longer. But then there was the issue of Sophia lying to everyone, including her sorority sisters, to protect Brody and me.

"For as long as we need to?" I offered as more of a suggestion than an actual answer.

She sighed heavily, probably because the solution wasn't a great one. But unfortunately, it was the only one. "'Kay," she agreed. "We'll keep it a secret for as long as we need to."

I couldn't resist rolling onto her, kissing her, feeling her squirm beneath me. "I like having you all to myself anyway," I said, but a knock at the door interrupted us. "Ignore it."

Both of us tried, we really did. But when the knocking continued, Sophia wiggled out from underneath me.

"I'll get it. Don't go anywhere."

I looked down at my erection, wishing it was getting the attention it deserved and hoping it would as soon as Sophia got rid of whatever demonic being had interrupted us. I expected her to return quickly after dismissing whoever was at the door.

What I did not expect was to hear her say, "Mom? Dad? What are you doing here?"

If there was ever a sentence that could kill a boner, that was it.

SOPHIA

I hadn't talked to either of my parents in a few weeks, and now here they were, standing at my—well, Brody's—door.

"Hi, Sophia. Can we come in?" My mom pushed past me before I could answer.

"Sure. It's good to see you guys," I lied.

I was scared shitless. A visit from them right now was akin to the FBI showing up to investigate a human trafficking ring I'd been running out of the apartment.

I hoped like hell they wouldn't find Drew in Brody's bed, because that involved one of two possible confessions: Drew was impersonating Brody, or Drew was a guy I'm sleeping with. Both were equally terrifying.

"It's nice to see you too," my dad said, bringing me in for a hug. My mom followed, and I noticed how ill at ease they both seemed. Nervous, even. Maybe the FBI was after *them*, and they'd come here to hide out.

My mom walked toward the small hallway that led to the bedroom, and I felt my heart jump out of my chest. Thankfully, she didn't leave the living room.

"Is Brody here?"

I hoped I wasn't silent for too long, but it was hard to get a sense of time when I had various possible answers and explanations running through my head. This was like one of those Choose Your Own Adventure books, only in this story, none of the endings were happy.

"No," I said because that seemed like the most logical answer. If I said he was here, they'd clearly want to see him. But what if they went snooping around because Brody had been ignoring them—which I'm sure he had—and they found Drew? I'd have no choice but to introduce him as my boyfriend.

"Do you know where he is?" my dad asked. "It's a little early for Brody to be up and out of the house."

"I think he's at work."

My mom's eyes widened. "Brody has a job?"

Of course not.

"Yeah. He works at the pizza place down the street." Why was I such a fucking moron? They'd just decide to go visit him there.

"It's nine in the morning," my dad pointed out.

"Oh, um, I'm not sure, then. He's probably around campus somewhere. Maybe he didn't come home last night. He could be at a friend's or something." That sounded more like Brody.

"We know what's going on, Sophia."

If I thought my heart was beating fast before, the pace of it now made me wonder if I should call 9-1-1 to report my heart attack before it became too late to save me.

"You do?"

They didn't exactly seem mad about it, which was definitely unexpected. Maybe they knew Brody would fuck up eventually. Or maybe that was just because they were talking to me. I definitely had something to do with covering for Brody's absence, but I was only an accomplice. Hopefully my parents would save their real rage for him.

"Social media is a modern-day truth serum," my mom

said with a sigh that seemed more coated in disappointment than anger.

I found myself feeling bitter about her reaction. She'd been madder when she'd found out I was running for president and hadn't told her. Brody always got off so easy. The moron must've posted a picture of himself in Europe while he was drunk or something.

"I was hoping he would be here when we got here, but we'll just wait for him to get home I guess."

She sat down on the sofa and looked to my dad. He took a seat next to her, leaned forward, and folded his hands. My dad schooled his features and exuded a calm exterior, but he couldn't quite hide the pensive set to his body.

"You're gonna wait for him?"

My mom ignored my comment and said to my dad, "I can't believe he didn't trust us enough to share this with us. That's what hurts. He is who he is. I just wish he knew how much we love him."

My dad smiled, but it was only the corners of his lips that lifted with it. Then he put an arm around her and rubbed her shoulder. "It'll be okay."

"I just can't help but feel like this is somehow my fault."

I could see the tears in my mom's eyes as she spoke. Tears for fucking Brody, who was on the other side of the ocean doing God knew what and posting a picture of it while I covered for his stupid ass. Fuck this.

"I can't believe you're not mad."

They looked offended. Speaking first, my father said. "Mad? Why would we be mad?"

"Why *wouldn't* you be? He's in another country, and you're acting like you caught him taking a drag of a cigarette in middle school."

"I thought you said he was at work," my dad said, sitting up a little straighter and removing his arm from my mother.

"That was a lie," I said. "Obviously."

What is wrong with them today?

Placing her palms together and bringing her hands up to her lips, my mom seemed to be considering her next comment before she shared it. I waited.

"Is he at his boyfriend's?"

It took me a moment for her question to register. "What? No. Knowing Brody, he's probably got like six French women in his hotel right now."

"It's okay," my dad said. "You don't need to cover for him anymore. Your mom saw the picture."

"What picture?"

Digging through her purse, my mom pulled out a folded paper and opened it. When she held it out to me, I took it quickly, wanting to see what the hell Brody had posted. But when I looked at the picture, I was surprised to see it wasn't of Brody at all. It was the picture we'd taken after the auction of all the bachelors and the people who'd won them.

Drew was standing next to me, but his head was turned enough that even I couldn't make out his face. It was also partially blocked by the guy in front of him. I wasn't even sure our own parents would've been able to tell it wasn't Brody. When I'd chosen which one to post on the sorority Instagram, I'd purposely chosen this one for that reason.

"I'm confused." At least that part wasn't a lie.

"So are we," my mom said. "Imagine having to find out from social media that your son is gay."

"Brody isn't gay," I said. "Why would this picture make you think that?"

"It wasn't the picture. It was the comments. Some boy named HoeyJoey tagged Brody and said something about how you bid on his 'boo.'"

"Just because a guy likes him doesn't make Brody gay." It almost scared me how quickly I came up with a response that made sense. I was really getting good at this lying thing.

"No, it doesn't," my mom said. "But then I called around and did some investigating. I didn't want to jump to any conclusions that weren't true, but the overwhelming verdict seemed to be that people on campus know Brody's gay." Sighing loudly, she looked to my dad. "We just wish he could've been as open with us as he was with a bunch of strangers."

"Jesus Christ," I said quietly. "Brody isn't gay. He's just . . . an idiot."

Straightening, my mom cleared her throat. "Can you please explain to me what's going on, Sophia Leigh?"

Neither of my parents were in the habit of using my middle name, and it only meant one thing when they did: I was in a heck of a lot of trouble. They were looking at me like I'd thrown a kegger while they were away for the weekend and charged underage kids fifteen bucks each to get in. Brody had actually done that a couple of summers ago, so I was familiar with that look.

"Actually, I think it'd be better if we spoke to the both of you together," my dad said. "Why don't you give your brother a call? We've tried a few times, but he never answers."

Though my father had masked his comment as a simple suggestion, I knew it for what it was: a directive I'd better follow. So I did.

With a deep sigh, I got up. "Let me grab my phone." I headed down the hall toward the bedroom, and once inside, I closed the door behind me.

Drew was lounging on the bed, playing on his phone. "Are they gone?" he mouthed to me just above a whisper.

"No," I said through clenched teeth. "They want me to call Brody. It's a long story. I'll explain later if they don't kill me first." My voice was hushed, but to explain why I was taking so long, I called out loudly, "I'll be out in a minute. Just gotta find my phone." I grabbed it off the dresser and whispered, "Put some clothes on," before turning back to the door.

When I opened it, my mom was standing outside. Pulling it closed behind me, I found myself practically up against her.

"Brody's in there, isn't he?"

"No, I'll call him. Watch."

"Brody," my mom said, reaching for the doorknob. But I stood my ground, hoping that the delay would at least give Drew the chance to get dressed.

"Is he back there?" My dad was up from the couch and was in front of me in an instant. "Let us in, Sophia."

I was proud of myself for waiting another ten seconds or so before finally stepping to the side so my dad could open the door. I braced myself for what he might see.

"Who are you?" he asked sternly.

Drew stood up—thankfully fully clothed—from where he'd been sitting on the edge of the bed, with a laptop open but probably not even turned on. Next to him lay one of his business textbooks.

"Drew Nolan," he said confidently. Smiling broadly, he reached out his hand. "You must be Sophia's dad. It's nice to meet you."

"That's right," said my dad, completely ignoring Drew's gesture. "Patrick Mason."

Drew slowly lowered his arm. "I didn't realize Sophia had plans, or I wouldn't have asked her to help me study."

"Studying, huh?" my dad practically grunted.

"Yes, sir."

"With Brody's MacBook?"

For as sharp as Drew was, my dad was sharper.

"He lets me use it."

"Are you his boyfriend?" my mom asked, looking almost excited at the idea.

Drew's eyes darted to me before settling back on my parents. "No?" Drew answered, obviously hopeful that he'd chosen correctly.

My dad kept his body squared to Drew's but turned his head toward me once again. "I don't know what the hell's going on here, but you better hope your brother picks up. We're not leaving until we find out where Brody is and why there's a strange man in his bed."

DREW

Mr. Mason was scary, intimidating in a way that went beyond Sophia's description of him. He couldn't have been over six feet tall, but his expression and posture created anxiety in me more than anyone's size ever had.

Not sure whether he was mad at Brody or the whole situation, I barely moved, let alone asked any questions as Sophia dialed his number. She held the phone so it was facing her, leaving her parents out of the frame completely.

I heard the FaceTime call connect, and Brody's voice immediately after. "What's up, little sis? How's college life?

The Greek goddesses let you back in the house yet?"

"I have a meeting with them in a little while, actually," she replied.

Was Brody picking up on the tension in her voice?

"Sweet. Let me know what happens."

It was more likely Brody was making conversation than it was that he actually cared about the result. Well, beyond wanting to find out when Sophia would be moving out of his apartment.

I heard a female voice giggle and Brody say, "I'm on the phone, babe. *Un momento, por favor.*"

"I see you've improved on your Spanish since high school," Sophia said, and I had to bite my tongue from laughing. Scared to make eye contact with Mr. and Mrs. Mason, I kept my gaze fixed on Sophia.

"Ha-ha," Brody said dryly. "Is Drew there? I wanna find out how my classes are going."

"Yeah, he's here," she said, adjusting the phone so Brody could see me.

I chanced a glance at Mr. Mason, who mouthed *Where is he?*

"What's my GPA looking like?" asked Brody.

"Good," I answered. Better to give as little information as possible and ask even fewer questions.

"Nice."

Just when I thought this whole thing couldn't get any more awkward, the dark-haired, bikini-clad woman next to him leaned over to kiss his neck.

One hard stare from Mr. Mason had me asking, "Where are you? Looks gorgeous there."

"Dude, you have no idea. The women, the view, everything

here is beautiful. If you ever get the chance, you definitely need to check out the Amalfi Coast."

"I'll keep that in mind," I said.

With that, Mr. Mason reached for the phone. As Sophia let it go from her hand, she muttered a quick, "Mom and Dad are here," before the Masons made face-to-face contact with their delinquent son.

"What?" Brody squeaked out.

"What are you doing in Italy, Brody?" Mrs. Mason said. "I've been worried about you."

"She's right to worry," Mr. Mason said, "because I swear to God, I'm going to kill you when I see you."

"Sorry, bad signal." Brody quickly tried to muffle the call with fake static he created with his mouth. "Hard to . . . er."

"You're on FaceTime, you fucking idiot," Mr. Mason said. "I can see you doing that."

"*¿Todo bien, mi amor?*" the woman asked.

"No," Brody said, which I at least knew meant the same thing in Spanish as it did in English.

Mr. Mason gritted his teeth. "Start talking."

Unfortunately, as his stare stretched from Brody to me and Sophia, I knew his directive was to all of us.

Brody tried convincing them he'd only been gone two weeks, but the lie detector known as the Masons determined that was a lie.

"We've been trying to reach you for over a month," Mrs. Mason said. "I thought you were avoiding us because you're gay."

"I'm not gay," Brody said, sounding more confused than he usually did, if that was even possible. "See?" I assumed he'd pulled the woman beside him again so his parents could see that he was not, in fact, gay.

"What I see," Mrs. Mason said, "is a selfish spoiled brat who's too lazy to ever take school seriously. *We're* the idiots to ever think you'd grow up." A tear crept into her eye, and I thought about how hard being a parent must be, especially when it was to a fuckup like Brody. Then she turned to me. "So what? You just had this boy going to your classes for you?"

Brody didn't answer.

"I'll assume that's a yes. Explains why you have good grades for once."

"Yeah," Brody said, and even I could hear the sadness in his voice. A part of me almost felt bad for the kid until I remembered he was the reason I was in this mess to begin with.

"You have a degree in business?" Mr. Mason looked me up and down like he was surprised that I could do so well.

"No. This is the first time I've taken any college classes," I said, my voice holding a similar sadness to Brody's. "I'm just a bartender. Thought it might be fun to see what college was like. Figured I could learn some things."

"Well . . ." Mr. Mason let out a disgusted laugh, and I wasn't sure if it was directed at Brody or me. Maybe it was meant for the both of us. "I hope you did."

I was sure even someone as dense as Brody knew his dad wasn't talking about academics.

Mr. Mason turned his attention back to his son. "I don't know what to say anymore or what to do." He rubbed his temples with his free hand. "A bartender did well in classes you couldn't even find the motivation to attend."

The way he said "bartender" made me wish I'd never told him what I did for a living.

"When are you coming home?" Mrs. Mason asked.

Brody was quiet for a moment, like he was truly contemplating the question and trying to answer as honestly as possible. "I'm not," he finally said.

"The hell you're not," their dad said, his voice rising.

Probably used to it, Brody seemed unaffected. "Are you coming to Europe to get me?"

It was more of an actual question than a challenge, and Mr. Mason didn't reply. Instead, he chose to end the call, not even bothering to say goodbye.

"I'll deal with him later." He rubbed a hand over his creased forehead in frustration before allowing his gaze to settle on me and Sophia. "I think the four of us still have some things to discuss anyway."

Not wanting to actually reply, I looked to Sophia to gauge her reaction.

"I know this is a mess, and I'm sorry," she said. "But I wasn't going to betray Brody's trust in me. You know we've never been close, but I feel like in some odd way this has actually brought us together a bit."

"Deceiving parents sometimes does that to siblings," Mrs. Mason replied.

"It wasn't like that," Sophia responded, and Mr. Mason insisted it was exactly like that. The family went back and forth for another few seconds until they all seemed to accept the conversation wasn't going anywhere. "Can we talk about this later?" Sophia asked. "I actually have a meeting at the sorority house that's kind of important."

Letting out a laugh that seemed more out of disgust than humor, Mr. Mason told her to go. "Why don't you drive her over, Kate?" he said, handing over the keys to his wife. "You can talk to Sophia on the way. I'd like to speak with Drew."

He spoke calmly, but his body held the same tension it had since he'd realized I was impersonating his runaway son. And speaking of running away, I wanted absolutely no part of talking to Sophia's dad, especially without her present. But something told me I had no choice. If I wanted Mr. Mason to think anything positive about me—and I really did—I had no other option than to man up and speak to him now.

Sophia looked to me like she was actually considering skipping the meeting if I needed her there, but there was no way in hell I'd let her do that.

"It's fine," I assured her. "I'll talk to you later."

"Sorry," she whispered, like any of this was at all her fault, and headed into the bedroom to get changed.

The Masons and I walked over to the living room and sat on the couch for a few awkwardly silent minutes before Sophia emerged.

"Ready?" she asked her mom.

A few seconds later, they were gone, and with the final close of the door, I felt like I was trapped in a lion's cage, hoping that if I stayed still enough, he wouldn't attack.

I wasn't normally the type of guy to remain quiet in situations like this, preferring to stand my ground and explain myself. But I knew no amount of explaining would help Brody, Sophia, or me, for that matter, so I chose to approach the impending conversation as I would a police interrogation. I'd answer what was asked of me honestly without elaborating any more than necessary.

We were both so quiet, so still, that I felt like the only movement in the entire room was the air passing my lips as I breathed. Finally, Mr. Mason looked up from where he'd been focusing on his hands folded in front of him.

"Tell me why you agreed to this," he said. "Why you'd give up whatever life you had to pretend to be someone you're not?"

I hated the way that sounded—like I'd sacrificed my identity to become someone else. I hated more that there was some truth to it. "I didn't really have much of a life to sacrifice, I guess."

"What were you doing before?"

"Bartending." Not wanting to give up any additional information, I offered only, "I still am."

He nodded and then cleared his throat. "That how you met Brody?"

I nodded.

"And he didn't offer you money?"

"No."

His brow furrowed, and he locked his stare on me like he was trying to determine if I was being truthful.

It suddenly became very important to me that this man know I was telling the truth. He would think what he wanted about me, but I wouldn't have him think I was a liar. Well, any more than he already did.

"I never had the chance to go to college," I said. "I'd always wanted to, though. Maybe just to prove something to myself. Or maybe to prove something to other people."

Mr. Mason's eyes widened. "Who else knows about this?" he asked, and I realized how stupid my last comment had been.

I was quick to answer. "No one." Except Carter. And there was no way I was pulling *him* into this. I'd be a liar before I'd be a rat.

He gave a quick nod. "Good." Then he settled back into the chair and stared at me for a few more seconds before standing, pulling out his wallet, and removing a check.

I didn't know why keeping blank checks in a wallet was a good idea, but then again, I knew nothing about how the wealthy lived.

"You're going to leave," he said, walking into the kitchen and pulling open drawers until he found what he was looking for.

Clicking the pen, he began writing. "Drew..." He looked up. "I don't remember your last name, and I don't really care to, so you can just fill that in."

What the fuck?

"Is three hundred enough?"

"What?" I figured he was giving me three hundred dollars to keep me afloat until I found an apartment of my own, and though the offer was considerate since he didn't have to give me anything at all, I still wanted nothing to do with taking this man's money.

"I'll make it four," he said.

"I don't want your money."

He stopped writing and looked up at me, his eyes blazing. "You don't have a choice." He finished writing the check, placed it on the edge of the counter, and put the pen back carefully in its place. "You're going to leave this apartment, Drew, and you're never going to speak to either of my children again. And you will never speak of this to another person. If anyone finds out about this, it'll ruin any shot my fucking idiot of a son has at making something of himself, should he ever decide to do the right thing. As it is now, I'll have to figure out how to get him excused from his finals."

I heard what he was saying about Brody, but I didn't focus on it. I was too caught up in thinking about a life without Sophia.

"No." I shook my head. "I understand that I can't pretend to be Brody anymore, and I won't fight you on that. But Sophia and I . . . " I'd never said the words I was about to say, but if I had any chance to convince Mr. Mason that my relationship with Sophia didn't stop here, this was it. "There's something between us," I said. "I love your daughter."

"Does Sophia know that?"

"I've never told her," I said softly.

Mr. Mason grabbed his coat and pulled it on, clearly not willing to bend. "Then you'll keep it like that," he said. It was a directive, an order not to be argued with. "Sophia's a good girl. She's smart and determined, and I'll be damned if I'm going to let her settle for someone with a sketchy background and no education. You'll just bring her down, and if you don't realize that, eventually she will."

And there it was. The lion had finally clawed at me until I couldn't fight back. At least not in any way that made me think I could win.

"You're no good for either of my kids, so stay out of their lives."

"You think I'm going to stay away from the woman I love for four hundred dollars?"

"No," he said, grabbing the door handle. "You're going to stay away from her for four hundred *thousand*." With that, he closed the door, leaving me standing in an apartment I wondered if I'd ever see again.

Mr. Mason was right about one thing: Brody was a fucking idiot.

Then again, so was I.

Chapter Twenty-Eight

SOPHIA

Standing in front of the door of my sorority, I tried to get my breathing under control. This was it. All the bullshit of the last couple of months had led me to this moment. I would either vanquish Aamee to the depths of hell where she belonged, or I would be able to free the kingdom so that we could live in perpetual sunshine and happiness.

I was clearly losing my mind.

I took one more deep breath and went inside. There was a steady murmur of voices coming from the large room where we held our meetings. When I walked into the room, all the conversations going on ceased as everyone's eyes fell on me. It was a tad overwhelming.

"Hey," I said dumbly, because what the hell else was I supposed to say? I'd been waiting for this decision for months, but now that it had arrived, I wanted to be anywhere but here.

"Hi, Sophia," Sam said, her voice friendly but professional.

I looked around at all the officers gathered at the front of the room and was suddenly overcome by how seriously they took all of this. They all stood there in cute outfits, perfectly pressed and tailored, with their makeup and hair done impeccably.

I'd thrown on jeans and a sweater of questionable cleanliness because of my parents' surprise visit and also because I'd been too busy fucking my secret boyfriend over the past few days to do laundry. Our priorities were so wildly different, and I wondered if they'd always been or if this was a relatively new development.

"Why don't you come sit over here? Aamee has called an emergency meeting to address some . . . concerns." Sam's eyes cut to Aamee when she spoke, and the look Sam gave her wasn't a kind one. If anything, Sam looked annoyed, which immediately piqued my curiosity.

I shot a look at Gina as I walked to my seat, but she shrugged in return. Getting no help from that direction, I settled into my chair and clasped my hands on my lap.

After looking around the room to make sure she had everyone's attention, Sam began. "Aamee came to me and alleged that the rules concerning the fundraiser weren't honored. She would like us to discuss the matter and vote whether anything improper has occurred."

I narrowed my eyes in confusion. "What's the allegation?"

Sam took a deep breath and faced me. She looked as if what she was about to say would pain her as she expelled it. "That you violated the rules by contributing money to your own fundraiser."

My head jerked back as if I'd been slapped. I turned my attention to Aamee. "Are you for fucking real with this?"

Aamee lifted her head high, but she didn't look at me as she spoke. "It's true. It clearly states in our bylaws that a sister running for president cannot unduly impact her own efforts. That includes donating to your own fundraiser."

I jumped out of my chair so quickly, I practically levitated. "I didn't do that to throw things in my favor, and you know it."

"How would I know anything? You've been combative and standoffish throughout this entire process. Traits, might I add, that aren't exactly appealing in a new president."

"I may have been that way to *you* because you're a manipulative jerk on a power trip."

"Okay, okay, none of this is helpful," Sam said as she got between us. I hadn't realized how close to one another Aamee and I had shifted, but we weren't more than three feet apart. Almost close enough for me to wring her neck.

"How much money did Aamee's fundraiser bring in?" I asked.

Sam looked to Kyla, who said, "Almost eight hundred."

Which was pathetic for something she'd had much longer than me to plan. Suddenly, I saw this for what it was. Aamee was afraid. Terrified really. Because there was no way I hadn't made more money, so the only thing she had left was to discredit me another way. It was such a sleazy way for her to behave, and I practically shook with rage.

"How much did I raise?" I asked through gritted teeth.

"Almost two thousand. Seven dollars short of it to be exact."

I looked at Aamee and sneered. "I could spot you the five hundred, and you still wouldn't have won."

"This isn't supposed to be decided solely on who brought in more money," Aamee argued. "It should be based on who's more fit for the job. And that isn't someone who violates the rules and has a scandalous relationship with her brother."

"For Christ's sake, will you drop the brother thing already? It's getting old," I replied, because it *so* was. I was tired of defending a mistake I wasn't even making. I didn't owe these people all my secrets. I didn't owe them anything.

And that thought . . . gave me pause. If I wanted to be their president, then I *did* owe them things. Maybe not to unleash every sordid detail for their entertainment, but I at least owed it to them to be honest. And while in this instance I couldn't be because the secret wasn't only mine to tell, I also didn't *want* to.

I looked over at Aamee. She was red-faced and shaking, but it wasn't from anger. Her eyes were red-rimmed, and I could see her furiously blinking back tears. And while she'd never win any presidential awards from me, at least she wanted the job. And deep down, I think she wanted to be good at it.

She had me beat on both fronts.

"Can I speak to Aamee alone for a second?" I blurted out, interrupting Sam and Macy as they addressed the rest of our sisters about conducting a vote.

"I don't think that's a good idea," Sam said.

"Please," I said, looking at Aamee. "I'll be calm and rational. I promise."

Sam looked to Aamee, who nodded, before saying, "Okay. We'll wait for you to get back to hold a vote."

I nodded and then turned and led the way into a small room we used for studying that was on the other side of the house. I heard Aamee's footfalls behind me and knew she was following me. Hopefully she wouldn't decide to seize the opportunity and literally stab me in the back. Once we were in the room, I moved aside so she could enter, and then I pulled the pocket door closed behind us.

Aamee took up a defensive position immediately, her arms crossed tightly across her chest, hip cocked, bitch glare in full effect. "What?" she asked icily.

I sighed heavily. "Can we not do this?"

"Do what?"

Gesturing at her, I said, "This. Despising each other was fun for a few months, but I'm kind of over it now. Can't you be?"

"Why should I be?" she asked, though she dropped her arms back to her sides. "You're the one who started this whole nightmare."

"No, it started because you kicked me out of the house for a bullshit reason. And it continued because . . . " I took a deep breath. This next bit was difficult to force out. "Because I was angry and hurt, and I wanted to hurt you back. But I'm over that petty bullshit now. Or at least I want to be."

She looked less like she wanted to bury my body in a shallow, unmarked grave, but she was still clearly wary.

"What *do* you want?" she asked quietly.

"I'm not sure. I'll tell you what I *don't* want. I don't want to take the presidency from you. I don't want to be someone who takes on a responsibility like that just so someone else can't have it. I don't want to be a bad sister."

Man, admitting that hit me on multiple levels. My clarity didn't only extend to wanting a better relationship with the girls in my sorority; I wanted a better one with my brother too.

Seriously, who the fuck ducked off to parts unknown and felt more comfortable discussing it with a stranger than his own sister? And while I'm glad Brody did what he did because it brought me Drew, it was still a symbol of just how messed up our relationship was.

Aamee's face showed hopefulness before shuttering

again. "Is this for real? I can get past a lot of things, but if you're fucking with me right now, I swear—"

"I'm not," I interrupted. "I promise. While the idea of being president has grown on me, I don't want it like this. And the fact is, it means more to you than it does to me. But I . . ."

When I didn't continue, Aamee said, "What?" in the softest tone she'd ever directed at me.

"Can you just promise you'll be fair? That you'll be the president that Zeta Eta Chi deserves?" I had to get the question out there. While I didn't want to place contingencies on my bowing out of the race, I wasn't going to go back to idly sitting by while Aamee was a dick to whomever she felt like mistreating. There had to be progress on both sides.

I could see her gearing up to argue with me—to defend herself against my words. But whatever internal battle she was fighting, the side that had her taking a breath and relaxing her posture won.

"Yes. I can promise you that."

Smiling, I extended a hand toward her. "Then I guess we have a deal."

She stared at my hand for a beat before offering me a small smile in return and grasping my hand. "I guess we do."

Our hands remained clasped for a few seconds, as if we were cementing the truce. When we broke apart, I moved to the door and slid it open. As we walked back to where our sisters were, Aamee said, "I guess this means you want to move back into the house."

"I wouldn't be opposed to the idea."

Her exhale was audible. "I guess. As long as you keep your bait-and-switch drama out of the house."

I swung my head in her direction and gaped. *Did she . . . ?*

A smirk played at her lips as she kept walking steadily forward.

"You know, don't you?" I asked, unable to keep the disbelief out of my voice.

"Whoa, are you giving me credit for knowing things now? My, how times have changed."

Sarcasm dripped from every word, but I couldn't think of a solid retort. I was too dumbfounded. A thousand questions were on the tip of my tongue, but I swallowed all of them. This was her chance to prove to me she could be different. That she *wanted* things to be different. While she'd been trying to make everyone believe I'd been fucking my brother, she hadn't exposed the actual truth.

Maybe she hadn't known it long enough to expose us. Or maybe she preferred to discredit me on a rumor that, while annoying, was too unbelievable to have real staying power. Only time would tell which it was.

And as we went in and told everyone of my decision, I was thankful I'd get the time to find out.

Chapter Twenty-Nine

SOPHIA

Even though I wasn't going to be president, I was still on a high from everything that had transpired, and I couldn't wait to go home and tell Drew all about it. Maybe it was a weird thing to want, but I was proud of myself, and I thought he'd be proud of me too.

I hoped my parents had either left or made themselves scarce. I needed to have an unguarded moment with Drew to tell him not only what I'd done at the sorority house but also how he'd impacted me making that decision—how he'd helped me become a better person.

I charged into the apartment and gave a quick look around, thankfully not seeing my parents anywhere.

"Drew?" I called.

"In here" came his voice from the direction of the bedroom.

It was all I could do to avoid sprinting down the short hall, though I was moving at a rate that could likely qualify me for a race-walking competition.

"Hey," I said, my voice loud and exuberant. Until I took a look around the room. "What's going on?"

Drew's back was to me as he put clothes into a large duffel bag. "Just packing up."

I should've anticipated this. It was logical that my parents weren't going to allow a stranger to stay in an apartment they were paying for. I walked over to him and slid my hand up his spine.

"We can find a hotel until we can sort out a more permanent solution."

Drew stood and stepped away, causing my hand to fall. I watched him go over to the dresser and grab some more of his things. As I looked around the room, I noticed almost all traces of him were already gone. A few bags were lined up by the door, and he was clearly gathering the last of his things.

"Drew?"

"Yeah?"

"Do you already have a place you can go?"

"Yeah. My parents said I could stay with them until I can sort out the situation with the guy who sublet my apartment."

"Oh. Okay. Well, I can help you take your stuff over there."

"That's okay. I got it." His tone was cold and brusque, and all the happy feelings that had been fluttering around inside of me evaporated.

I tried to remind myself that this was a difficult situation. It had only been a few hours since we'd been lying in bed discussing the future of our relationship, and then my parents had barged in and ruined everything.

I sat down on the bed. "At least the semester is almost over. There's no way my parents will blow the whistle on Brody and ruin the grades you've earned him. So, you'll be able to attend the last few classes and take the finals. Though maybe taking finals isn't exactly a positive," I joked, hoping it would break the weird tension between us.

"Your dad said he'd handle getting Brody excused for the rest of the semester. I'll text Brody later and see what he wants me to do. We had a deal, after all."

The way he said the last sentence sounded odd—bitter almost. But I didn't want to focus on the negative.

"And then we'll be free of school for a few weeks," I said. "We can hang out without that added stress weighing us down."

Drew finished tucking the last few items into his bag and zipped it up before carrying it over to where his other bags sat. He stood there for a second, facing away from me, before whirling around and rubbing a hand over his jaw.

"I don't think that's a good idea."

My stomach dropped, but I held the rising panic at bay. "You don't think what's a good idea?"

"Us. I think we just... I think we need some space." His eyes were everywhere but on me, which pissed me off.

"Really? You certainly didn't seem to want much space this morning. Or over the last couple of days. What's changed?" It was a stupid question. I knew a lot had changed. But even though some waves had popped up, that didn't mean we had to capsize the whole fucking boat.

"The last few days, hell the last few *months*, haven't been reality," he said. "But reality sure as hell came knocking today. And I can't ignore that."

I felt like my entire body could radiate through the wall. I wasn't sure if it was rage or despair that was making me tremble or if it was a combination of the two. My feelings were so big and loud that I couldn't parse them out and get to the driving force behind them.

"They *have* been real. Christ, the past few months have been a total disaster. And we've weathered that storm. We can weather this one too. Sure, my parents aren't thrilled about what's been going on, but none of that really has to do with you. They're pissed at Brody and me, but they'll get over it. And if they don't ... " I shrugged.

"If they don't, what?" he asked.

"Huh?"

"What will you do if they don't get over it?" He might have been dodging my gaze before, but his eyes were locked on me now. My answer to this question was clearly important, but I wasn't sure what he wanted to hear.

"I won't have to do anything. They *will* get over it. With all the shit Brody's put them through over the years, they've become nothing if not resilient."

Drew shook his head slowly. "You're so naïve."

His words made my spine stiffen. I stood from where I'd been sitting on the bed and faced him. "Excuse me?"

"You just ... expect life to always go the way you want it. That it'll bend to your will. And maybe that's because it always has. Maybe that's the difference between the haves and the have-nots. Life just unravels before you like a red carpet, while I have to pretend to be someone else to even find out where the carpet is."

"That is ... the strangest metaphor I've ever heard. And it's bullshit. I work hard. Don't diminish what I've gone through because you think it gives you ammunition to use against me. Maybe we're fighting for different things in different ways, but we're both fighting our own battles the best way we know how."

"Right. And this is the best way I know how."

"And what way is that?" I was sorry I asked as soon as the words were out of my mouth because I was sure I wasn't going to like the answer.

"By leaving. By ending this before we get too deep into it."

Tears prickled my eyes, but I fought them back. I wanted to rail at him that I was already in deep, but he clearly didn't feel the same, and I didn't want to give more of myself away. If he was content to break the connection between us, he could damn well do it without knowing he was breaking me in the process.

"By running away, you mean. By quitting. Giving up."

He looked at me for a moment before replying in a quiet, controlled voice. "Walking away doesn't mean I'm quitting. Sometimes the path you're on isn't the right one for you and you have to change course. That isn't cowardly. It's smart."

"Oh, come on, Drew. You didn't have any of these feelings before my parents showed up. How can a couple of hours have changed things for you this much?"

He took a couple of steps closer but brought himself up short as if he hadn't realized he was moving closer. "I don't expect you to understand. And I'm sorry that I can't . . . be who you need. Who you deserve—"

"What makes you think you aren't?"

He shook his head slightly. "I don't belong in your world. And what's more, I don't want to be there."

I scoffed. "You sound like my dad."

"Doesn't make me wrong."

"You are, though. So wrong."

"Then I guess I'll have to live with that mistake."

"So will I."

He gave me a sad smile. "I think you'll be just fine. In

fact, I know you will."

"If this conversation has taught me anything, it's that you don't know me at all."

He reached out, his fingertips coming into contact with my hair before he tucked an errant strand behind my ear. "I really hope that's not true." In the blink of an eye, he was stepping away, moving toward his bags and hefting some into his arms. "I wish things could be different."

"That's bullshit. You could *make* things different by making a different choice."

"Maybe. But this is the only choice I know how to make."

"That makes me really sad for you."

He laughed, but it was humorless. "I'm sad for me too. Goodbye, Sophia."

I didn't say anything as I watched him walk out of the room, laden with bags. I stood unmoving as I heard his footsteps creaking around the apartment as he probably made sure he wasn't leaving anything behind.

It wasn't until I heard the front door close that my body sagged and tears began to leak from my eyes and stream down my face. I could taste the saltiness of them on my lips, but I didn't wipe them away. Instead, I let myself embrace the pain of this moment. These were the only tears I was going to give Drew Nolan.

Because, seriously, fuck him.

Epilogue

DREW

Four weeks later...

I wiped the bar down for the thousandth time since my shift at Rafferty's started two hours ago. The place was a ghost town due to the forecasted snow. Even Max had stayed home.

I tried to busy myself behind the bar, cleaning bottles and straightening things up to keep my mind occupied, but it was no use. And as had been the case anytime my mind had wandered over the past few weeks, my thoughts immediately went to Sophia.

What was she doing? How had everything worked out with the sorority? I felt bad that I hadn't asked how all that had gone. I hoped it worked out for her, however that might have looked.

Unable to resist, I pulled out my phone and pulled up a picture of us—one we'd taken at the costume party. It was pathetic, but whatever. Jesus, I missed her.

I expected the ache of losing her to have started to dull by now, but there was no lessening of the intensity with which I missed that girl. But I'd made my choice, and now I was stuck with it, for better or worse.

Funny how I'd been convinced it was for the better when I'd walked out. I wasn't so sure anymore.

"Hey, Drew."

Sean's voice startled me, and I slipped my phone back into my pocket before turning to look at him.

"Hey. How's it going?"

Sean blew out a breath. "Snow's starting to come down heavier. If no one's here by now, I doubt anyone will show up. You might as well take off."

"For real?"

"Yeah, I'll hang out for a while in case anyone shows. I know you only have that damn bike. Might as well get home before the roads get too bad."

I couldn't deny it—the fact that he was concerned about me felt nice. "Thanks, man. I appreciate it."

"No worries. Get out of here before I change my mind."

"I'm going," I said with a laugh. The fact that I was going home to a crowded house wasn't the most silver of linings I could've hoped for, but I'd deal. I had a few leads on cheap places I could rent or people who were looking for a roommate. In another week or two, staying at my parents' place should be a distant memory.

And maybe once I was back on my own, things would start to feel more normal again. Maybe I'd be able to start getting over Sophia and forget about all the things I couldn't have.

SOPHIA

"Merry Christmas!" Carter yelled as he stood in my doorway with a Santa hat on, thrusting a present at me.

"What's this?" I reached out to take the poorly wrapped package from him.

"A Christmas gift for the best tutor a guy could've asked for."

I toyed with the ribbon as I looked at him. "Well, now I feel like a jerk. I didn't get you anything."

"You got me through psychology. That's gift enough."

I smiled, one of the only real ones I'd managed since Drew left. "Still. Thank you. Come on in," I said as I opened the door farther.

He walked over to the couch and sank back into it, and I joined him after I closed and locked the door. Giving the box a little shake, I asked, "What is it?"

"What are you, five? Just open the damn thing."

"Okay, okay." I slipped a finger between a gap in the paper and tore it open. Then I lifted the lid on the box and peered inside. "What . . . is this . . . Did you make me a collage?"

"Yup. You like it?" Carter's eyes were wide, and he seemed to be close to bouncing on the sofa. The fact that he seemed to care so much whether I liked his gift warmed me.

My eyes drifted over the pictures he'd taken over the course of the semester and had printed onto a canvas. My breath caught when I saw pictures of Drew on there.

I'd left out the details of what had happened between Drew and me. It was too painful to rehash and, quite frankly, a little embarrassing too. I had no idea if Carter had spoken to Drew since he'd left, and I honestly didn't want to know if Drew had kept that relationship while disregarding mine.

My throat grew tight as I let a finger lightly skim over a picture of all of us at Aamee's costume party.

"I wasn't sure about putting those on there," Carter explained, his voice the softest and gentlest I'd ever heard it. "But I figured that they were still good times, even if it ended. Did I mess it up?"

I shook my head, unable to trust my voice at first. After swallowing the emotions down, I said, "No. It's perfect. I love it."

Carter smiled at that and opened his mouth to speak, but the shrill ring of my phone interrupted him. Looking down, I saw my dad's name.

"One sec," I said before answering. "Hi, Dad." I stood and walked into the kitchen to get a bottle of water for Carter and me.

"Hi, Soph. You all packed up?"

I looked around at the apartment that seemed so empty without my stuff hanging around. I'd begun sleeping at the sorority house again but had left a few of my things at Brody's that I wanted to grab before going home for the holiday break.

I'd told Carter to meet me there in order to keep things peaceful with Aamee. Tomorrow, my dad was driving down to pick me up for winter break, and while he was keeping the apartment for Brody—who was supposed to be coming home in time for Christmas and to resume his own identity for the spring semester—I'd be heading back to the sorority house.

"Yup. All set."

"Good. And still no sign of that *boy*, right?"

Rolling my eyes, I answered, "No, I have not seen Drew.

And you'd think you'd be a little more grateful to him. Brody just got the best report card of his life." Why I was defending Drew was beyond me, but nothing I was saying was untrue.

"Yes, well, thank heavens he was good for something. At least he was smart enough to get good grades and know when to leave well enough alone."

I froze at that. "What do you mean, 'leave well enough alone'?"

"What? Oh, nothing. I'm just glad he's out of our lives is all."

I opened my mouth to call my dad on what was clearly bullshit, but Carter ran over to me and thrust his phone in my face.

"Hang on a second, Dad," I said, putting him on mute. "What is that?" I asked, squinting at the picture that was too close to my face. I pulled back a bit. "Why are you showing me a picture of an accident?"

"Look right there," Carter said, his voice sounding panicked as he pointed at the screen. "Isn't that Drew's bike?"

I looked harder at the picture for a second before my eyes widened in alarm. "Oh my God," I whispered.

And then I did the only thing I could think of. I hung up on my dad and got my coat.

ALSO IN

The Love Game

SERIES

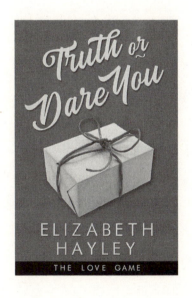

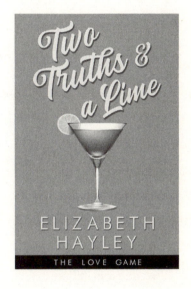

CONTINUE READING

The Love Game

SERIES

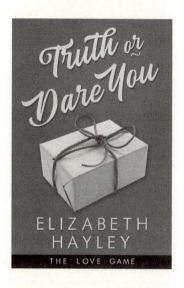

After tragedy strikes, Sophia Mason finds herself thrown back together with her ex fake-brother/boyfriend Drew. But this time she's going in with her eyes open and her mission clear: she'll help Drew get back on his feet and then show him the door. Simple...right?

Drew Nolan's spirit is almost as broken as his body. Asking Sophia to help him seems cruel after the way things ended between them, but she doesn't give him much choice—something he's extremely grateful for.

When Sophia's brother, Brody, reappears, their lives become even more of a circus, but they all manage to settle into their own version of normal—a normal that involves starting a venture of questionable ethics in the eyes of the university. As Sophia and Drew help get the business off the ground, it becomes impossible for them to deny the feelings that still exist between them.

But when the going gets tough and Sophia risks getting kicked out of school, will Drew remain by her side and support her, or will he run again?

Also by
ELIZABETH HAYLEY

The Love Game:
Never Have You Ever
Truth or Dare You
Two Truths & a Lime

Love Lessons:
Pieces of Perfect
Picking Up the Pieces
Perfectly Ever After

Sex Snob
(A Love Lessons Novel)

Misadventures:
Misadventures with My Roommate
Misadventures with a Country Boy
Misadventures in a Threesome
Misadventures with a Twin
Misadventures with a Sexpert

Other Titles:
The One-Night Stand

Acknowledgments

First and foremost we have to thank Meredith Wild for always believing in our writing and inviting us to be part of the Waterhouse Team. We're thankful that you thought of us for a rom-com series and that you trust in our humor.

To our swolemate, Scott, thanks for making the editing process smooth and for always trusting us to get a story where it needs to be. You're always there to provide insight when we need it, and you've helped make our books the best they could be.

To Robyn, thank you for answering our million and one questions and for stepping in and taking control of things when we were floundering. We're sorry we're such disasters sometimes.

To the rest of the Waterhouse Press team, you simply kick ass. Thank you for everything you do to help us be as successful as we can. You're an amazing group of people, and we're lucky to have the honor of working with you.

To our Padded Roomers, you all are such a tremendous group of people. It's tough to find people as crazy as we are, and we've truly found our tribe with you. Thank you for everything you've done for us, such as posting teasers, sharing links, reading ARCs, writing reviews, and making us laugh.

We don't deserve you, but we're damn glad to have you.

To our readers, there's no way to accurately thank you for taking a chance on us and for your support. Thank you for letting us share our stories with you.

To Google, thank you for providing the means for us to research things including, but not limited to, fraternities, sororities, marketing degrees, alcoholic drinks, dean responsibilities, business class topics, college codes of conduct, Gen Z lingo, and popular clothing trends.

To our sons for inspiring the last names of our main characters. Our lack of originality strikes again.

To Elizabeth's daughter for being a spitfire and inspiring the way in which she wrote Sophia's character.

To our husbands, we know it's not easy. Thanks for hanging in there. We honestly don't deserve you.

To each other, for pushing one another forward when we stall. The ride hasn't been easy, but it's sure as hell been a lot of fun. On to the next.

About

ELIZABETH HAYLEY

Elizabeth Hayley is actually "Elizabeth" and "Hayley," two friends who love reading romance novels to obsessive levels. This mutual love prompted them to put their English degrees to good use by penning their own. The product is *Pieces of Perfect*, their debut novel. They learned a ton about one another through the process, like how they clearly share a brain and have a persistent need to text each other constantly (much to their husbands' chagrin).

They live with their husbands and kids in a Philadelphia suburb. Thankfully, their children are still too young to read their books.

Visit them at AuthorElizabethHayley.com